LADY *of* VENICE

SIOBHAN DAIKO

For Lili

CHAPTER 1

Italy
June 1989

I pushed open my bedroom door and my stomach gave a sudden lurch. Something was burning; I was sure of it. In the corridor, morning sunlight filtered through the shutters, but there was no sign of a fire. The passage was clear of smoke, yet I could smell an acrid odour. *Could it be bleach?*

A frisson of cold stirred the air.

'Lorenza!' came a ghostly voice.

I almost jumped out of my skin.

'Who's there?' I whispered, my heart thudding.

Snorts reverberated from behind the closed door. Aunt Susan, Dad's sister, could snore for Wales just like Dad. Maybe what I'd heard was simply an echo?

Slippers flip-flapping, I made my way along the corridor and down the spiral staircase. In the kitchen, a fat tabby cat wound its body around my legs. I bent to stroke the smooth fur, catching the scent of roses from the vase on the table.

Everything seemed normal down here; I must have been imagining things.

I straightened up and took in my surroundings. The open-plan room looked out at a wide veranda fronting the ground floor. There was a fireplace between the cabinets, and a sitting area with a sofa, an armchair and a television. It was a lived-in kitchen, well-used and comfortable. Not like the "shoebox" where I prepared my own meals in London.

I gazed through the picture window at a narrow road hugging vineyards and cornfields. Dawn light illuminated a range of hills in the distance. An ancient fortress-like building sat on the highest crest, and below the fort nestled the small town of Asolo. A place for writers, musicians and artists, by all accounts. Would I find the peace I was seeking here?

'Lorenza . . .'

The whisper, so plaintive, came from right next to me, and a shiver ran up my spine. 'Who is it?'

Silence.

Feeling a tad ridiculous, I repeated the question.

Nothing.

How weird…

I went over to the bookshelf and picked up Auntie's latest novel. *The Duke's Mistress— A Romance by Susan Finch*. I loved reading and couldn't wait to lose myself in it.

Tingling with anticipation, I carried the book to the table. I let out a gasp; my foot had knocked against something rough… a jagged piece of wood, about six inches long, blackened by fire. Had the cat brought it in? I ran my finger along it… cold as a tomb. With a sick feeling in my belly, I picked it up and threw it into the grate. Was that what I'd smelt?

No. It had burnt out long ago . . .

'Lorenza.'

The word hung in the air.

A sliver of ice slipped down my spine.

With a yowl the cat ran from the room, its tail fluffed out to twice its normal size.

Floorboards creaked above my head and my heart skittered.

'Is that you, my lovely? You're up early,' Auntie said in her Welsh lilt as she came down the stairs in an old cotton dressing-gown that hugged her portly figure. She pushed frizzy grey hair back from her forehead, dislodging a pair of tortoiseshell-framed glasses.

I knitted my brows. 'Something woke me, and I couldn't get back to sleep again.'

Auntie stared at me myopically. 'A bad dream?'

'I don't think so.' I narrowed my eyes. I was cured of the nightmares, I hoped. Those dreadful visions of flames and death. Smoke pouring through the blackened tunnels. The panic and the choking and the searing in my lungs.

'*Lorenza . . .*'

Like a soft echo.

I swallowed the sudden lump of fear in my throat, and asked, 'Did you hear that?'

Auntie switched on the kettle. 'Hear what?'

'Someone's whispering.'

'I didn't hear anything,' she said, settling her glasses onto her nose. 'It must be the wind.'

I peered through the window, but the olive trees outside were completely still. I glanced at the fireplace; no sign of that piece of wood I'd thrown in earlier. I told myself not to be pathetic. There had to be an explanation for the whispering. Someone outside could be calling out, *Lorenza*, or my ears might be playing tricks on me. Not my eyes, though. I was sure I'd seen that piece of burnt wood. And I'd definitely touched it.

'Where's Gucci Cat got to?' Auntie asked, pouring boiled water into the teapot. 'He's usually here in the mornings, begging to be fed.'

'He was in the kitchen when I came down, Auntie. Don't worry.'

'Oh, that's a relief,' she beamed. 'We could go to Asolo after breakfast, if you like.'

'Perfect! I'll take my sketchpad and try to capture some of the scenery.' Again, I felt a breath of cold air and rubbed my arms. 'Isn't it a little chilly in here?'

'Not to me it isn't. Quite the opposite, in fact. Early June can be as hot as mid-summer,' Auntie said unblinking. 'You're just tired after your journey last night. I always feel cold when I'm tired.'

I forced a smile. 'Maybe...'

Half an hour later, we set off in Auntie's Fiat 500 and soon we were sitting at a table on the outside terrace of the Caffè Centrale... sipping frothy cappuccinos in the warmth of a glorious, sunny day.

I studied the building with frescoed walls on the other side of the cobbled piazza. The sunshine lit faded outlines of a battle scene, knights on horseback carrying lances... ghosts from centuries past. But wasn't something missing? Shouldn't there be an external staircase leading to the first floor? No. This was my first visit to Asolo. I had to be wrong. My mind was playing tricks on me, that's all.

A fountain graced the centre of the square, a column with grooved shafts at its base, and a barrel-chested pigeon had bobbed down to drink from the flow. The winged Lion of St Mark was surveying the scene from the top of the pillar. *Symbol of the Venetian Republic.*

My skin tingled and a fluttery feeling invaded my insides.

How the hell did I know that?

I tapped the coffee spoon on the side of my cup.

I'm tired. Just tired. Must be something I've read about.

The scrape of a chair on the tiled terrace interrupted my thoughts. A tall dark-haired man dressed in faded denim jeans and an open-necked white dress shirt was approaching our table.

'*Buongiorno*, Susan.' The man bent and kissed Auntie's cheeks, his tanned face a stark contrast to her pallid complexion.

'Luca. What a lovely surprise!" She cooed. "This is my niece, Fern. She's staying with me for a few weeks.'

I held out my hand.

He swept his eyes over me. 'Haven't we met before?'

'I don't think so.' I would have remembered meeting this man. He was probably in his early thirties, judging by the slight recession in his hairline. Not much older than me. And devastatingly good-looking (he wouldn't look out of place on the cover of one of Auntie's novels).

Not that I was interested.

Far from it . . .

Something passed through me as his warm palm enfolded mine. Something like a mild electric shock. Hard to describe, but it made me feel light-headed. I grabbed hold of the table to steady myself.

'Let's leave walking up to the Rocca for another day.' Auntie pointed toward the old fort at the top of the hill. 'The weather is too hot for the hike. Why don't we visit the Queen's Castle then call it a day?'

A smile tugged at my lips. 'The Queen's Castle? Did Asolo have a queen?'

'Queen Caterina Cornaro,' Luca said, taking the seat next to me and stretching out his long legs. 'Daughter of Venice. Married off to the King of Cyprus. Persuaded to abdicate by the Republic and given the fiefdom of Asolo in 1489.'

'Luca's an expert on the subject,' Auntie said in an impressed tone.

I shot him a curious look. 'Are you a historian?'

He was unlike any of the fusty old historians I'd met when I'd gone to the History Club at university...

Luca's smile made his deep blue eyes crinkle at the corners. 'An architect, but I'm involved in restoration work. I met your aunt at a talk I gave in the local museum. I'm not such an expert on the Queen,' he chuckled, 'however, I do know about the castle.'

'I've got a book about Caterina Cornaro at home.' Auntie's lips pursed. 'Quite academic, but interesting all the same.'

I laughed. 'Well, that's my vacation reading sorted, then. Come on, Auntie! The castle is waiting for us.' I turned to Luca. 'Your English is brilliant. I wish I spoke Italian half as well.'

That would be an achievement considering I only know a few phrases.

'My mother's English.' Luca grinned. 'I grew up bilingual and I was educated in England. I'm going to the castle too, so I might see you up there.'

'Great,' I said, unhooking my handbag from the back of the chair. 'Hope to catch you later.'

I got to my feet, and followed Auntie across the road, my long skirt billowing around my legs. Vacation clothes… the ones in which I felt most comfortable. I glanced to my left. The Venetian plain stretched beyond my gaze; the silhouette of a church tower etched against the clear blue sky. Something about it tugged at my memory. *What?* I shook my head and caught up with Auntie.

'In Asolo, you should walk with your nose in the air.' She took me by the arm. 'Look at those arched windows and purple petunias cascading from the balconies!'

'It's stunning. So well-preserved.' I loved how the colours of the buildings harmonised with each other in shades of cream and apricot. And the shop signs were discreet, not like in towns back home. 'If I walked with my nose in the air without you to hold onto,' I smirked, 'I might end up falling flat on my face.'

Auntie snorted out a laugh. 'Indeed. Only do so if sure you're safe. Goes without saying…'

She led me up a short steep incline, under an archway to a high terrace. Then she stopped abruptly. 'Goodness.'

'What's wrong?'

'I've just thought of the solution to a plot problem. It's been niggling at me for ages.'

I stared at her. 'That's good, right?'

'Yes, but I need to get it down before I forget.' She rummaged in her handbag. '*Duw!* I've left my notebook in the car. Will you be all right while I go and get it?'

'I can tear you off a sheet from my sketchpad if you like.'

'Thanks, love, but I need to check through my notes. I'll meet you on the terrace.'

A quiver of unease passed through me as I waved her off. The tables sprawling across the patio, shaded by ivory-coloured umbrellas, seemed alien to this place.

Of course, everything would be different, I told myself. I was used to the drizzle of London and red-bricked houses with grey slate roofs, the drone of jetliners on their way to Heathrow, the hunched crowds hurrying along pavements, and shops screaming sales or unbeatable offers at every corner.

I decided to climb the steep steps to the ramparts and admire the view. At the top, I retrieved my sketchpad from my bag and contemplated the green terraced gardens glistening in the bright sunshine.

Without warning, the colours intensified, almost blinding me. I quickly returned my pad to my bag and shaded my eyes from the intensity.

Dizziness buzzed in my head, and my knees began to give way.

My hand went to the parapet, but it wobbled under my fingers.

Christ!

Without warning, the light had changed, and the vibrant colours had become washed-out, over-exposed like an old photograph.

This is so bizarre.

Suddenly, I was floating, looking down on the scene from above the castle wall. I tried to set my feet onto the stone, but all they encountered was thin air.

Oh, my God.

The sunlight had fractured and splintered like glass shards.

The tall building had transformed into a two-storey structure.

A regal lady and her attendants, mounted on magnificent horses, were passing under the portcullis.

I had to be dreaming. The wasn't real. Except, I could hear the hooves clattering on the cobblestones and the voices of the people.

I shut my eyes and opened them again.

The building had morphed back into its 1989 state.

Only the faint clop of horseshoes on cobbles resonated in my ears.

I inhaled the lemony scent of caper plants growing through cracks in the ancient wall.

The wall which had appeared much newer only a few seconds ago.

CHAPTER 2

*L*uca

I saw the English girl sitting on the ruined rampart of the castle. Dressed in a voluminous skirt and a gypsy blouse, her long hair a riot of curls, she reminded me of a hippy. What was her name? Something botanical, wasn't it? Could it be Heather? The girl seemed miles away. *Oh, shit!* She was swaying and looked as if she was about to fall. I ran up the steps and managed to grab hold of her before she toppled from the wall. The girl slid to the foot of the parapet, and I shook her gently.

'Put your head between your knees,' I said as she came to. I patted her shoulder and experienced that sense of recognition again. *Jesus!* I eyed her white face and the sheen of perspiration on her high forehead. 'Are you all right?'

'I think so,' she said softly.

'You shouldn't be sitting here. It's dangerous. Especially if you're not feeling well.'

'I'm fine. Really, I am." She shrugged. 'Last night I didn't sleep well, and I suppose I must've dropped off just now.'

'You were literally dropping off this wall and it's quite a long way down on the other side. I think you were on the point of fainting.' I frowned. 'You were totally out of it, you know. Where's your aunt?'

'Gone to fetch something from the car.' The girl took a deep breath. 'Please don't worry. I'm perfectly all right.'

'Are you sure we haven't met?' I couldn't help staring at her. She had an unforgettable face. A prominent nose slightly spoiled the symmetry of her features… not that it made her ugly… and her blonde hair could only be described as wild, but there was definitely something alluring about her.

The girl's gaze rested on my chest, then travelled up to my face. Green eyes. Quite lovely. She smiled at me, her lips curving in such a delightful bow-shaped way that I wanted to reach out and brush my fingers across them.

Not in a creepy fashion— more like in admiration.

'I'm sure we haven't met,' she said firmly.

I nodded but wasn't convinced. Could I have seen her at some party in London? It didn't seem appropriate to ask.

The girl pointed at the castle buildings. 'I was wondering about the structure at the time of the Queen.' She tucked a curl behind her ear.

'There's a drawing in the Civic Museum showing what it was like before demolition in the early 1820s.' I led her toward the terrace.

Best get her sitting down before she passes out again.

'Such a shame,' she sighed. 'I mean, that we can't see the original today.'

I glanced at her, trying to detect a note of irony in her voice. My friends often accused me of going on and on about the castle, but she appeared to have a genuine interest in what I had to say. The pallor had returned to her face. 'Have you got time for a drink?' I asked.

Without waiting for an answer, I took her to one of the tables at the café on the patio and signalled the waiter. *'Un Fernet Branca per la signorina ed un caffè macchiato per me.'*

'You're very kind,' the girl said. 'What did you order for me?'

'Something to pick you up. A mixture of alcohol, cordial, and herbs.'

'Oh,' she caught her bottom lip with her teeth. 'Thank you.'

It didn't take long for our drinks to arrive. The girl took a sip and her nose wrinkled. 'It tastes terrible. So bitter.'

'Knock it back! You'll feel better afterward,' I smirked. 'It's an old remedy for fainting.'

'Anyone would feel better after they'd stopped drinking this,' she said with a throaty laugh. 'But I'm not sure I did faint, actually.'

'What do you think happened, then?'

The girl put her glass down, picked it up, and placed it back on the table. 'I'm not certain, to be honest. When I was sitting on the rampart, I had this incredible... oh, I don't know, exactly.' She shifted in her seat. 'I felt as if I'd been here before, even though I know I've never set foot in this place.'

'Maybe it looks familiar because you've seen some photos?'

'Could be.' The girl appeared to be struggling to find the right words. She lifted her shoulders and eyed the clock tower. Shaking her head, she turned back to me. 'Do you work in Asolo?'

'My office is in Treviso, but I have an apartment here.' I shot a glance at the sketchpad poking out of her bag. *She must be an artist.*

'Lucky you! I've got a flat in Islington and work in the City.' The girl frowned again, momentarily, then relaxed her expression.

'I prefer small town living. Not that Treviso is a big city. I have an affinity with Asolo. Always have done.' I thrummed my fingers on the armrests of my chair. 'If you're in Asolo until the end of the month, then you'll be here for the re-enactment. To celebrate Queen Caterina Cornaro's court,' I said with unabashed enthusiasm. 'A group of us dress up in Renaissance costumes and there are dances and street parties. The whole town joins in.'

'Sounds like fun. Will you perform the *saltarello?*'

I lifted an eyebrow. 'I'm surprised you know about a dance

from the 15th century. It's a tricky one, so we tend to leave it out of the performance.'

The girl tossed her hair back from her face. 'Must've seen a TV programme or read about it somewhere. I'm not a dumb blonde, you know.'

'I didn't think you were,' I said with a laugh. Should I ask about her sketches? But, before I could do so, footsteps crunched on the gravel and Susan Finch came marching up to the table, her short chubby legs enveloped in baggy track-suit bottoms, and her mouth covered with tell-tale crumbs showing she'd indulged in a pastry or two on her way past the Caffè Centrale.

'My dear,' she squealed. 'You look as if you've seen a ghost.'

'I'm fine. Just a funny turn, Auntie,' the girl said. 'Thank God Luca was here.' She smiled. 'He managed to grab hold of me as I was about to fall off the ramparts.'

'Goodness! What a stroke of luck you saw her.' Susan shot me a grateful look. 'Would you like to come to dinner the day after tomorrow? Fern and I would love it. It's the least we can do.'

'I'd be delighted.' *Fern… the girl's name at last.* 'But I really didn't do much. Fern should see a doctor, though.'

'We'll stop off at the hospital on our way home,' Susan said briskly. 'To get Fern checked over. Best to be safe than sorry.' She paused. 'We'll expect you at around eight o'clock on Friday evening, then?'

'*Mille grazie.* Thank you so much.'

Watching the two women ambling arm in arm down the path, I clapped a hand to my forehead.

Cazzo!

I'd forgotten I was supposed to spend Friday evening with Mother.

CHAPTER 3

I was sitting in the kitchen, sipping from a glass of mineral water while Auntie prepared our evening meal. At the hospital, after an interminable wait and several tests, the doctors had said I'd fainted as a result of high blood pressure and needed to make sure I avoided caffeine. Probably all that coffee I'd drunk while waiting for the flight at Heathrow. *Thank you, four-hour delay!* Not to mention my breakfast tea and the cappuccino at the Caffè Centrale. I'd been a caffeine junkie for years, and now I'd have to limit my intake to one coffee and one tea a day.

I'd braced myself to hear the ghostly whisper when I'd returned to Auntie's, yet the only sound was the echo of church bells emanating from the village, and the noise of a motorbike revving past on the road. I must have imagined the whisper; that drop I'd felt in the temperature probably had something to do with my blood-pressure and feeling faint. There could be no other explanation. My weird experience in Asolo had been my caffeine-loaded brain playing tricks on me. Nothing more.

I took in a breath and there it was again: the faint smell of burnt wood. I wrinkled my nose and put it down to farmers burning stubble in the fields.

Auntie was opening a jar of sauce. 'Spag bol okay?' she asked.

'Perfect.' My mouth watered. I hadn't eaten a proper meal since the day before yesterday.

Could be another reason why I'd felt light-headed…

Steam rose from a pot of boiling water, and Auntie tipped a handful of pasta into it while the cat purred loudly at her feet. 'I'd offer you a glass of wine,' she said, picking up a bottle of Bardolino. 'Except, you need to line your stomach first.' She pulled the cork then wagged a finger at the cat. 'Shoo, Gucci. You've been fed already. Now where are my specs?'

'They're on top of your head, Auntie,' I smiled. She was certainly a one-off, but I loved her so much. Inadvertently, I thought about the man I'd met this morning. 'Luca seems a nice guy. How did he end up going to school in the UK?'

'His family's very wealthy and can afford private education. He was at Eton, you know. Comes from one of the oldest families in the Veneto. In fact, I think they number a couple of Doges, rulers of ancient Venice, in their ancestry. Italy's a republic now, of course, so no one can call themselves a count or countess with any legitimacy. Otherwise, Luca would be Conte Goredan.'

'His mother's English?'

Auntie nodded. 'She's a widow. *La Contessa*, as the locals still like to call her. A lovely lady. I met her when Luca gave his talk at the Asolo Museum.'

'Interesting. But why did you invite him to dinner? I mean, it was kind of you. Only you didn't have to…'

'I just wanted you to have a friend nearer to your own age.'

Hope Auntie isn't setting me and Luca up. If she is, she has no chance.

We ate in companionable silence and with the last forkful of pasta, my eyelids drooped.

'An early night for you, Fern.' She picked up the plates and took them to the dishwasher. 'I'll go to bed soon too.'

I was so tired I could barely haul myself up the stairs.

The following morning, I was in the kitchen having breakfast with Auntie. 'Why don't you take the car and go exploring?' she suggested, her mouth full of toast. 'Just remember to keep on the right side of the road.'

'I'd like to visit Asolo again. I'm dying to paint it.' My fingers twitched. I couldn't wait to take out my colours and lose myself in creativity. Art therapy. It had started as a way of "facing my demons", but now it had become almost as essential as breathing. A surprise to both myself and the therapist I was seeing for grief counselling.

I helped clear the table, then went to get my things from my room. The drive from Auntie's village, Altivole, took about twenty minutes. I found a park, then reached for my rucksack. After gazing up at the Rocca, its fortifications etched against the azure sky, I decided not to go there today; I couldn't face the climb. I'd have a leisurely stroll and find a quiet place where I would paint.

Within minutes, I was ambling down the Via Canova, the sun warming my bare arms, guidebook in my hand. Reading that I should "glance up Vicolo Belvedere, at the corner of the bakery", I did so. The book said there'd once been a Jewish Ghetto there.

A mansion painted the colour of terracotta rose up on my left. Apparently, it used to belong to a famous Italian actress. I strolled under an archway and caught sight of an elegant palazzo with gold lettering on a wooden sign saying *Hotel Villa Cipriani*. I peered through the wrought-iron gate into a lush garden, planted with an array of salmon-pink geraniums.

Next door stood an old house with a balcony, mullioned windows, a portal, and a massive doorway with a shutter and bolts. Recognition rang like a bell, but I furrowed my brows and told myself to keep focused.

There was nothing familiar about the small church on my left. Putting the guidebook into my rucksack, I stepped into the building and sat on a pew at the back.

My breath caught.

I know this place, but something about it is different.

An image swam into my mind, of another church, of mourners in black and a coffin at the altar, the wooden box containing the charred remains of my fiancé, Harry. My chest tightened so much I could barely breathe. Warm tears ran down my cheeks; I brushed them away with trembling hands and stared at the altar.

The faded frescoes were brightening as the roof began to squeeze down on me.

The colours had become even more vivid.

I closed my eyes and grabbed hold of the pew in front. Only it was no longer the wood of a pew, but the stone of a castle parapet, rough against my fingers. Music lifted from the park below . . . and the sound of singing.

My head swam with dizziness.

I squirm, feeling lost, but it is my own singing that I hear and I'm delirious with it.

Who am I? Where am I?

For a moment I'm confused, as if floating in a daydream. Then I'm back where I belong. I'm Cecilia and it is the year of our Lord 1504. My world is as it should be, and I sing along with my sister Fiammetta while she plucks her lute in the shade of the cherry tree. The rhythm never falters as the tune rises and falls. When Fiammetta sings, Orpheus could not fail to be astounded at her skill; she can keep perfect harmony on her instrument, bringing melody to the inflections of the song. No wonder she's the Queen's darling.

We sing of the bitter sweetness of love and I take hold of my sister's hand. 'I'll miss you when you are wed.'

'My dear. At court you'll be too much in demand to think of me.'

Think of me. These three words soar in the breeze with an echo. *Think of me. Think of me.* Something makes the skin on my arms prickle and I spin around. A shadowy figure floats at the top of the castle wall. I look again, but all I see are the usual caper plants; the parapet is empty. The moment passes, and I'm caught up in singing once more. Fiammetta plays a different tune; I screw up my eyes to remember the words and the melody.

'Shall we dance?' I ask, tired of singing. 'I need more practice.' I love to dance. To twirl until I fall over with the dizziness of it. I can't wait for the time when I shall step out with a handsome suitor, whom I don't yet know, but who will adore me as I'll adore him. Even more than dancing, however, I like to draw – covering paper with black chalk representations of the people and landscape of Asolo. So much more enjoyable than endless embroidery.

'Have you learnt the *saltarello*?' My sister inclines her head toward me.

'It is the most difficult of dances and I've yet to master it. Fiammetta puts down her lute, holds my hand high, and counts the five beats. We move our feet gracefully, right, left, right, left, then execute a short jump before repeating the movement by starting the sequence on the opposite foot. We go over the steps again and again until Fiammetta, playing the man, bows, and I drop into a deep curtsey, perspiration dampening my armpits.

The rough lawn is springy beneath the soft soles of my shoes and I sit down, my skirts billowing around me. I run my hands through the grass, plucking at the pink valerian flowers and lifting them to inhale the vanilla fragrance. The delicate scent reminds me of something, but the memory eludes me.

Fiammetta's dark hair cascades in a long braid down her back and curls escape to frame her face. My breath catches, and I try to hold the picture in my mind. When she is married, she'll live with her husband, of course; she will have no time for me. The compensation will be that I'll take her place at court and will make frequent visits to Venice. I only vaguely remember the city where we were born. I was barely a child of five when we were dispatched here after our parents died in the plague.

'Will you not miss the Queen's parties in her palace on the Grand Canal?' I asked my sister.

'Why would I wish to be there? I'm promised to Rambaldo, who loves me.'

Rambaldo Azzoni Avogadro, that nobleman from Treviso, is

too ugly for her, but he's wealthy and doesn't need a bride with a dowry. Even so, the Queen has been generous with her wedding gift to Fiammetta: a small villa on the road to Venice.

My dreams of a handsome suitor are mere fantasies, however. I push the thought from my mind; I will not dwell on it. Who knows what the future will bring? Lying back on the grass, the warmth of the sun caresses me and dispels my disquiet. Horse hooves clatter on the cobbles and the bell in the clock tower strikes the hour.

Fiammetta tugs at my sleeve. 'You have grass stains on your kirtle, Cecilia. Remember, we are soon to go with the Queen to sing the Te Deum. You need to dress appropriately.'

Standing, I brush down my dress before sprinting up the steps to the building where I've lived for the past ten years. The Queen is there, and I drop into a deep curtsey. 'Are you ready for your debut, child?' she says.

A smile spreads over my lips. 'Yes, Domina.'

I run to change my attire. Today, after luncheon, I shall join the court at her country villa at last. The castle in Asolo is too cramped and crude for the Queen's tastes and she only visits when necessary. Excitement sparks in my chest, and I feel I'm about to explode with happiness.

'Sit still,' Fiammetta gives my arm a shake. 'You're supposed to be praying, not fidgeting.'

My eyes fly open and I peer at the frescoes, confused by their brightness. I clutch my psalter to my chest. What am I doing here? Then, I remember. The church of Santa Caterina. We arrived here a few moments ago.

From my left comes the most melodic voice, deep and true. A young man, with dark brown hair flowing to his shoulders. Bowing my head, I pretend to ignore him, while taking surreptitious peeks. He stands next to the Queen in the opposite pew. My gaze travels to his mouth and my heart flutters.

What am I thinking, staring at a man so boldly?

I can't help it. For once I feel as beautiful as the other ladies. Over my shift, I'm wearing my kirtle, with the sleeves of my shift pulled through the slashes in puffs along the arm. The latest fashion. My over-gown of pale blue satin is sleeveless and laced at the front. I stroke the material and blush with pleasure. 'It is a gift from the Queen for my debut.

How kind she is!

After the service, we progress up the hill to the castle, where a meal has been prepared. The heady perfume of roses in vases on the long wooden tables mingles with the aroma of roasting beef. My mouth watering, I take my seat beside Fiammetta; I ate little at breakfast and hunger twists my belly.

Fiammetta nudges me, 'That man is staring at you,' she says, breaking off a piece of bread and stuffing it into her mouth. 'Looks like you've made a conquest. Except, I wouldn't be too pleased. He's an artist, a womaniser, and he likes to drink.' Fiammetta's eyes take on a dreamy expression, even though she's to be married soon. 'So handsome. I do believe he's known as Zorzo from Castelfranco.'

'I don't like him,' I say. Best not reveal what I really think. His smile fascinates me, as do his full lips that turn up at the corners. *Wish I could feel that mouth on mine*. I give a start, shocked at my thoughts, and cut a slice of meat with my knife. I can't help feeling a stab of jealousy that he, a man, can be an artist, whereas I, a woman, can have no such hope.

The strumming of a lute interrupts my thoughts. It is that deep, melodic voice again, singing, 'Subtle beauty of the golden tresses, can you see that I am dying for you?' I flick a look at the musician and his eyes meet mine. I huff and glance away.

If you think I will succumb and become one of your women, Signor Zorzo, you'd better think again!

I do not let myself observe the artist further, although every word coming from him seems to be directed at me. 'Breeze, blowing that blonde curling hair, stirring it, and being softly stirred in return, scattering that sweet gold about, then gathering it, in a lovely knot of curls,' he sings. I've worn my so-called tresses loose today, not encased in a hair-net. I hate to dress my hair, there's far too much of it and I think it my worst feature.

Oh, foolish Cecilia! I realise that the artist is singing a sonnet of Petrarch's set to music, not his own words. He could be addressing them to any of the ladies assembled here, although I'm the only blonde besides the Queen. *Domina! Of course, he's serenading her.* I'm such an ingénue…

Finally, the time has come to depart, and we make our way to the courtyard. The stable-boy, his smile revealing blackened teeth, hands me my horse's reins. I stroke my grey steed's soft velvety nose and his sweet hay-breath makes me sneeze. I've named him Pegaso. Only recently schooled, he's young and full of life. Pegaso's bristles tickle my wrists, and I laugh as the boy helps me up. Sitting astride with my dress spread out behind me, I'm ready to ride at the back of the procession.

The townspeople have come out to watch, and I sense their delight at the sight of us for we are wondrous to behold. The Queen leads the parade on a splendid black destrier; no milksop palfrey would suit her. She expects her ladies to be like she is, and to equal the knights in their equestrian skills when they join the hunt. Even though Domina is no longer young, she's energetic and radiates an inner beauty and intelligence that have made her court the place where writers, poets, artists and musicians congregate from miles around. I can't wait to be a part of it and, at the same time, tremble that I might not be worthy.

Three young courtiers are ready to accompany us. They're wearing new-style doublets, so short you can see their bulging codpieces. I regard the men from beneath my eyelashes and recognise one of them. It is the artist; he catches my gaze and I make a face at him. Zorzo from Castelfranco nudges his companions, who fall about with laughter, and the heat spreads to my cheeks, which redden to bright scarlet, I'm sure.

We cross the square and head down the hill. The sound of singing spills out of the tavern. From an upstairs window come the shouts of a housewife, yelling at her children to stop staring at us and do their chores. On the corner, at the farrier's, echo the clash and clamour of pincers and hammers. Women gossip by the fountain where they are washing their clothes. The church bell tolls, calling the faithful to mass.

I'm not sad for I shall return to Asolo from time to time as the court moves between castle and villa. If the Queen pleases, she'll take me to Venice when she goes to visit her family. I smile at the prospect of seeing my birthplace and staying in a magnificent palace on the Grand Canal.

Without warning, the skin at the back of my neck prickles. I catch a strange man staring at me. His skin is pale, and his hair is black like a witch's cat. The sun beats down hard on me, but frost coats my body.

Telling myself not to be fanciful, I focus on keeping my seat. Pegaso has been spooked by the crowds. He rears and prances from side to side. I'm at home in the saddle and can gallop across the fields toward the foothills of Monte Grappa without any difficulty. However, controlling this excitable creature in the midst of all the confusion is beyond my skill.

Maria Santissima!

I lose my seat and tumble from my saddle. Pinpricks of light, and the world around me sways as if it were a tapestry coming away from the wall.

My head was spinning. I felt a tap on my shoulder and turned around. A woman in strange dress was looking at me, concern radiating in her eyes

'Are you ill?'

'Ill?'

Why should I be ill?

'You were swaying. I thought you were about to faint.'

The frescoes had faded, the ceiling had levitated, and the church was empty except for me and this stranger, who was wearing what could only be described as men's clothing, albeit the strangest masculine apparel: straight beige pantaloons and a tight black doublet. Definitely a woman, from her shape. She had long, dark brown hair pulled back from her face and knotted at the nape of her neck, and some sort of tincture above her deep blue eyes. Something only courtesans wore.

Make-up.

The awareness was like a punch on the arm, shocking me into the twentieth century, and I took in a shaky breath.

'Oh,' I said to the woman. 'Please don't worry. I was just… daydreaming.'

'I'm Vanessa Goredan.' The woman held out her hand. 'Pleased to meet you.'

The Contessa! I introduced myself. 'I met your son yesterday. He's having dinner with my aunt and me tomorrow evening.'

'Ah! So you're the reason he changed his plans,' the Contessa said with a laugh.

'Changed his plans?'

'Not to worry. He can see me any time. You're still a bit peaky. Let me offer you an *aperitivo* at the Cipriani.'

'Thank you.' I shuddered at the thought of another drink like the one Luca had given me yesterday. 'I'd love a glass of sparkling water.'

'And you shall have one,' the Contessa said, rising to her feet.

We strolled up the road and into the elegant entrance of the hotel, richly carpeted and lined with display cabinets showcasing expensive jewellery. Feeling underdressed, I glanced down at my scruffy sandals and smoothed my skirt. I almost wished I was wearing my summer work outfit of linen trousers.

The enclosed veranda opened onto the gardens I'd spotted earlier. A bald man was coming toward us, dressed in a dark dress suit, white shirt, and grey tie. He bowed before the Contessa, kissing her hand. 'We are honoured by your presence, Madame.'

'Giuseppe,' she gave a delighted laugh. 'Ever the charmer! We'll sit in the garden as it's such a lovely day. This is Fern, a friend of my son's. Please ask the waiter to bring a bottle of *acqua minerale frizzante* and some of your delicious pastries.'

I sat next to the Contessa at a table under a large umbrella on the patio. 'The manager here oozes charm from every pore,' she said, 'but he's a nice man and keeps this place running like clockwork.'

'It's beautiful.' I breathed in the scent of honeysuckle growing up the side of the building. 'Seems old, but not as old as the church.'

'You're interested in history?' She glanced at me. 'I believe it used to belong to Robert Browning, the English poet, back in the 19th century, but it was built in the mid-16th.'

I sat back and closed my eyes, the logical part of my brain fighting with the illogical events of the morning. What I'd experienced in the church had been beyond illogical, though; it had been completely, mind-blowingly incredible. I turned to the Contessa and said, 'I can feel the past here in Asolo. It could be my imagination. Except it's so vivid, it's as if I'm there.'

'Are you psychic?' She raised a brow.

I laughed softly. 'Not at all. I've always thought anything like that a load of old rubbish.'

'I wouldn't dismiss the spirit world, Fern. As Shakespeare said, "there are more things in heaven and earth, Horatio, than are dreamt of in your philosophy".'

A rush of embarrassment washed through me. 'I'm sorry, I didn't mean to offend your beliefs.'

'No offence taken. But I'm certain that the dead can manifest themselves to us. Our villa, for instance, has a presence in it. Not a malevolent one, mind you. Sometimes, I hear the sound of a lute. Comforting, in a way.'

What would she think if I told her I'd not only heard a lute but had seen the musician himself? She'd think I was bat-shit crazy, that's what.

'I'm researching our family tree,' the Contessa added. 'Only I haven't come across the lute-player yet.'

I picked up a small doughnut, sugar scattered on top, and bit into it. *Custard-filled. Delicious.* I eyed Luca's mother; she was leaning forward, staring into her glass, her long elegant fingers spread around the top. 'Is your home in Asolo?' I asked.

'No, it's halfway between here and Bassano. I'm only in Asolo today as I've been to visit an old lady, Freya Stark, the

English writer and explorer. She lives near the Santa Caterina church and was a friend of my mother-in-law's.'

'How interesting.' I tried to make my voice sound knowledgeable. I had no idea who the writer was.

The Contessa's eyes met mine as she put her glass down. 'You must come and see our villa one day. It's quite famous.'

'I'd like that.' I pressed the pastry crumbs on my plate with my finger. 'There's so much to see around here, and I'm only in Italy till the end of the month.'

'Have you been to Venice yet?'

'It's on my "to do" list.'

A whispered sigh of approval stroked my cheek.

I lifted my hand and brushed it away.

The air seemed to crackle around me. *Stay focused on the present, Fern!*

I fixed my gaze on the Contessa. 'I'm looking for a good spot to do some painting. Can you suggest somewhere?'

'Why not stroll up to the Sant'Anna cemetery? There're some wonderful views.'

'Is it very old?'

'Dates back centuries.'

'Oh, maybe not,' I said, remembering that the girl in my vision— if that's what it was— Cecilia, had mentioned the year 1504. 'Is there anywhere only dating from, maybe, a couple of hundred years ago?'

Luca's mother gave me a questioning look. 'Why not stay here? The gardens would make a lovely subject. I'll clear it with Giuseppe for you, if you like.'

'Thank you.'

'I meant what I said about visiting the villa. I'd love it if you could meet my daughter. Luca's sister, Chiara.' The contessa sighed. 'She's got herself involved with the wrong crowd at university. They go around distributing leaflets about how the Veneto should become independent of Italy. I just hope they aren't about to become terrorists.'

'What a worry for you!'

And it must be, or she wouldn't be sharing it with me, someone she's only just met.

'It's that boyfriend of hers, Federico, I'm sure of it. He's got her twisted around his little finger. Luca and I keep telling her how unsuitable he is, but the more we try and convince her the more she turns to the boy. It would be nice for her to meet someone sane like you.'

Not that sane…

Within minutes the Contessa had arranged a small table overlooking the valley and a glass of water for my paintbrush. Then she took her leave, assuring me of an invitation to dinner via her son.

I opened my rucksack and took out a small board. I frowned. Had I been suffering from hallucinations? *Not exactly.* After clipping paper onto the board, I started to work. Spreading water onto the paper, I wondered if I could be reliving a past life.

Ridiculous. There's no such thing as reincarnation.

I added paint to my palette, a small plastic tray. Maybe the young woman, Cecilia, was a projection of myself? I began transferring the scene in front of me onto the paper: the cypress trees, the vineyards and the olive groves. There were definitely some similarities between me and her— the same hair and build and something about Cecilia's personality that reminded me of myself before…

That's it! Must be something to do with the fire, some bizarre warp in my brain related to the trauma I'd suffered.

I dried my brush on the old rag I kept in my bag, then scuffed it and rubbed it on the palette. Time to add some leaves. *And time to get a grip on yourself, Fern!*

CHAPTER 4

'You should have an afternoon nap, my lovely,' Auntie said, picking up the plates and taking them to the dishwasher after we'd eaten. 'Then we can go for a stroll and I'll show you what's left of the Barco. It would make a fabulous setting for one of your watercolours.'

'Barco?' I asked, handing her a wine glass,

'Caterina Cornaro's country estate. There's part of the east wing still standing, and this house is built near to where the west wing once stood.'

A chill sliced through me. Cecilia had been about to set off for the Queen's villa when her horse had spooked, and she'd taken a fall.

With a sigh, I poured myself a glass of water and took it up to my room. There was a packet of valerian tablets on my bedside table, and I swallowed two. Stretched out on my bed, I stared at the wall opposite. Auntie had framed a watercolour I'd sent her of Westminster Abbey. I'd sold the same print to a greetings card company only last month, with the promise of further commissions as soon as I could come up with them. Art was what had saved my sanity after I'd lost Harry.

Sudden pain pierced me.

He'd been everything I'd ever wanted, and he'd died because of me.

Tears prickled, but I bottled up my unhappiness. It was something I'd got used to doing; if I'd let them flow, I wouldn't have been able to stop.

Don't think about Harry!

Don't think about what you did!

Don't think about how he died!

Sleep came eventually, and the next thing I knew Auntie was calling from outside my door.

'Wakey, wakey!'

I so loved her old-fashioned expressions.

I rubbed my eyes and glanced at my travel clock. Five pm. I'd slept for over three hours. No wonder I still felt groggy. 'Give me a minute,' I called out.

In the bathroom, I stared at my reflection, but it had started to blur.

I squinted, and the image wavered like a ripple across a pond.

'*Lorenza…*' The whisper tickled my neck.

I spun around.

No one.

I looked at the mirror again and let out a gasp.

Another woman was staring back at me.

The woman had the same colour hair as mine, and there was something about her that was familiar. She had my mouth and the shape of her face was like mine, also the curve of her lips and the arch of her eyebrows. Her eyes were different, though… deep brown whereas mine were green. And she was much younger than me.

I blinked and caught my own refection. The apparition, if that's what it was, had disappeared.

With determined steps, I returned to my bedroom, holding the image in my mind. My sketchpad was on the desk and I grabbed it along with a pencil. It only took a couple of minutes to produce a rough outline of the face, even though my hands were shaking and my heart thudding. I stared at the result. I'd sketched a self-portrait. Pure and simple.

Just my imagination getting the better of me.

Again.

I let out the breath I'd been holding, closed the pad and put it into my rucksack along with the rest of my sketching pencils.

Auntie had said the Barco was worth painting.

I'll make a start on something today and try to forget all this weirdness.

I was a rational person; I'd never given in to occult imaginings before, and I wasn't in any fit state currently for all that silliness. At school, when my classmates had messed about with Ouija boards and tarot cards, I'd been the level-headed one who'd talked them out of their fantasies.

I'll carry on being level-headed now.

Crickets screeched in the low bushes beside the dusty road as I strolled with Auntie toward a group of buildings. The air was oppressively hot and sweat beaded my hairline.

'It seems we're in for a thunderstorm,' Auntie said, pointing at the bank of clouds gathered over the distant mountains.

Within minutes, she was pushing open a gate to what looked like an abandoned farmyard. I trailed behind, my heart fluttering.

I know this place.

On my right, I spotted faded frescoes of a hunting scene. Ladies and knights on horses, giving chase to a deer. Something stirred in my memory, and a picture came into my mind of strong arms holding a paintbrush.

I glanced in the direction of the far end of the building. Where were the fish ponds, the gardens, and the peacocks strutting about with their tails fanned? The courtyard should be peppered with courtiers or at least their servants, the air redolent with the scent of herbs and spices from the kitchens. All I could see were cornfields. And what had happened to the towers and fortifications?

My legs dragged and soon Auntie had left me behind. Almost in a dream, I sat on the balustrade below one of a set of five rounded columns. They reached to roof height and were mirrored on the opposite side of the building, creating an open area like a patio.

A loggia, that's what it's called . . .

I took out my sketchpad, but my head had started spinning and that buzzing I'd experienced this morning echoed in my ears.

'Cecilia!'

I swivel around and let out a gasp.

'Dorotea! You gave me a fright!'

'I don't know why that should be,' Dorotea mutters. She pouts in that annoying way of hers. 'There's nothing frightening about me.'

'It is true that she is pretty, with her chestnut-coloured hair and milk-white complexion. She's one of the Queen's ladies like me, but Dorotea flaunts herself before the court, constantly pulling down her gown to show off her plump breasts, lumpy like pillows. I glance down at my own chest. There would be no point in my doing the same. My bosoms are as small as my fists.

'I have searched for you everywhere,' she says. 'Why are you sitting here?'

I peer around and give a shiver. I had been feeling lost for some unfathomable reason; the world about me had crumbled and changed. But now everything is as it should be, and I tell myself not to let fantasies rule my mind. 'I was daydreaming,' I say, slipping the sheet of paper and black chalk into my pocket.

I will not show my work to anyone.

Dorotea lets out a dismissive laugh. Far be it for her to ever have her head in the clouds or even do anything the slightest bit creative. 'Domina requests our presence,' she says. 'There's to be a banquet this evening. For the Hapsburg Emperor and his wife.'

We make our way upstairs to the Queen's chamber and Dorotea whispers, 'Pietro Bembo will also be at the feast. He proposed a liaison last time he was here. I would love to be his mistress.'

I glance at her, torn between disapproval and jealousy. The Queen insists her ladies keep their virtue, and I have done so. Except Bembo, her kinsman, is possessed of such wit and good looks that Dorotea has sought his attention. I pray she will not be hurt, for his station is higher than hers and this can only be a dalliance on his part, especially as he is a cleric. I sigh to myself; it would be wonderful if he decided to read from his discourse on love. He wrote it on the occasion of Fiammetta's wedding, and I long to hear it.

I miss my sister. Fiammetta is expecting a child— as she should be after a year of marriage. I pull at a loose strand of hair. What is it like to lie with a man? The thought makes my chest squeeze and the blood pulse between my legs. Yet I know that I would not give myself to any man who flattered me; I'm hoping for marriage.

Stupid Cecilia, your life is here with Queen Caterina. No one will want you as you are poor and, even if the courtiers compliment you on your beauty, and your bloodline is noble, none of them will take you to the altar.

It has been the greatest surprise of my twelve months at court that men should consider me beautiful in spite of my small bosoms.

As if reading my thoughts, Dorotea says, 'Isn't it about time you took a lover, Cecilia?'

'M… m… me?'

'I have seen the gleam in men's eyes – even Bembo's – yet you seem oblivious to their admiration. What are you waiting for?'

'I'm not waiting.' I cannot tell Dorotea of my hopes for a good marriage like my sister, and of going to my wedding night pure. Dorotea would think me naive; she would not be wrong, perhaps. 'The Queen keeps me close to her. There has not been the opportunity.'

'Not true and you know it,' she says, and her laughter echoes up the stairwell. She pinches my cheek. 'This fair flesh will fade before too long. How old are you now?'

'Sixteen,' I cannot keep the irritation from my voice. Who is she to talk to me this way? Only one year older, and the daughter of a local aristocrat who has fallen on hard times, she has much in common with me.

Except for her easy virtue.

'Let's hurry,' I say. 'Domina doesn't like to be kept waiting.' And I bite my tongue before I let it give her a piece of my mind.

The wooden stairs have been polished until they gleam, and the soft soles of my shoes make no sound as I follow Dorotea to the landing. 'Just a moment. I need to wash my hands.'

There's a washstand at the end of the corridor and a jug of water beside it. I glance at my reflection in the mirror and let out a yelp. A strange woman is staring back at me. Her hair is uncovered, and it is unruly like mine. The woman has a look of me, except her eyes are green. I glance behind me, yet there's no one there. And when I gaze in the mirror again, it is only myself that I see. *Very strange!* I didn't take any wine at lunch, so I can't blame my vision on drink. Only a figment of my imagination, I decide.

I wash the black chalk from my fingers, turn on my heel, and go to the Queen. She smiles when she sees Dorotea and me. 'My sweet girls,' she says. 'What took you so long?'

We drop into deep curtseys and, as I rise, I feel as if I am not really there but looking at myself from a great distance. The same feeling that I had when I was sitting in the loggia. *How odd!* Pure whimsy, I tell myself and brush the feeling aside. Yet, a chill squeezes my heart at the same time.

'Fetch my best pearls,' Domina commands. 'And I would like to wear cloth of gold this evening. In honour of our visitors.'

Running a comb through the Queen's thinning hair, I wonder about the Emperor and his wife, Bianca Maria Sforza, the daughter of the Duke of Milan. Is she beautiful?

'Ouch,' Domina says. 'Take care!'

'Pray forgive me,' I mumble, dropping into another curtsey. My poor queen has suffered so much from my ineptitude when dressing her. She has a soft spot for me, however, thank the Holy Virgin, and always excuses me.

The banqueting hall next to the loggia is large, with three long tables making the three sides of a square. We sit at the central table. Musicians tune their instruments in the gallery at the far end.

I gaze around at the assembled company and let out a gasp. Seated at the right of the Empress, is a man I am sure I have seen before. He's short and thin, his face is pale, and there is a scar on his left cheek. With a shudder, I turn my glance to Bembo, on the Queen's left. Fair-haired and light-eyed, he is the complete opposite of the stranger. Bembo speaks in Tuscan, the language in which he writes. I can follow his discourse without difficulty, for I have studied the great writers of that province. Nevertheless, I wish he would not show off so. I would prefer him to speak Venetian.

'Well, Bembo,' Queen Caterina says. 'You think we should all be conversing in the tongue of Florence, do you?'

'In every town in Italy the mode of speech is different from everywhere else.' His smile is lopsided. 'Yet Florentine is the language of Petrarch, and this is the model I take for my writing, for it is the most lucid and elegant. Do not call this Tuscan, but Italian.'

'There is no such thing as Italy,' she huffs. 'Even the Borgia Pope failed to conquer us all and form one state.'

Bembo gives her a steely look. 'Not so. There is strength in unification. Italy needs to face up to the French and the Spanish.'

'I agree,' the Emperor Maximilian interjects. I remember he was unable to stop the French king from conquering his wife's city of Milan four years ago. I eye his beaky nose and loose, fleshy lower lip. An ugly man and his wife is scarcely a beauty either, with her receding chin.

'Hmm,' the Queen responds, ever gracious. She is a daughter of the Venetian Republic; I know all talk of a unified Italy is an anathema to her. 'When do you print *Gli Asolani*?' she asks Bembo, changing the subject.

'Soon, Domina.'

'Then I shall reserve judgement on the lingua franca until I have read it.'

And I too.

My attention is distracted by Zantos, the Queen's dwarf, who is prancing in front of us, juggling five golden balls. Far be it for him to crack vulgar jokes. Domina grants us such liberty that, with the exception of Bembo (who holds her affection in spite of his argumentative nature), we all consider that the most pleasurable thing possible is to please her, and the most displeasing thing in the world is to earn her displeasure.

The food comes, and I try to behave in a ladylike fashion and nibble. Yet, I'm hungry (I have a greedy streak), and want to eat until I am stuffed fit to bursting. For the antipasto there's a caper, truffle and raisin salad in pastry, as well as a second salad of greens with citron juice and anchovy. There are also radishes carved into animal shapes, little cream pies, *prosciutto* of pork tongue, boar pies, smoked mullet, and gilt-head bream. I help myself to everything.

The first hot course arrives. I can't resist the capon fritters sprinkled with sugar, the roasted quails and pheasants, the pigeons in puff pastry, the meatballs, veal, carp, turbot and shrimp. I chew my food slowly, remembering how the beef was always tough and overcooked in Asolo, not like the fine fare we eat at the Barco, where the Queen employs the best chefs. The castle in Asolo was rough and rudimentary; my home for so many years, it now seems like a lifetime ago.

I'm fairly groaning by the time the third course arrives: partridge, rabbit, turtledoves, sausages and more fish. The fourth course consists of a rice pie and I barely take a mouthful. I wish I'd copied Queen Caterina; she eats so daintily and merely picks at the morsels she cuts with her trencher knife. Suckling pig follows then peacock, only now I feel sick. I allow myself a few vegetables for the sixth course then almonds in syrup to finish.

The meal seems to go on forever, but my attention has been caught by the young man who sits quietly at the end of the table. The artist, Zorzo from Castelfranco. He has been absent from court this past year, engaged with commissions in Venice. It has been the greatest disappointment of my early months here that the painter had departed, for he fascinates me.

Signor Zorzo says little to those on either side of him, and simply observes us all. *Maria Santissima!* He is so handsome. I'm struck by his attractiveness, for there is no other word to describe his countenance— his regular features, sun-darkened skin, and eyes fringed with long, dark lashes.

After dinner, the Emperor and his wife retire, for they have a long journey tomorrow. The court parades to the Queen's rooms. There we sit in a circle arranged one man, one woman, one man. She announces, 'It is my wish that you should begin the games this evening, Cecilia.'

'Surely not I.' Shocked, I am, for this is the first time she has made such a request of me. I catch the artist looking at me. Could I be mistaken, or did he give me a wink?

'It has been a year since your debut, my dear,' she says. 'I believe you have grown in maturity and wisdom. Please commence!'

I rack my brains for some witty proposition and all I can think of is, 'Why not have each of us suggest some game he likes that has not been played before; and then the choice will be made of the one that seems worthiest of us?' I turn to Bembo and ask him to state what his proposal will be.

He replies, 'You must tell yours first.'

'But I've already done so.' I smile at the Queen, 'Domina, I beg your help in ordering him to do what he is told.'

She laughs. 'So that everyone will obey you, I give you my authority.'

Bembo bows his head to me. 'I would like our game to be that each of us should say whether, if the one he loves has need to be angry with him, he would want the reason for her anger to be found within her or in himself. This way, we shall establish whether it is more painful to give displeasure to the person one loves or to receive it from them.'

Probably something he has written in *Gli Asolani*, I think, but I do not voice my thoughts.

I make a sign to Dorotea that it is her turn, but Domina

interjects. 'Since Lady Cecilia is unwilling to give herself the trouble of suggesting a game, it is only right for the other ladies to enjoy the same privilege and also be exempt from making any effort this evening, especially as we have so many men with us that there is no danger of running out of games.'

'Very well then,' I say, taking in Dorotea's smirk. I glance at the pale-skinned man with the scar on his cheek, whom I now know is Lodovico Gaspare, a visitor from the court of the Duke of Ferrara. He inclines his head toward me and grins, his teeth white but uneven.

'The game I would like played this evening is that each of us should say what quality he would most like the person he loves to possess. Then, since everyone must have some defect, what fault he would choose as well.'

The Queen claps her hands. 'An excellent game,' she says, in her low soft voice. 'The best. Cecilia, you must tell us what you think.'

I stare at her, tongue-tied. Then I blush and stutter, desperate to come up with something. She nods her head. 'Dear girl, I should not have asked you. What knowledge do you have of love?'

It is the way Domina speaks to people that I most admire; it is always with such charm. How could anyone not wish to delight her? I've let her down, I feel, and sit in silence as the rest of the court carries on the game.

Finally, the Queen stands, and it is as if a thread has passed from the ceiling to her head so erect does she hold herself. 'Come, child,' she says to me, 'Take me to my chamber.'

Her words ring in my head. *Child.* So true, for that is what I am until a man lays with me.

Oh, that it could be my future husband…

'Did you see the way he was staring at you?' Dorotea asks as we undress in our room above the stables after the Queen has retired. 'If only Bembo would look at me that way!'

'What do you mean?' My mouth gapes, like one of the fish in the pond at the centre of Domina's garden when I crumble bread across the surface. Surely the artist's glance at me was not that obvious?

'If his eyes had been tongues, they would have licked you,' Dorotea giggles.

My cheeks burn, but at the same time pleasure thrills through me.

The next day I can hardly contain my excitement. When the time comes to dress the Queen's hair, my fingers tremble so much that I drop the comb again.

'Goodness me, sweet girl,' she says. 'You're even more clumsy than usual. Whatever is the matter?'

I apologise before going to my room and attending to my own toilette. I change my over-gown to one of deep pink and steal a glance at myself in the mirror. No strange woman there, so I stick my tongue out at my reflection. Then I remember I'm supposed to act like a lady. Sometimes I find it hard to put aside my childish nature.

'There! See him eating you with his eyes!' Dorotea points at Lodovico Gaspare and disappointment wells up in me. She hadn't meant the artist at all. I glance around for him, but he isn't here. 'They say he's extremely wealthy,' Dorotea adds. 'He could set you up in a fine house with your own servants. Think about it, Cecilia. Do not turn your nose up at such a man.'

If she knew my secret desire for a husband, she would laugh in my face.

Tonight, we dance the *pavana*. Simple and slow. Lodovico Gaspare takes my hand and leads me onto the floor in procession with the other dancers. We step forwards then move apart, again and again.

'Tell me about Ferrara,' I say to him when the dance brings us together.

'What do you wish to know?'

'Is it like Asolo?'

He laughs. 'Not at all. Ferrara is much bigger and far noisier. There are many walls and gates encircling the moated city, which is crossed by long, wide roads. Every day there seems to be another new building. At the centre rises the Duke's castle, a miracle of construction.'

The dance moves us apart and I wait until we meet again before saying, 'I think I would like Ferrara, but my favourite city of all is Venice.'

A scowl passes across his face, then he composes himself; I must have imagined the frown. Something about him makes me nervous, but I put it down to his *ferrarese* accent and his stern countenance. When he suggests a breath of fresh air outside, I ignore the tickle of disquiet that strokes my chest and agree. We step into the loggia and sit on the balustrade.

Lodovico Gaspare intrigues me; he's not like the other courtiers. Reckless, I know, but I tell myself he will do me no harm. I find it exciting to have an admirer, even if that person does not make my heart flutter in the same way as does the artist.

The cool night air is a soft caress against my throat. Crickets chirp from the garden shrubs and the new moon cuts a thin sliver of silver in a sky that swells with stars. I know I should not be alone with a man who is not my betrothed. He will think me shameless. Yet Dorotea's words ring in my head, and I cannot help feeling flattered that a man should look at me in the way she described. Surely, he is a gentleman and will treat me like a lady?

I shiver as I feel again that sense of dislocation, as if I am regarding myself from afar. There's a shadow on the other side of the terrace. Lodovico Gaspare takes my hand and lifts it to his lips. The shadow moves forwards and bows.

Zorzo from Castelfranco!

Heat rushes to my face and I start to feel faint.

My head was spinning.

'Fern, are you all right?' Auntie rushed up to me. 'I thought

37

you were behind, but when I looked behind, I couldn't see you anywhere.'

The feeling was ten times worse than waking in the middle of a dream and being unable to distinguish between reality and that dream. My stomach heaved. I'd been whooshed through hundreds of years of history, and now I felt sick. 'I'm sorry.' I glanced down for my sketchpad. *It must have fallen out of my hands.* 'I was miles away.'

'That you were. I was going to suggest we go home. Look at the sky!'

I peered at the dark thunder clouds and folded my arms around my body, suddenly cold. Fat drops of rain splattered the dusty path. I hurried with Auntie as quickly as her chubby legs would allow. By the time we'd arrived at the house, a squall was sheeting across the cornfields, the vineyards, and the olive trees, plastering my hair to my face.

'Run upstairs and get changed into something dry,' Auntie puffed as she closed the front door. 'I'll put some soup on before I do the same.'

In the bathroom, I stared at my reflection.

My reflection, not Cecilia's.

What the hell has been happening to me?

Something beyond a daydream had taken place in the Barco. I still felt nauseated and faint from the jolt back to the twentieth century.

Pull yourself together! You are NOT Cecilia, you're Fern.

The girl was in my head, though, her annoyance festering that I'd left her behind, her neediness. *Need for what?* I glanced down, half-expecting to see my legs swathed in a long gown, still remembering the weight of it, the feel of the heavy brocade and the tightness of the bodice over my breasts. I shook my head. *Am I going insane?*

A grumble of thunder echoed. Lightning streaked the darkened sky outside the window. A quiver of fear twisted my stomach. *Don't be silly, you're perfectly safe.* I reached for a towel and dried my hair. Shivering, I stepped out of my soaking wet skirt and pulled on a pair of jeans and a sweater.

Down in the kitchen, Auntie handed me a wooden spoon. 'Stir the soup for me, my lovely, while I go and change.'

The aroma of simmering vegetables was mixed with something else. Burnt wood. *Shit*! My heart thudded. Another rumble of thunder echoed, much closer than before, followed by a loud crack like a gunshot, then sudden darkness.

The damn lights have gone.

In the glow from the gas flame under the saucepan, I could make out a faint outline moving in my direction.

The hairs on my arms stood on end.

A flashlight glowed.

Auntie!

'The power company always shuts down the grid during a storm like this. I've no idea why.' She lifted a candle holder down from the shelf. After fumbling in a drawer for a box of matches, she lit the taper. 'Put this on the table, love, and I'll serve up the soup.'

I sliced a chunk of bread and helped myself to some cheese. 'This is delicious,' I said, the rich taste coating my tongue. *A memory. I've eaten this before.*

'It's called Asiago and comes from the mountains behind us. We could go up there one day, maybe.'

'That would be nice.' A chance to get away from here. Away from the smell of burnt wood. Away from associations with fire.

Another peal of thunder crashed, followed by a zigzag of lightning. A sudden cacophony reverberated, sounding like thousands of pebbles lashing the side of the house. 'What's that?'

'Hailstones,' Auntie said. 'Can you help me close the shutters? If you shut the ones upstairs, I'll fasten those down here. We don't want any broken glass. Take the flashlight!'

I ran up to Auntie's room first. The bathroom was next, and then I scurried into my own bedroom. The wind had blown the window open; through it, I could see fireworks being launched into the darkness. *Fireworks!*

Grasping the latch, I tugged at the frame. A hailstone, big as a golf ball, caught me on the finger and I yelped.

Back in the kitchen, I asked, 'What's with the fireworks?'

'Oh, the farmers think the explosions will break up the hail, so it doesn't damage the grapes.' Auntie smiled. 'Talking of which, let's have a glass of wine to cheer ourselves up.'

She fetched the already open bottle from the counter and poured. I took a sip. *That's better. No need to worry.* 'I think I'll stay at home tomorrow. And do some painting.'

'Good idea, love. I'll get on with my writing. Don't forget that Luca is coming for supper.'

I glanced at her. 'Need any help with that?'

She patted my hand. 'I'll cook roast beef and Yorkshire puds to remind him of England. Perhaps you can make a nice English trifle?'

'Of course.' I turned away from her, pain coursing through me. Trifle had been Harry's favourite. I swallowed the sudden sorrow in my throat.

Oh, Harry!

CHAPTER 5

$\mathscr{L}$*uca*

I stirred my coffee, replete with the fine food served up by Susan and Fern. The dinner had been a surprise; from my experience, the English tended to overcook their beef. Not that Susan was English; she'd announced proudly that she was Welsh. I'd never been to Wales and had no experience of the food there…

Even though I had a British passport as well as an Italian one, my preferences were geared toward the local cuisine. But, to give credit where it was due, Susan's Yorkshire puddings had been as light as air, and Fern's sherry and raspberry trifle had enticed me into having two servings. I rubbed my stomach. 'Thank you for a delicious meal.'

'You're most welcome,' Susan said. 'It's nice for Fern to have someone around who's closer to her own age than me, although perhaps you're a little older than she is.'

A cough came from the other side of the table. 'I'll be thirty on my next birthday,' Fern huffed. 'Not that much younger than you, Luca, I'd guess.'

I grinned. 'Three years. I suppose we're both part of the baby-boom generation.'

Susan levered herself out of her chair. 'Well, I'm feeling a bit tired. I'll leave you two baby boomers to load up the dishwasher. Just make sure you lock the door and shut the lights before you come up to bed, Fern.'

I watched Susan shuffle over to the wrought-iron stairs. The proverbial eccentric British woman. I liked her for the fact that she didn't seem to care what others thought about her. The way she dressed, for instance, and her unkempt hair. Not the sort of person I'd imagined would be a highly successful romance writer. Maybe she lived vicariously through her characters?

I got to my feet and reached for Fern's coffee cup. 'Lead me to the kitchen sink.' I let out a self-deprecating laugh. 'But don't try and give me an apron.'

It felt companionable, standing next to her as we stacked the dishwasher. Throughout the dinner, I'd tried to draw her out. She'd listened to me talk about my work yet hadn't said much about herself. How to find out if she had a boyfriend? Could I come right out and ask? *Don't be a fool, Luca! She's only here for a few weeks.* Fern didn't strike me as being the sort of girl who'd be up for a vacation fling, or any sort of fling for that matter. Best to keep it casual. 'My mother asked me to remember her to you,' I said.

'She was lovely to me in Asolo when I had another of my "funny turns".' Fern paused. 'I think it was more than that, actually.'

'Oh?'

She wrinkled her nose. 'Can you smell anything unusual?'

I sniffed. 'No.'

'Well, I can. Not all the time.' She picked up a cup from the sink and twisted it in her hands. 'Occasionally, the odour of burnt wood in this house is really strong.'

I thought for a moment. 'I've heard that sometimes people smell things which remind them of a particular experience.'

'That could be it.' She frowned down into the cup. 'I was at Kings Cross Station when they had that tragic fire.'

'God! How awful! Were you hurt?' I asked, shocked.

'No, I was on the escalator, saw the fire, and ran back down again.' She twisted the cup, staring at her hands. 'I suffered a little physically from smoke inhalation. And a whole lot more mentally from the trauma.'

Her fingers were shaking, and I took the cup from her. 'I'm so sorry. What a horrible experience.'

'And now I think I'm going crazy,' she said, her voice rasping. 'I've been having the weirdest visions since coming to Italy. It's like I'm being possessed by some sort of restless spirit.'

I fought to stop myself from staring open-mouthed. 'What do you mean?'

She shook her head. 'You'll think I've lost it.'

'I won't think anything of the kind,' I half-lied.

'Remember when you told me about Caterina Cornaro?' Fern met my gaze.

I nodded. *Where's this going?*

'I think I'm reliving a life as one of her ladies.' Her breath caught, and she looked away from me. 'I'm scared I'm having some sort of breakdown,' she added quietly.

Holy hell! I was an architect; I believed in hard evidence not fantasy. For the second time in a few minutes, I was lost for words. I chewed on my lip. 'Would you like to come for dinner tomorrow night and talk about this with my mother. She's a tad otherworldly, for want of a better word, and won't be at all shocked by what you've told me.'

'Whereas you are?' Fern asked quietly.

'I'm surprised, more like. It's not the sort of thing I've come across much. Indeed ever, to be honest.' I gave her what I hoped was a reassuring smile. Her eyes had taken on a "rabbit caught in the headlights" expression. I touched her hand. She jumped back as if she'd been stung.

'I shouldn't have said anything.' She folded her arms. 'You must think I'm more than a little insane.'

'Of course, I don't.' I adopted a reassuring tone. 'Trauma does strange things to people. For example, someone who survived a fire may smell smoke when they feel anxious.'

'You're probably right,' she said with a sigh. 'But it's more the visions than the odour of burnt wood that I find disturbing. They seem so real.'

'Please tell me about them.'

Maybe by talking, she'd lose that "scared rabbit" look.

We returned to the kitchen table and I listened while she told me about what she'd experienced in Asolo and at the Barco. It didn't sound like anything she could have read about or seen in a film. There hadn't been any movies made about Caterina Cornaro, as far as I was aware, and the books wouldn't have described such detail. I needed to go to the library and find out more about this kind of psychosis. If that's what it was. Had to be. The alternative was unthinkable.

'So, you see,' she said. 'I'm a bit fragile at the moment. But I'd love to come to dinner. I'm sure Auntie will be happy for me to take the car, and she'll be glad of an evening on her own to devote to her reading or writing.'

'I'll pick you up.' *Couldn't risk her having one of those visions while driving.* 'Would seven o'clock be a good time?'

'Thanks, and apologies again for laying all this on you.' A smile curled her beautiful bow-shaped lips. 'Talking about it has helped, actually. And it will be good to get away from here tomorrow. Your mother might be able to offer some suggestions about how to block Cecilia from my mind.'

'I'll prep her beforehand.' I rose from the chair and held out my hand. 'Good night, Fern, and thank you for an interesting evening.'

She saw me to the door and closed it behind me. I sat behind the wheel of my Alfa and shook my head. Fern was damned attractive, beautiful even, but she was clearly suffering from post-traumatic stress. I was playing with fire even considering helping her, except there was no question of my stepping back. She had drawn me into her orbit like a moth to a flame and there wasn't a damn thing I could do about it.

CHAPTER 6

*T*he villa stood in solitary grandeur in a sea of green fields. Auntie had mentioned it had been designed by the sixteenth century architect, Andrea Palladio. I did a double take at the sight of such beauty. And wealth. Remembering Vanessa Goredan's understated elegance, I'd put on something smart: one of my work outfits, a pair of white linen trousers and a navy-blue cotton blouse. I'd struggled with my hair after washing it and had tamed it by getting Auntie to help me with a loose braid. Hopefully, I wouldn't look too out of place.

All the way to the villa, I'd argued with myself about whether to tell Luca not to say anything to his mother. Then I'd remembered he was going to prep her beforehand. How embarrassing to have blurted everything out to him last night. I barely knew him, yet I'd shared something that would categorise me as crazy by anyone's standards.

Gravel crunched under the tyres of Luca's red Alfa Romeo convertible as he parked up. Two chocolate brown Labradors bounded toward him, wagging their tails. He introduced them as Jason and Sam. After stroking their silky ears, I walked with him up a wide ramp with a gentle slope. A flight of steps led up to the loggia at the centre of the villa, which took the form of a portico crowned by a gable that made me think of a Greek temple front. It was awe-inspiring. *No other word could describe it.*

'See those,' Luca said, pointing out the two colonnaded wings at each side of the main building. 'They originally housed the grain stores, which needed to be under cover.'

'What sort of grain?' I asked, staring at the most beautiful so-called storage areas I'd ever seen.

'My family introduced the cultivation of corn here' He pulled in a deep breath. 'Now it's grown all over the Veneto and has become a staple in the form of polenta.'

'Polenta? That's what the Americans call grits, isn't it?'

His smile was easy. 'Similar, but polenta is made from ground yellow corn and is much coarser.'

I tilted my head toward him. 'Do you still grow it?'

'Yes. And we also have vineyards and our own wine label. My brother, Antonio, has taken over running the estate since our father died. We no longer store the corn here, by the way, but have built barns over there.' He pointed to the left. 'The offices and family accommodation are now in the wings. The original living area is open to the public three days a week, and far too swanky for us. I'll give you a quick tour of the *piano nobile* then we'll go out to the garden.'

'Sounds like a plan,' I smiled.

He led me into a large, square room, richly decorated with frescos. 'You can see why we don't live here. It would be like living in a museum.'

'So beautiful,' I said, my feet sliding on the smooth marble floor. The walls were decked with paintings of gods and goddesses indulging in rural pursuits. It was unlike any house I'd ever been in, and unease spread through me.

I'm way out of my comfort zone here.

Outside the window, I could see a private garden with mani-cured lawns and flower-beds. An umbrella shaded a table on the patio in the corner. Trailing geraniums tumbled from urns, and red roses crowded a bed hugging the honeysuckle-smothered wall. About ten times bigger than Auntie's patch, and Mum and Dad's country garden near Chepstow in the UK. It was more the sort of place Cecilia was used to, living a life of luxury in Caterina Cornaro's Barco, than what I'd experienced up to now. The lump of unease had lodged in my throat and I swallowed hard.

'My mother's waiting for us.' Luca took my hand. At his touch, the tension within me evaporated. A friendly gesture, not a come-on, and reassuring for its naturalness.

'How lovely to see you again,' Vanessa Goredan said, glancing up from her seat as we entered the garden. The Labradors had flopped down at her feet, and both rolled over for me to tickle their bellies. 'Please take a seat," her face broke into a smile. 'Luca will fetch us a bottle of Prosecco and we can toast your first visit to the villa.'

I pulled out a chair and sat on the soft cushion. The air was filled with the jasmine scent of honeysuckle. *No odour of burnt wood here.* 'Thank you for inviting me, Contessa Goredan.'

'Please, call me Vanessa,' her voice purred. 'Now, tell me. Luca mentioned that you've been having strange visions. I thought something was going on when I saw you swaying in the church the other day.'

'Didn't want you to think I'd gone crazy. If someone had told me a couple of days ago that they'd experienced what I've been experiencing, I would have thought they'd totally lost it.'

'I can assure you I won't think anything like that.' Vanessa's eyes met mine. 'Remember the lute-player I told you about?'

'Yes…. Okay…' I released my pent-up breath and told her everything – from the ghostly whispers in Auntie's kitchen to my strange experiences in Asolo and at the Barco; they didn't sound as weird as they had done when I'd blurted out my concerns to Luca last night. 'What do you think?' I asked Vanessa when I'd finished recounting the whole sorry saga.

She eyed me with a thoughtful expression. 'Well, in my opinion you're lucky.'

'Lucky?'

'I mean to have been given the chance to re-experience the past so vividly.'

'I don't feel lucky. I feel… I feel as if I've become some sort of conduit.'

'Possibly,' she said. 'Cecilia seems to be using you to tell her story.'

'But why? And why me?'

'Is there something you might have in common with the girl?'

I creased my brow, trying to come up with an explanation. 'The only thing I can think of is that Cecilia has ambitions to be an artist. She likes to draw.'

'That could well be why she's selected you.' Vanessa tapped her chin. 'What about this odour of burnt wood? Luca said you were at King's Cross when they had that awful fire. Perhaps fire is another thing you share?'

I clasped my hands to hide their trembling and my heart gave a stutter. 'Cecilia might have been in a fire?'

'She could well have been. Most of the Barco was destroyed by fire in 1509. Perhaps she was caught up in it?'

Fear pierced me. 'I don't want to relive a fire.' I suddenly felt sick. 'There must be some way I can block Cecilia from my mind...'

'If she's a restless spirit, it might be a good idea to call on the local priest and ask him to bless your aunt's house,' Vanessa said calmly. 'If you wear a cross around your neck, it might afford you some protection.'

I let out a gasp. 'Do you think Cecilia wants to harm me?'

Vanessa shook her head. 'Quite honestly, I don't know what to think, my dear.' Her eyes followed a bumblebee dipping and darting over the flower bed. 'Have you talked to your aunt about what's been happening to you?'

'Not yet. I'm planning to tell her. Just haven't got 'round to it...' No point in explaining my reluctance. Auntie couldn't hear or smell what I'd heard and smelt in the house; she probably wouldn't believe me. 'How's your family tree research coming along?' I asked Vanessa to change the subject. I didn't want to talk about Cecilia anymore; things were moving too quickly for me to process.

'Oh, it's terribly complicated.' Vanessa said brightly. 'I've managed to go back to the start of the nineteenth century, which is as far as the records here at the villa go. I'll need to visit Venice and search there next.'

'A little like looking for a needle in a haystack,' I laughed.

'Very much so,' Vanessa said, standing. 'Luca must have gone to the stables to see his sister. She's always messing about down there. I'll be back in a minute with the Prosecco.'

A horse whinnied in the distance and I closed my eyes. The sun had moved 'round so that I was no longer shaded by the umbrella. I rubbed my arms. Why were they suddenly cold? The crow in the tree to my left gave a mournful caw. Then the chair beneath me started moving, my legs astride in voluminous skirts instead of stretched out in front of me. Holy shit, I was riding a horse; I'd ridden a lot when I was a teenager, but this was incredible. The world around me took on an iridescent brightness and my head swam away from my body.

Pegaso is fighting the bit; he wants to gallop, except we're at the back of the hunt. Queen Caterina and her knights are giving chase to a deer and we've left the confines of the Barco. Turf flies up around us. The hounds are baying and the horns sound as we cross a wide field; we've come far. Pegaso prances from side to side and I give up trying to hold him back.

He gives a surge and we're going like the wind. *Patatatum, patatatum, patatatum.* Soon we are neck and neck with Lodovico Gaspare. I've heard he's a cavalryman for the Duke of Ferrara; he certainly rides like one. He glances at me and beams, revealing his uneven white teeth. Something in me recoils and longs for another man's smile, the turning up of a mouth at the corners, but I have not seen the artist for months.

The chase is long, yet I do not tire. Finally, up ahead, the deer doubles back on its own tracks and runs through a stream as it tries to hide its scent. We come upon it and the dogs surround it. I stare at the magnificent hart with beautiful antlers; the animal heaves in exhaustion. I wish that it could be saved, yet I know it would be impossible.

Lodovico Gaspare dismounts and approaches the beast,

raising his sword. I can't look. The horns blow the *morte* in celebration. Domina directs one of the huntsmen to cut the deer apart and divide the meat. The crows in the trees by the stream start cawing for the carrion.

I'm surprised to find that I am crying. Why is this? I've never cried before at the death of a hart. Hunting is a part of my life at the court. I love galloping across a field, Pegaso and I together.

The scene around me takes on a strange aspect. It's as if I'm gazing at a painting and not part of reality anymore. I have felt this before and don't like it. I blink as if it might dispel my unease, except it makes things worse and now my vision is blurred as sorrow for the deer fills my eyes.

I jolted back into the twentieth century with a lurch. I wiped my tears and gazed at the field beyond the garden. There was a stream shaded by willows. Could it be the same stream where that magnificent animal had been hacked apart? I could still smell the blood and nausea swelled my gut.

Footsteps echoed on the flagstones and I turned toward the sound, still feeling dizzy. Luca was approaching, carrying a tray with a bottle and three glasses.

'Has it happened again?' he asked, concern in his voice as he put the Prosecco down on the table. 'You've gone as white as a sheet.'

I hugged my arms. 'I don't think I've gone completely crazy, although some of what I'm experiencing could be attributed to trauma, I suppose. There's usually a smell, or a sound that triggers it. Your mother thinks Cecilia might have been in the fire that destroyed the Barco.' I chewed my bottom lip. 'I don't think I'm imagining her… she's too real.'

He steepled his fingers. 'And you're scared by her?'

'Well, wouldn't you be?' I couldn't help the sharpness in my tone.

He held up his hands. 'Of course.'

'I'm sorry, I didn't mean to snap at you. I can't help being fascinated by her,' I said more calmly. 'I'm torn between wanting to know what happens to her and not liking the way she takes over my mind.'

'So, it's not the girl who scares you.' He met my gaze. 'It's the fact that you can't control when you're having these flashbacks.'

'Sounds as if you believe me.' I pulled at a loose strand of my wild hair.

'Fern, I never doubted *you* for one minute.' He reached for the wine. 'However, whether Cecilia is a figment of your imagination or not is something I still need to get my head around.'

'Oh.' I felt my eyes drawn to the area across the field where I was sure I'd seen the deer killed. *Where Cecilia had seen the deer killed*. I had to find a way of separating myself from her. Damn difficult, though, when my thoughts had meshed with hers. 'Maybe I should leave Italy.' I suggested reluctantly.

Luca gave me a searching look, then pulled the cork from the bottle. 'Wouldn't that be running away?' He filled the three glasses.

'You're right, of course. Besides, I love it here and I'm not due back at work until the end of the month.' My words came out in a rush. 'It's just that I can't keep going on like this. It's dangerous. I mean, I could be driving along a road then suddenly find myself back in the past.'

'To be honest, I had the same thought myself,' he blew out a breath. 'You need to find a way to control these visions. As far as I'm aware, they seem to happen when you're alone.'

'That's true. So far. Are you suggesting I should never be by myself? That would be hard, particularly as I like my own company and, in fact, thrive on it usually. Especially when I'm painting.' I lifted my glass and took a sip of Prosecco, savouring the sparkling fruitiness.

The sound of voices alerted me to the arrival of Vanessa, who was coming down the steps to the garden with a tall dark-haired girl, dressed in riding breeches and a white t-shirt. Luca stood and pulled out two chairs. 'This is my sister, Chiara,' his smile was warm. 'She's been looking forward to meeting you.'

'Hello.' Chiara took a seat and raked her eyes over me. She

turned to her brother. 'You're right. Fern *is* like the girl in *The Tempest.*'

'*The Tempest*? What's that?'

'I was going to tell you, but smart ass here jumped in before me,' Luca chuckled. 'It's a painting by Giorgione. I'll take you to see it in the Accademia Gallery in Venice, if you like. The resemblance is uncanny.'

'Don't we have a picture in one of our art books?' Vanessa interjected.

'We do. I'll go and fetch it.' Luca pushed back his chair and got to his feet.

I watched him set off across the patio. His broad shoulders tapered to a slim waist and his jeans hugged his firm buttocks.

I gave my head a shake to clear it of inappropriate thoughts. 'I used to ride when I was younger,' I said to Chiara for the sake of making conversation.

'Oh, then you must come out with me sometime.'

I gave a wry laugh. 'Not sure I'm up to it anymore.'

'It's like riding a bicycle. You don't forget.' Chiara pressed her lips together.

'Fern can ride Magic. He's a lovely old boy and calm as anything,' Vanessa said, re-filling my glass. She went on to praise the virtues of the horse and told me about her successes at show jumping when she was younger. 'Ah, here's Luca.' She glanced up as her son approached. 'Did you find the book?'

'No. It seems to have gone missing. I was only looking at it the other night, too.' He shrugged.

'Don't worry,' I said with a smile. 'I was planning on visiting Venice, so I can see the painting while there. Are you sure you can spare the time, Luca? I mean, I'm quite capable of going by myself.'

His mouth turned up at the corners and a feeling of recognition passed through me. No. Not recognition. Attraction. And it was wrong. Too soon, too sudden, too much of a betrayal. I couldn't allow myself to be attracted to Luca.

'I'm due for a day off,' he said. 'I'd love to show you my favourite city.'

'What about you, Chiara?' I asked his sister. 'Would you like to come with us?'

'No way! I was at university in Venice. Had enough of the place to last a lifetime.' She grimaced.

'Wow! That must have been a fantastic experience.'

'Not when there's a high tide and you have to wear long rubber boots to get around,' she groaned. 'Thank God my student days are over.'

'Chiara's taking a break from her studies.' Vanessa frowned. 'A hiatus.'

'I can't see the point of endless exams,' Chiara muttered.

'What were you studying?' I asked, genuinely curious.

'English. It was easy for me, of course. But I found it boring.' Her gaze bounced from me to her mother and back to me again.

'Did you go to school in England like Luca?' I ventured to ask.

'Yes. But I couldn't face university in England, unlike him. I found the weather far too depressing.'

'With hindsight, that might have been a better choice.' Vanessa's voice had turned shrill. 'You wouldn't have met such extremists.'

'They're not extremists,' Chiara huffed. 'The Veneto is being suffocated by Rome.'

Vanessa waggled her finger at her daughter. 'We won't discuss that now. It's impolite to talk politics during a social occasion.'

'You're so old-fashioned, Mum,' Chiara laughed. She got to her feet and said to me, 'I meant what I said about coming for a ride. It's a great way of seeing the countryside.'

I could only nod. There was no way I would get on a horse, I said to myself. Not after my strange vision only minutes ago…

Vanessa shot Chiara a stern look. 'Aren't you staying for dinner?'

'Sorry, but I'm meeting Federico. I told you this morning, didn't I?'

'Ah, I'd forgotten. What time are you coming home?'

'I'm twenty-one not eleven.' Chiara said determinedly. 'I'll be home when I'm home.'

'While you live under my roof, you'll follow my rules. I want you back by midnight.'

'Yeah… yeah,' Chiara's smirk belied her promise. She was clearly rebelling against her background, trying to find her place in the world.

Vanessa's gaze followed her as she headed out of the garden. 'I apologise for my daughter. She's becoming quite impossible. First, she drops out of university. Second, she runs around with all sorts of wrong people. I don't know what to do with her.' She sighed. 'Dinner should be ready now. Let's go into the dining room.'

Luca stood and held out his hand to me. Again, his touch felt unthreatening as he led me into the family's rooms in the right-hand wing of the villa. Furnished in what I guessed were Italian country antiques, it had none of the opulence of a stately home, even though a maid had prepared our meal and waited on us at the table. I immediately relaxed.

After a starter of *prosciutto* with melon, washed down with a lightly chilled red wine, the maid served us thinly sliced grilled fillet steak with roast potatoes and salad. While we ate, Vanessa and Luca told me about the history of the villa, which had been in the Goredan family for centuries.

Luca's brother and his wife joined us after dinner for coffee. Antonio had the same blue eyes as Luca, and he chatted to me about the family business. His wife, Michela, appeared shy, barely saying a word. They lived in a house on the estate and had three young children: two boys of eight and six, and a girl of three, whom they'd left in the care of their English nanny.

At around eleven, Luca drove me home. 'Thanks for a wonderful evening,' I said as he pulled up in front of Auntie's house. 'I like your family. Antonio's wife is very reserved, though, isn't she?'

'They've been married for ten years and even now she's somewhat in awe of *La contessa*, as she still calls her.'

'Oh, why's that?' I blinked.

'Antonio met her at Padova University. Unlike me, he opted to study in Italy. She comes from a family of factory workers. Mother isn't a snob, of course, and does everything she can to put Michela at her ease. The problem isn't my mother but Michela. I don't think she'll ever change.'

'Some people are natural introverts, I suppose.' I paused. 'Are you sure you can spare the time to take me to Venice?'

'Of course. I'll pick you up at eight on Tuesday morning.' He leaned over to kiss me on both cheeks.

I pecked his cheeks in return, a friendly Italian gesture, catching the spicy scent of his after-shave.

He leapt out of the car and opened the door for me before I had a chance to do it myself.

'Good night, Luca,' I said. 'Thanks for a lovely evening.'

'It was a pleasure, Fern,' he smiled.

I waved him off as I stood in the doorway.

He was nice.

He was far too nice for someone like me…

CHAPTER 7

*J*feel drowsy in the warmth of this early summer's afternoon as I sit on the stone lip of the fishpond. The Queen and the rest of the court are taking a post luncheon nap. I couldn't sleep and tiptoed out here as soon as Dorotea was snoring next to me in the quarters we share.

I trail my fingers in the lukewarm water, green like the moss that grows up the statue of a cherub with feathery wings, which graces a plinth in the shade of the cypress tree. Golden carp swim in lazy circles, nibbling at my thumb, and a dragonfly dips down for a drink before flitting away again. I think about the painter and wonder when I shall see him next. I hear footsteps on the path; I blush and lift my gaze. Not the painter, but the man from Ferrara, Lodovico Gaspare. Oh, how I wish he wasn't seeing me with my cheeks so pink; he might think I'm blushing for him…

I stand and we make our reverences, Lodovico bowing and doffing his hat. I curtsey and keep my eyes downcast so that he should not consider me forward.

'Will you go to Venice with the Queen next week?' He asks, lowering himself to sit on the stone bench by the pond.

I perch next to him. 'To her palazzo on the Grand Canal.' I'm unable to keep the excitement from my voice. I have heard that

Signor Zorzo's studio is in a *campo* nearby, and, as he isn't at court, he might well be there.

'Ah,' the man from Ferrara frowns. 'I depart tomorrow to attend the Duke.'

I've heard such stories of the Duchess of Ferrara, Lucrezia Borgia, and ponder whether to ask Lodovico about her. In the end, my curiosity gets the better of me and I say, 'Is it true she did "know" the heat of a bed with her brother?'

Lodovico glances from left to right. 'Those were but rumours put about by Cesare Borgia's enemies.'

I'm not interested in politics and request more information about the Duchess instead. Lodovico appears pleased to spread the gossip. 'They say she did "know" Francesco, Marquis of Mantova, but that "knowledge" has ended since he came down with the pox, and now she has become the lover of Pietro Bembo.'

'Oh.' *Poor Dorotea – she will not be able to compete with a duchess.* 'And does the Duke not mind?'

'As long as she brings forth sons of his blood, and runs the household well, he's happy to look the other way.'

'And what does he see when he looks?' I have heard rumours of Alfonso, Duke of Ferrara's, many affairs.

The man from Ferrara roams his eyes over me. 'No woman as beautiful as you.'

Cecilia, you should not have spoken of the heat of bedrooms.

I pretend to be shocked, deliberately opening my eyes wide and letting a hand fly to my mouth.

Maria Santissima! Lodovico leans in and tries to kiss me.

I twist my face away, repulsed by the fishy stench of his breath. *He should have picked his teeth after lunch!*

He persists, and puts his arms around me, pulling me against him.

I wish I had never thought this man fascinating, and I'm filled with disgust. Not only does his mouth stink of fish, but his lips are like fishes' lips, thin and flat and bony.

I push my hands against his chest. He takes them in his and

pins my wrists together. 'Hush, Lady Cecilia. I presume this is your first time. Relax and it will be easier for you.'

Easier? What does he mean? Surely, he'll not take me here in the open? Am I about to lose my maidenhead? 'No,' I say. 'Not here.' He's so much stronger than me that I won't be able to stop him if that's his intent.

Lodovico Gaspare laughs mockingly. 'My dear, I did but mean your first kiss. You want me to make love to you?' His thin lips curl in a smile that makes me recoil.

'No. Of course not,' I splutter. 'I'm a maid and will remain so until I'm wed.'

'Glad to hear it,' he says with another laugh, the straight white scar on his cheek shining. 'And you shall have an even more spectacular wedding than your sister, I hope. In the meantime, let me caress you. I've been longing to taste your sweetness. Don't deny me!'

He pulls me to him again, untying the laces on my sleeves so that my shoulders are bared, and he slobbers at them like a hungry beast.

Heartbeats racing, I flail at him with my fists.

He doesn't seem to notice and his bony mouth travels down to my chest.

Summoning all my strength I push at him again.

Finally, he lifts his head and I catch sight of the spittle on his lips and the hotness of desire in his eyes.

'I said to relax.' Desire changes to anger in his expression. He takes my hand and places it on his codpiece. 'Can't you feel how much I want you?'

I let out a cry and whip my hand away. 'No!'

This is a nightmare, I tell myself. I will wake and all will be well. I close my eyes and count to three.

One, two, three. I woke with a start and gulped in the cool night air. I was in my bed at Auntie's but disgust still festered in my stomach— a revulsion so palpable I could taste it. I'd been dreaming, but it had all seemed so real. I could still smell Lodovico's fishy breath and it was making me gag.

A knock sounded at my door, and Auntie poked her head around. 'Are you all right, Fern? I heard a shout.'

'I'm fine. Just a dream, that's all,' I said, my throat scratchy. 'Please don't worry.'

'Hmm.' She gave me an uncertain look. 'I'll make you a cup of camomile tea. Come downstairs.'

In the kitchen, she handed me a warm mug. My teeth chattered as I lifted it to my mouth. I sat on my usual chair and sipped, my mind flitting between what had happened to me as Cecilia and the comforting reality of the woman in front of me, who was adding sugar to her drink and opening a tin of chocolate chip cookies. 'Was it the usual nightmare?' she asked.

I shook my head. The memory of Lodovico's fishy lips on mine was making my stomach churn again. Had he gone on to force himself on Cecilia? It was all so weird; I couldn't continue like this— keeping my dreams and visions from Auntie. I had to tell her.

'I'm not dreaming about the fire anymore.' I put my mug down. 'Something really bizarre is happening.'

'Tell me what's wrong, love,' she said in a kind tone. 'I'll see if I can help.'

Haltingly, I recounted everything I'd told Vanessa and Luca, adding the latest incident. However, the more I talked, the more I became aware of how weird I was sounding. Auntie's expression was indecipherable and soon I began to falter. 'You think I'm crazy…'

'No, I don't.' Her eyes were huge behind her glasses. 'I think you're still suffering from what happened two years ago. Somehow, your mind has become confused.'

I shook my head. 'But it seems so real.'

'I'm sure it does.' She paused. 'Be sensible.' Her Welsh lilt was even more pronounced than usual. 'We can't relive past lives. It's physically impossible.'

'How could I know so much about life hundreds of years ago if

I wasn't actually living it? I do know it sounds impossible. I've had that argument with myself, believe me. It's just that I can smell things, taste things and even touch things, and be touched by them when I'm there.' I shuddered. 'You can't do that in a dream.'

Auntie reached across and patted my hand. 'You must have read about it in a book or seen a film. And now your imagination is getting the better of you.'

'No. I don't think so.' I leaned away, creating space between us. 'It's far too vivid. I couldn't possibly know so many details unless I've actually been there. Cecilia *is* real; she's not just in my mind.'

'Something has upset you; I agree. Tomorrow I'll take you to the hospital and we'll see if they can prescribe you something.'

Heat rose behind my eyelids. 'I don't want any more medication, Auntie. I'm done with all of that. There's nothing wrong with me.'

'Really?' Her expression reflected her doubt.

'I don't want to see a doctor. Next thing I'll have a "mentally ill" label slapped on me again, and I'll be declared unfit to work. I went through all that last year. I'm over it.' I made an X sign with my hands.

'Are you sure?' Auntie lifted an eyebrow.

'Absolutely. I know how it must seem, but I'm not making this up.' I fingered my mouth, still bruised from Lodovico's advances. I felt exhausted and crushed by Auntie's disbelief. 'I'm sorry to have woken you up. Let's go back to bed. I feel fine now.'

'If you say so,' she said, taking my cup from me. 'Try not to dwell on the past, Fern. You have your whole life ahead of you and you must live it fully.'

I followed her up the stairs, my feet dragging.

If only it could be as easy as that…

⁓

Upstairs, I took my valerian tablets and slept dreamlessly. When I woke, the taste of Lodovico had gone. Bright sunshine lit the garden, illuminating the olive leaves and the small white flowers that would later become fruit. Auntie suggested I go for a walk after breakfast, so I set off down the road. The closer I got to the ruins of the Barco, the more I felt anxiety prickling my spine. I turned around and strode in the opposite direction, past the row of houses beyond Auntie's, deciding to head for the centre of the village.

The sun warmed my shoulders; I took off my denim jacket and bundled it into my rucksack next to my sketchpad. A water-colour sky, washed with blue, and, beyond the fields soared the Asolani hills, the towers, and the turrets of the town itself. *Such light!* My fingers itched to paint it.

A street market was in full swing when I arrived at the main square. I sat for a while at a café and contemplated the hustle and bustle, so different yet at the same time so familiar. Brightly coloured vegetables piled high; cheeses of every shape and variety, their rich, greasy aromas tickling my nostrils; scaly fish displayed on crushed ice, mouths gaping and eyes staring blankly. *No!* Nausea swept over me. *Focus on the now! Keep your mind in the present!*

My ears tuned into the cries of the vendors competing with the shouted conversations of the shoppers, haggling over every Lira. A young couple were holding hands and exchanging kisses at the next table, their backs to me, and a group of elderly men were playing cards at the table beyond. Life going on as usual. No one out of place.

Auntie had to be right– it was physically impossible to go back and relive the past. There was no need for me to see a doctor and absolutely no reason for any strong medication. My herbal tablets were perfect; I'd slept like a log after I'd taken them last night. Soon this vacation would be over; I'd return to my work as an accounts' manager at City Bank in London and get on with my life. It was time to move on. I'd never forget the fire and what had happened to Harry, it would mark me forever, but I'd cope with my angst by losing myself in my job and my art.

I took some change from my purse and went to pay for my

cappuccino. As I squeezed between my table and the next, the young woman who'd been exchanging kisses with the young man looked up. 'Chiara,' I said, recognising Luca's sister. 'Hello!'

She introduced her boyfriend, Federico, who flashed a crooked white-toothed smile at me. *Lodovico's smile.*

My pulse leapt.

Past and present had smashed into each other in a warped collision.

All I could do was stand and stare, while every instinct screamed, *Get the hell out of here!*

Chiara was gazing at Federico in adoration. The young man gave me a lazy smile, curling his thin lips in a way that was all too familiar.

I clenched my fists and brought my trembling hands under control. This couldn't be Lodovico, pursuing Cecilia down the centuries. Such things didn't happen. He was just Chiara's boyfriend who, on closer inspection, looked nothing like Cecilia's antagonist. Much better-looking, in fact. Federico's skin was lightly tanned whereas Lodovico's had been pale. Chiara's boyfriend's sun-streaked brown hair was spiked up with hair-gel and the only thing he had in common with Lodovico was a thinness about the lips. 'Pleased to meet you,' he said.

The hairs on my arms tingled. *That voice!* The timbre of it was exactly the same. *Don't be ridiculous! The dream from last night is still with you, stirring up your imaginings.* Yet when Federico's eyes rested on me, I felt the sharp stab of hatred. This young man was dangerous, I was sure of it. No wonder Luca was concerned. Federico's whole aura radiated a need to control other people, much like Lodovico had tried to control Cecilia. 'Well, it was lovely to see you again, Chiara, and to meet you, Federico,' I said quickly. 'I should be off now, though.'

Luca's sister scarcely registered my leave-taking she was so enthralled to the young man, but Federico smirked at me and his eyes lingered on my body as if they were undressing me. *The creep!* I turned on my heel and made for the bar, where I settled my bill.

Half an hour later, I arrived at the front gate of the house. It was still early, and Auntie would be tapping away at her typewriter. The vista of the hills lured me on, and I found myself walking in the direction of the Barco as if I was being reeled in by an unseen cord. I knew this place; it was in my soul. I sat on the same balustrade in the loggia where I'd sat before, only this time instead of that feeling of trepidation my heart was singing. The faded frescos on the far wall shimmered in the sunshine and I could feel Cecilia's presence. Closing my eyes, I let myself drift...

The swelling between Lodovico Gaspare's legs disgusts me. At my touch, it moves like a snake. Does he want to stick it into me? I push him so hard this time that he falls back. I seize my chance, gather my skirts and run to the loggia. The far wall is covered with scaffolding, and there is Signor Zorzo, perched at the top, dipping his paintbrush into a pot.

I can see the *cartone* stuck to wall on the left of him, a drawing of Queen Caterina on her destrier with the outline pricked out so it can be transferred to the wall in charcoal. I know how frescoes are created. My whole being cries out to learn more as the desire to paint surges through me. The artist clambers down the ladder and we make our reverences to each other. How I long to throw aside this politeness between us. Instead, I keep my gaze averted and say, pointing to the fresco, 'How do you do that? Can you show me?'

'You?' He sounds surprised.

'I draw, but I would like to learn the techniques of painting. There is no one here to teach me.' I cross my arms in front of my chest. 'If I had been born a boy, I would have been apprenticed to a master just as you were to the great Bellini.'

'Oh, so you know all about me, do you?' His voice is soft, and a smile crinkles his eyes.

I stamp my foot. 'Only that you are conceited, and arrogant, and laugh at me for wanting to be something I can never be.'

'Ha! To be a true artist you need a burning in your soul. If you burn with the desire to paint, Lady Cecilia, you will do so whatever hindrances are put in your way.'

'Please, teach me. I can be your pupil in secret.'

He bends to gather up his paintbrushes, saying nothing. *How dare he ignore me!* 'Let me show you my work,' I plead.

'Only if you will pose for me. I have longed to paint you ever since I first set eyes on you.'

'When?' I ask, unable to keep the eagerness from my voice. Finally, someone will show me how to develop my skills.

He peers between the columns of the loggia. 'There's time to make a start before the court wakes up. The light is good this afternoon. Follow me.' He slings a bag over his shoulder with one hand, takes *my* hand with the other and leads me outside. I look around, checking for Lodovico Gaspare, but he's nowhere to be seen. Honeysuckle scents the air and the call of a cuckoo echoes from the lime trees beyond the rose bower. The Queen has planned this garden for enjoyment and there are stone benches on the other side of the bushes, hidden from the sight of anyone who might be gazing from a window… the perfect place for us.

Signor Zorzo pulls a wooden frame from his carrier and leans a small canvas against it. He picks up his brush and dips it into the pot of paint he has also taken from his bag. I long to have colours to work with; I'm so bored with black chalk. Will the painter be true to his word and transmit some of his knowledge to me?

He grasps his brush and, with deft strokes, brings forth the outline of my face. Within minutes, it seems, although it must have taken longer, he has finished. 'I can complete it in my studio in Venice,' he says.

'Might I visit you there? I go with the Queen next week.'

Signor Zorzo appears thoughtful for a moment. 'Arrange for quarters overlooking the canal. I'll fetch you at night in my boat. You'll be my muse.'

A bubble of happiness forms in my chest. I go to him and put my arms around his waist, caring not if I'm being forward. My gesture comes from the heart. Our lips meet, and I rejoice at the softness of his mouth, the sweetness of his scent. He lets out a moan and our tongues entwine. The feeling is delicious at first, then becomes more intense as my body starts to burn. He pulls away. 'We must stop. The hour of the afternoon rest is over.'

The strangest feeling comes over me. I'm being watched again by a shadowy figure. I want to hide from whoever it is who spies on me and bury my head in the artist's rock-hard chest. Instead, he bows and tells me to wait for his call. He leaves me unaccountably bereft, heat billowing between my legs and disconcerted by a strange brightness that makes the world shimmer around me.

I closed my eyes against the bright light and took in a deep, shuddering breath as I became Fern once more. I could still feel desire pulsing through me, fighting with my guilt. How could I betray Harry like that? I touched my lips, still moist from Zorzo's kiss. *How the hell could that be?* I rested my hands on the balustrade of the loggia and rubbed my palms on the rough, lichen-encrusted stone. Crickets and sparrows chirped in the undergrowth and the breeze blew a tendril of hair into my mouth. I tucked it behind my ear.

My entire body throbbed, and I thought not of Harry, but of Luca. Something about his mouth reminded me of the artist. Their height was the same. However, Luca was slim whereas Zorzo could only be described as a bear of a man. Despite their differences, there was a likeness between them, a familiarity I found disturbing.

Tomorrow I was going to Venice with Luca, to see the painting. How amazing it would be if the girl in *The Tempest* turned out to be Cecilia. Did she have a life with Zorzo? Part of me wanted to find out, and the other part was completely terrified.

CHAPTER 8

$\mathcal{L}$uca

I glanced at Fern sprawled in the passenger seat. Soon after we'd set out from her aunt's she'd fallen into a deep sleep. Must be exhausted, the poor girl. She was wearing her hippy garb again — a floaty embroidered white skirt, and a white lace blouse hanging sexily off her shoulders. She'd left her hair loose and, on her lap, she was clutching a cloth shoulder bag which wouldn't have been out-of-place in an Indian bazaar. *Jesus!* She was certainly original. None of the women I'd dated in recent years would have been seen dead going out without having had their hair styled by a hairdresser or wearing the latest designer outfit.

I smile to myself at Fern's quirkiness, and, taking the ring road around Treviso, I thought about her visions. I'd gone to the library yesterday, and had looked up psychotic depression, discovering that it could lead to delusions and hallucinations. However, these were negative, self-critical, self-punishing and self-blaming episodes. What Fern had been experiencing was something totally different. Incredible as it seemed, she might well be slipping back into the past and seeing the world through Cecilia's eyes.

I gripped the steering wheel and focused on my driving; I would have liked a nap myself. Last night, I'd experienced the strangest dream. Something about a race against time. I'd lurched awake, panic surging through me as I'd tried to figure out where I'd been going in such a hurry, why I'd been going there, and what had caused such extreme anxiety. Then I'd tossed and turned for the rest of the night.

The motorway from Treviso wasn't busy and half an hour later I was pulling into the assigned spot in the multi-storey car park at the end of the causeway that led to Venice.

Fern woke with a yawn. 'Hope I didn't snore . . .'

'You slept like an angel,' I said, jumping out to open the door. But she'd already got out by the time I reached her.

She walked with me down the flight of steps to the ground floor, and we made our way to the water-taxi rank. After giving the driver instructions to take us to the Accademia, I sat next to her on the plush seat at the back of the gently rocking boat. A breeze was blowing her tangled hair back from her face and she was staring around, that "rabbit in the headlights" expression in her eyes again.

'It's so much busier than I remember,' she said in an awe-struck tone.

'I thought this was your first visit here?'

She shook her head and I caught the conflict in her expression. 'Another flash-back?' I asked.

'Not really. Just a conviction that I know this place. Parts of it, I mean.' She twisted her hands together. 'God, I must sound crazy to you.'

'Crazy? You?!' I smiled.

'I'd forgotten how beautiful it is. Was.' She shielded her eyes as we cruised up the Grand Canal. 'I can see the decay now. Where the tide has eroded some of the buildings. Still amazing, though.'

She gazed around in amazement as our water-taxi took a shortcut down the Rio della Croce. We turned right at Ca'

67

Foscari to arrive at the landing stage in front of the Accademia Gallery. I paid the boatman and handed Fern ashore, refusing her offer to help with the fare. 'No way,' I said. 'This was my suggestion and my treat. And we can take a gondola ride later, if you like.'

Delight lit her eyes. 'If I like! That would be perfect.' She bit at her lip. 'Please let me treat you to lunch, though. I know how expensive water-taxis and gondolas are.'

'Listen, Fern.' I set my jaw. 'Today you're my guest. It's the least I can do when it was me who proposed we come here. Next time, you can invite me… and we'll do things differently, okay?'

She nodded her agreement and strolled with me across the small piazza and up the marble steps to the museum. It was cool inside and echoing with the babble of foreign languages. *Tourists. Unavoidable.* I bought our entrance tickets and said, 'Before we view *The Tempest*, let me show you something.'

Within minutes we were standing in front of Gentile Bellini's *Procession of the True Cross*. Fern stared at the painting, her face pale and rigid. 'It's so familiar,' she whispered.

I took her hand. 'Come, have a look at this one.' I led her to *The Miracle of the Cross at the Bridge of San Lorenzo*. 'See the woman at the bottom left of the picture? Historians believe that she's Queen Caterina Cornaro.'

Fern eyed the figure dressed in black. 'Yes, it's her,' she said in a shaky voice. 'Oh my God! I think that's Fiammetta, Cecilia's sister.' She pointed at the first in a line of women to the left of the Queen. 'I'd know her anywhere.'

'Wow,' I said. I'd studied this painting when I'd taken a History of Art course at university. 'See how richly frescoed the buildings were then.'

'I know. And the figures in the painting seem to have been frozen forever in a moment of time,' Fern released a long, slow breath. 'Just like what's happening to me, only the reverse.'

'We need to find out why.' I took her hand again. 'Let's go and meet Cecilia, your nemesis.'

'Nemesis?'

'Well, who else could she be? A ghost, maybe? Not a figment

of your imagination, I realise that for sure now. Your reaction to the painting convinced me.' And it had. Fern's familiarity with the characters depicted by Bellini couldn't have been faked. 'Cecilia wants something from you, Fern. We need to find out what that is, so that she can be at rest.'

'Do you think it could have something to do with Giorgione?'

'Giorgione, Big Giorgio. *Zorzone* in Venetian dialect. Was Cecilia's Zorzo a tall man?'

'Huge.'

'One of the most enigmatic painters in history. So little is known about his life. You're amazingly lucky to have "met" him.' We stopped in front of a painting approximately three feet square. 'Here's *the Tempest,* supposedly his most important work,' I announced.

'Luca, I didn't "meet" Giorgione,' Fern said firmly, staring at the naked lady on the canvas, nursing a baby. 'Cecilia met him. I do see a resemblance between her and this woman, and yes, her face is a *little* like mine.'

'Her pose is unusual,' I observed. 'Normally a baby would be on the mother's lap when suckling. I wonder why Giorgione has positioned the child at the side of the mother?'

'The woman seems as if she's recently given birth. Look at her flabby tummy! She's gazing directly at the viewer.' Fern leaned forward. 'This must be one of the strangest paintings I've ever seen. Incredibly haunting, in a way, although I can't say why.'

'Apparently it was Lord Byron's favourite for the fact that it's so ambiguous,' I said matter-of-factly. 'Viewers can make up their own interpretation of the symbolism.'

'I'd like to buy a print of it. Do they sell them here?' She pointed to the male figure in the picture. 'He seems to have been dropped into the scene, not a part of it at all. And he looks a bit like Zorzo.'

'Art historians have suggested he could be a soldier, a shepherd, or a gypsy,' I said, remembering what I'd learnt on that History of Art course. 'X-rays of the painting have revealed that in the place of the man, Giorgione originally painted another female nude.'

'Wonder who she could have been?' Fern peered at the painting. 'The depiction of the landscape is stunning. And the gathering storm reminds me of the one we had the other night. See how the sky is lit! There's a real feeling of foreboding. As if there's about to be a terrible disaster.' She shivered. 'Is there a shop here where I can get a copy?'

'Of course. I'll take you there.'

We descended to the entrance level and, after Fern had bought a print of the painting and a book about the artist, I said, 'We can take stroll to the restaurant. It's not far.'

Hand in hand, we left the tourist trail behind, to wander through the hidden *calli* and across the small bridges spanning a network of tiny canals. Fern gazed around as if captivated. She took her camera from her bag and framed some shots of the strings of laundry hanging from the windows above. We came across a couple of boys, kicking a football in a deserted square. Then we crossed to a darkened alleyway, so narrow we could almost reach out and touch both walls with our outstretched hands. We emerged into the sunshine of a *campo*, where umbrella-shaded tables cried out for us to take a break and enjoy an *aperitivo*. I signalled the waiter and ordered *Bellinis*.

'Excuse my ignorance,' Fern said. 'But what are Bellinis?'

'Prosecco mixed with peach juice. Invented by Giuseppe Cipriani, the founder of Harry's Bar,' I informed her. 'I'll take you there the next time we visit Venice.'

'Oh, is that anything to do with the Cipriani Hotel in Asolo?'

'The Cipriani family used to manage it during the late sixties and early seventies. Now it belongs to an international chain.'

I took her hand again.

Out of the blue, she snatched it back from me.

I almost fell off my chair. 'Sorry,' I apologized. 'Didn't mean to upset you…'

Her brows pulled in, and her eyes locked with mine. 'I really like being with you. I just don't want you to get the wrong idea.'

'Oh?'

Where was this going?

'Remember I told you I'd been in the King's Cross fire?' She stuttered out a breath, then breathed in deeply and stuttered out another. 'My fiancé . . . Harry, he . . . he died in it.'

'I'm so sorry. How tragic...' The words seemed trite in the circumstances.

A lone tear ran down her cheek; she wiped it away with the back of her hand. 'I'm not ready for another relationship,' she murmured. 'I apologise if I've led you on. You've been so kind to me.' Her voice was quiet, but her tone determined.

Ha, Luca. She's knocked you back before you've even kissed her. Your punishment for all those girls you've kissed and ditched in the past. Well, to be honest, more than kissed . . .

'Can we be friends?' she asked hesitantly.

'Wouldn't have it any other way,' I lied, disappointment lodged in my chest. Our drinks had arrived, and I lifted mine in a toast. 'To our friendship.' I clinked my glass with hers. 'Can you tell me what happened? To Harry, I mean . . .'

'We'd arranged to meet in the ticket office and go for dinner nearby. I blame myself as I'd made him wait.' She glanced away, her lip trembling. 'If I'd caught an earlier train, we'd both have been out of there before the station went up in flames.' She met my gaze, and I caught the grief in her eyes. 'I'd worked late, even though the account I was setting up could have waited until the following morning. Wanted to impress my boss. So selfish of me . . .'

'You weren't to know,' I said reassuringly. 'It's lucky you weren't on the concourse with your fiancé.'

'I almost was.' Her mouth formed a straight line. 'I think I told you before, I was half-way up the escalator. Well . . . suddenly.' She shuddered, and her expression clouded. 'Suddenly the steps were on fire, and I looked up and the ceiling was in flames too.' Her voice cracked. 'Pieces of debris were crashing down . . . So, the only thing I could do was run back to the platform.'

'It must have been terrifying.' Again, I was lost for words. I touched her hand, and, this time, she didn't pull it away. Her trembling fingers wrapped themselves around mine.

'The tunnel was filled with dense smoke. I could barely see. People ran up and down, hammering on the closed doors of the trains as they crept past.' She shut her eyes, visibly shaken. 'Finally, one of the trains stopped and I jumped on.'

'Thank God for that.'

She could have died…

'I turned on the TV as soon as I got home and saw all the black body bags lined up outside the station.' Tears welled, and she brushed them away again. 'I've been in therapy ever since. That's when I started painting; it's been my salvation.'

What could I say? 'Ah! Good, good. You clearly needed something to focus your mind.'

'When I smelled burnt wood in my aunt's house and heard that ghostly voice calling to me, it brought it all back.' She shuddered. 'Remember me telling you that your mother thinks Cecilia might have died in the fire that destroyed the Barco?'

I could only nod.

'The burnt wood I keep smelling could be a vestige of the past, and I'm convinced that's what happened to her.'

'You can't know for sure,' I said, trying to inject optimism into my tone. 'It might not have.'

She visibly shook. 'I'm terrified of fire, Luca.'

I squeezed her fingers. 'Don't forget all that happened nearly five hundred years ago. You're perfectly safe.'

She drained her glass and said, 'At least let me pay for these drinks.'

I pushed myself to my feet. 'Absolutely not. I'll settle up. Then we can go for some lunch.'

With heavy steps I made my way toward the bar.

She wants to be friends. But I want so much more…

CHAPTER 9

I sat back in my chair. Luca's reassurances had almost calmed my fears, except I hadn't told him everything. There was something I'd never told anyone – not even my therapist. It festered inside me, poisoning my life. I'd never, ever be rid of it, and, one day, I'd be called to account for it.

Not today, hopefully. Today I was in Venice, and there was something about this place that called to my heart and soul.

I watched Luca walking toward the entrance of the café, his long legs covering the distance in easy strides. He was so different to Harry— who'd been blond, of medium height and stocky. I was attracted to Luca, of course I was, and I'd had to swallow the lump of unexpected yearning in my throat when he'd willingly agreed to be "just friends".

With a sharp pang, I remembered the instant attraction between myself and Harry. I'd met him when I'd set up an investment account for him after his uncle had died and left him two hundred thousand pounds. Harry had been cautious with money and insisted I find a safe home for his inheritance. I'd done that for him, and then he'd invited me out to a swanky restaurant. We hardly ate anything, so intense had been the sexual chemistry between us. Back at his place, supposedly for a night-cap, we'd barely stepped through the front door before we were practically ripping each other's clothes off. And it had been like that for most of the three years I'd known him. That is until…

Damn! That buzzing sensation was back in my head. I gripped the edge of the table so hard my knuckles turned white. Paint was flaking off and had caught under my fingernail. *This is what's real. Hold onto it!* I swivelled my gaze toward the far side of the square and let out a gasp. There, in the corner, shaded by the church campanile, was Zorzo's studio.

My eyes lost focus and the world around me disappeared.

I manage to get myself assigned to a small room on the ground floor of the Queen's palazzo. Practically a store cupboard, except it's perfect for my purposes. Dorotea is surprised that I don't want to share quarters with her upstairs on the *piano nobile*, and she regards me with suspicion. I hope she won't guess my motives.

Domina's Venetian home is on the Grand Canal in the San Cassiano district. I've been here before, of course, only now there's more purpose to my existence than the last time I visited the city. The painter said that he'll fetch me in his boat this night. I find myself shivering with anticipation.

The evening meal seems interminable, even though the court is tired from the journey. *Such a palaver! So many courses!* I'm too excited to eat. Finally, we retire, and I wait. And I wait. And I wait. If he doesn't arrive soon, I fear I'll collapse with disappointment.

There's a rattle of pebbles on the window and I jump up from my mattress. I beam a smile of pure happiness. Signor Zorzo is below me, his small craft bobbing on the emerald-green water. 'Come, Lady Cecilia,' he calls out.

I grab my cape and mask, and then tiptoe across the floor. The painter has nudged his skiff against the landing stage, and I step aboard. He stands at the stern with a set of oars in his hands while I perch at the prow, my identity hidden by the white *Bauta* with square jaw and no mouth, worn by Venetians all times of the year when outdoors. If I'm seen, no one will know me.

Signor Zorzo rows us past the Campo della Pescaria, and then under the wooden Rialto bridge. Venice is magical tonight, its pearly palaces shining under a full moon, its chimney pots reaching for the stars. Excitement blooms within me. I know I shouldn't be out alone with this man, except I can't help myself. I'm like a bee to his flower; he makes me feel important. I'll pose for him and, in return, he'll teach me to paint. I trust his promise; there's no reason for me to suspect otherwise.

'We've arrived,' he says, tying up by some steps. In one bound, he's ashore holding out his hand. My own is like a child's compared with his. The warmth of his touch surprises me, and I let out a small gasp. 'Do not fear,' he says, misinterpreting my exclamation. 'I shall treat you with the utmost respect.'

I feel the heat in my cheeks and glance away from him. If only he knew how much I long for him to crush me against his strong chest, and to feel his lips on mine once again. I should keep to my resolve and remain a maid until my wedding day. *Much better!* My maidenhead will be checked by doctors before I go to my bridal bed, as is the custom. *You are a fool, Cecilia! Who will want to marry you? You have no wealth.* My shoulders sag.

The painter's studio is at street level. Windows give onto a *campo*, dark shadows outlined by the moonlight. He has set up tallow candles around the room and holds a taper to them from the fire he has kept burning in the grate. 'Please sit here.' He indicates a stool. 'I'll paint you first. Then I'll give you some instruction on the use of colour.'

The chair has been positioned on a small platform so that my eyes are level with the painter's. I remove my mask and cape, which he takes and hangs on a hook by the door. 'Loosen the stays on your sleeves. I'd like your shoulders bare. And remove the net from your hair. It is too beautiful to hide.'

My fingers tangle in my ribbons as they tremble at my shamelessness. If the Queen saw me now, she'd banish me from her court. Yet I can't resist wishing to please this man, who looks at me with admiration and, at the same time, honours my virgin flesh. What they say about him being a womaniser cannot be true. Or perhaps he doesn't consider me woman enough?

I steal a sideways glance at him. He has rested a canvas on a wooden contraption, which, I've found out, is called an easel. He holds a twin-headed stick in his hand and is sketching in the highlights and lowlights of my portrait.

'Stay still, *dolcezza*,' he admonishes. 'You're fidgeting.' He has called me sweetness, but not in a lover's voice. He has used the same tone an uncle would use with a niece. The painter must think me such a child, even if he can't be more than ten years my senior.

Keeping my gaze on the far wall, I let my mind wander. What would Dorotea do to show this man that she's ripe for plucking? *No, Cecilia! You mustn't think like that! You need to keep your purity.*

The artist picks up a palette, the wood curving in such a way that it seems as if some beast has bitten a chunk out of it. He clips on his swag of brushes and his pot, with what I presume is a mixture of linseed oil and turpentine. I'm envious as I study him, wishing I had his abilities.

At length he has finished. 'Are you thirsty, Lady Cecilia? Would you like some wine?'

I nod my agreement, get up from the stool and wander over to the easel. He hands me a goblet and I stare at the canvas. Not only has he caught my physical characteristics, he seems to have caught my spirit as well: the flash of defiance in my eyes, the stubbornness of my chin. I'll never be as great an artist as this man. 'My art is nothing compared with yours,' I say.

'Let me be the judge of that. Did you bring anything to show me?'

'No. I rushed out when I heard you call and left my work behind.' I decide there and then not to let him see what I've accomplished thus far. Better to learn from him first.

'Come, let me show you my paints and explain the language of colour.'

He leads me to the far wall, where there's a grindstone and glass jars containing vivid powders. 'These are liquefied with oil, drop by drop.' He picks up his brushes and caresses them lovingly as if they were women's tresses.

'What are the brushes made of?' I ask, although I know the answer already.

'Horsehairs wrapped with waxed string onto sticks, or small clumps of squirrel fur forced into bird quills which are then inserted into narrow wooden batons.'

'How interesting,' I say, with a flutter of my eyelashes.

'The brushes are graded according to the size of the bird that suffered to provide them: crow, duck, small swan, large swan…'

I put my hand to my mouth. 'They aren't alive, surely, when they're de-feathered?'

The artist laughs and indicates his collection of colours, showing me the most precious ultramarine blue, ground from lapis lazuli, and cerulean, as transparent and luminous as the lagoon. Cobalt needs the addition of lead white to maintain intensity, whereas indigo, dark blue-black like the night sky, should be used for background work. He goes through all his other tints, talking of them as if they were old friends. My head is spinning by the time he has finished.

'Come, *dolcezza*,' he says. 'I must take you back to the Queen's palazzo. Can you feign sickness tomorrow? I shall come for you in the morning. We can make a start on your lessons.'

I realise that if I do nothing, he will not kiss me, and I have been thinking of nothing else for hours. So, I plant myself in front of him and place my hands on his chest. I raise my head and, finally, his lips meet mine and he kisses me so deeply I'm dissolving. My body becomes liquid in his embrace, and the feeling is wonderful.

Finally, he pulls back and gazes into my eyes. 'Lady Cecilia, you have my heart.'

What does he mean? I want to ask, but he grabs my cape from the hook by the door and wraps it around my body. 'Come,' he says. 'The hour is late.'

Back in San Cassiano, I collapse on my bed, my entire body throbbing. Eventually, I drop off to sleep, with the memory of his kisses in my thoughts. Some hours later, although it seems like only moments, Dorotea is shaking me. 'Wake up, Cecilia!'

I groan and open my eyes. Then I clutch my belly. 'I have my monthly pains,' I lie. 'Can you manage without me?'

'We shall have to, won't we?' she huffs.

A smile bubbles up from within me. I gulp it back down again and make an effort to look indisposed. 'I shall be better momentarily,' I say. 'Must be the journey here that has upset my humours.'

'Domina has just told me we go to her villa on Murano tomorrow. She has invited the Marques of Mantova for a *pranzo*.' Dorotea shakes a finger. 'You had better be well enough by then.'

I peer up at her from my pillow, only something strange is happening. The edges to Dorotea's body are blurring and she starts to fade.

Then I feel someone shaking me.

Shake, shake, shake. I wished whoever was doing that would stop. It was most rude of them.

'Are you all right?'

'Zorzo?' I reached for his hand and found my own enveloped in a bear paw. What was Zorzo doing in my room?

'It's Luca,' the voice said. 'You've had another one of your episodes.'

'Who?' His tone was familiar, but my mind struggled to place the name. I opened my eyes, then closed them again, blocking out the sight of a stranger with hair cut shorter than I'd ever seen anyone wear and strange, dark eyeglasses. I pulled my hand back.

'Luca,' the man repeated.

Recall whooshed through my mind, whirling around like surf on a beach before retreating and leaving me giddy.

'Luca . . .' I ran trembling hands up and down my arms.

Of course.

I'd come to Venice with Luca.

We'd gone to the Accademia and I'd seen Giorgione's painting. I remembered staring at the naked lady, remembered seeing Cecilia staring back, remember Luca calling her my nemesis. I remembered the bolt of familiarity as I'd contemplated the two other paintings by Bellini. Remembered the cocktail I'd drunk had been named after him. Remembered staring at this square and seeing Zorzo's studio, the place where love had flowed through my veins for the first time. *Not your veins, Fern. Cecilia's. Your first love was Harry, wasn't it?*

Suddenly, the blood rushed from my head and I swayed. I wanted to be back with the painter; my soul ached for him.

'Here, take a sip of water,' Luca said, grabbing the bottle and glass from the next table and ignoring the startled expressions of its occupants.

'I'll be fine. It always feels like this when I come to. Just give me a minute.'

'Are you sure?'

'Absolutely,' I said, sipping from the glass and swallowing my anguish. 'Maybe you should apologise to those people…'

Luca clapped a hand to his forehead. '*Scusi,*' he said to the startled elderly couple. He handed the half-empty bottle back and ordered another one for them. After paying for it, he held out his hand to me. 'Some lunch will make you feel better.'

I kept my hand in his, telling myself we were walking alongside canals and crossing bridges, and, if I had another so-called episode, I didn't want to fall into the water.

My hand feels safe in his. Protected. Cared-for.

I stopped myself from thinking silly thoughts, and soon we'd arrived at the Trattoria alla Madonna, where we ate a delicious meal of fish risotto, followed by grilled sea bass and green salad served with chilled white wine. I filled Luca in about what had happened between Cecilia and Zorzo. He listened, nodding but keeping his thoughts to himself. 'I'll show you San Marco,' he said when we'd finished our lunch. 'It's definitely worth a visit.'

After crossing the Rialto Bridge, we made our way through a labyrinth of small streets heading to the heart of the city, passing designer shops selling everything a tourist with money could wish for. The closer we got to St Mark's, the more my nerves jangled.

Keep focused! You'll be all right.

Of course, I'd seen pictures of the square, but the real thing took my breath. The Basilica's columns and domes shone in the afternoon sunlight, in radiant mounds and pleats, in golden extensions and undulating surfaces.

'It's amazing.' I stared at the familiar clock tower on the left. All the other buildings around the piazza were newer than in Cecilia's time, as was the bell tower (although it was in the same place and the loggia at its base jogged my memory). The Doge's Palace appeared to have changed little, even though I'd read in Auntie's book on Venice that it had suffered from a fire in the late 16th century. *So many fires!*

Luca led me up the steps to the arched portals of the church and in we went. A queue of people in front was making slow progress but I didn't mind. Light leapt and twirled from myriad minute surfaces of refracted gilt. The aroma of incense and candlewax filled my nostrils. A millennium of worship in this place. *And Cecilia came here and saw what I'm seeing now.*

Above me and at every angle, strange gleaming mosaic figures danced in a cloth of gold: lions, lambs, flowers, thorns, eagles, serpents, dragons, doves. It was an incredible sight, both terrifying and soothing. Emotion welled up, and I squeezed Luca's hand. *No need for words.*

When our visit was over, we stumbled out into the sunshine. The square heaved with tourists, cameras clicking and pigeons swooping to peck at the corn held out to them. 'Let's have a drink before heading home,' Luca suggested.

We sat at an outdoor table. *Florian's.* A friend at work had warned me about the prices here. Luca was being far too alpha about not letting me pay for anything, but I knew what to do.

A waiter was hovering. *'Due calici di Prosecco,'* Luca ordered.

I stared at the clock-tower and squirmed in my seat.

'Everything all right?' he turned and asked me. 'No flashbacks?'

'No. Just a deep conviction that I've been here before.'

'I was wondering about something.' He shuffled his chair closer. 'Have you considered that you might be possessing Cecilia?'

The weirdness of the notion had me gaping at him. 'What do you mean? Cecilia lived almost five hundred years ago. I'm still alive.'

'I've been reading up about it. There's a theory that past, present and future are all happening simultaneously but in parallel dimensions. Perhaps there's been a blip in the space-time continuum,' he added, eyeing the musicians tuning up on a podium. 'And if that's the case, who came first: you or Cecilia? You tell me she seems to be aware of you occasionally.'

I frowned. 'I've seen *Back to the Future* too, you know. It's just fiction.'

'No. The theory actually originated with Einstein's concept of space-time.'

'What about your theory she was trying to tell me something, get me to do something for her so she could rest in peace?'

Luca shrugged. 'Whatever it is, I just hope you'll be all right. I must admit I was worried about you earlier on. You were in what I can only describe as a trance.'

'Please don't worry,' I said determinedly. 'I doubt Cecilia wants to harm me. I'm still not sure about your parallel dimension idea, though. Seems a bit farfetched...'

'And being possessed by a woman who died half a millennium ago isn't?' He laughed.

'Touché!' I smiled and sipped the rest of my Prosecco, gazing around and absorbing the magnificence of St Mark's Square. Then I said, 'Just need to use the facilities. I'll be back in a minute.'

'*Va bene.* Okay...' He stretched out his legs and leaned back in his chair.

I stood and went inside. On my way past the bar, I asked for the bill and settled up. I'd need a second mortgage to pay for it when my credit card statement arrived, but I'd made my point. I just hoped Luca would take it in the right spirit.

Back at the table, I said, 'Hope you don't mind. I've paid for our drinks. It's the least I can do.'

He chuckled, getting to his feet. 'Not at all. The gondola ride is on me, though. I insist.'

'That would be lovely.' I fell into step beside him. We strolled hand-in-hand toward the lagoon and again recognition rolled through me as I stared in wonderment at the island on the other side of the basin. A church campanile, like an enormous pencil, pointed skywards as if about to write a message. 'I know I sound like a cliché. But I'm overwhelmed, Luca, it's all so beautiful.'

He lifted my wrist to his mouth and brushed his lips to my pulse. 'This is my favourite city,' he said proudly.

My heart fluttered, but I resolutely ignored it. Just the Venice effect, I told myself. This place is incredibly romantic.

The afternoon sky had started to fade to a smoky blue and the sun was casting a wash of gold over the buildings. Gondolas rode the waves, tethered along the waterfront before us. Luca approached one of them and negotiated with the gondolier. I stepped onto the boat and sat next to him on a plush red seat in the centre.

'This part used to be covered up in the past, I think.'

'To preserve the modesty of young women like Cecilia. She's quite a rebel, by the way,' he smirked. 'Sneaking out to see her painter at night. She would have been kept indoors in those days, as only courtesans could walk about freely. I wonder if Cecilia managed her meeting with him?'

'Well, I'm not about to find out,' I said with determination. 'It's not every day you get to see the Grand Canal by gondola. I'm going to make the most of every minute.'

Cecilia and her artist could wait.

Of course, I wanted to find out if my nemesis had learned to paint.

All in good time, though.

I reached for my camera. For now, I'd focus on enjoying this amazing experience and bask in the incredible beauty of Venice.

CHAPTER 10

Luca

With a groan, I scrutinised the pile of paperwork on my desk—estimates to send out and quotes to get in. Routine stuff, which I could easily handle on autopilot, but it had mounted up. I was in the office this evening, working overtime. I thought about Fern and our gondola ride yesterday, remembering her smiling softly, taking everything in and clicking away with her camera. When we'd passed under the Rialto Bridge, she'd grabbed hold of my arm and I'd held resolutely onto her to keep her in the present.

Jealousy rolled through me as I imagined her spending time with the painter. *Not her, but Cecilia. Even so…* I shook my head and picked up another sheaf of papers. God, it was hard to concentrate. Fern's visions and where they appeared to be leading were at the forefront of my mind.

After work, I drove home to my apartment, then sat on the terrace with a glass of chilled Chardonnay, gazing at the view of the mountains. Would Fern be up for a drive through the hills and dinner at a trattoria tomorrow evening? *There's only one way to find out.* I went to the phone, rifled through my address book, and dialled Susan's number.

Fern answered and said she'd be delighted, thanking me again for the visit to Venice yesterday. I felt ridiculously happy she'd agreed to see me, then remembered I should ask if everything was all right.

'Fine. Cecilia has left me in peace,' she said reassuringly.

'Well, that's good to hear,' I said, relieved. 'What have you been doing today?'

'Auntie and I went to the market in Bassano. I bought myself a new pair of sandals.' I heard the enthusiasm in her voice. 'We had the best pizza I've ever eaten. The town is gorgeous. I'd love to go back there soon and paint a watercolour…'

'I worry about you driving on your own… What if you have a flash-back?'

'Unlikely in a car. I've realised it only seems to happen when I'm in a place associated with Cecilia. I'm planning a visit to Murano the day after tomorrow.' Her excitement came down the phone line. 'That's where my so-called nemesis' story will continue, I think. I've decided to go with the flow, as they say. I really want to find out what happened to her and solve the mystery of why she's singled me out.'

'Will you be okay on your own?' My gut clenched with concern. There was no way I could take another day off work to look after her.

'Auntie will come with me. Not that she'll be much help; she's convinced Cecilia is a figment of my imagination. She loves Venetian glass, though, and would like to buy some in Murano for her collection. I'll take my sketchpad and sit by a canal while she goes shopping.'

'Okay.' I'd warn Fern to be careful when I saw her tomorrow. 'I'll pick you up at seven, then.'

'Perfect.'

I hung up and ran my fingers through my hair. How the hell was I going to keep my relationship with Fern on a friendly footing? I'd never been "just friends" with a woman in my life. That said, I'd never managed to commit myself fully to any of them either. Fern was different, however. She called to something buried deep within me. Something unquantifiable, but fundamental.

The following evening, I pulled up outside Susan's house and rang the bell. Fern answered the door. I was stunned by her unique beauty; she was wearing a light green gypsy blouse that brought out the emerald in her eyes. I was pleased she hadn't embraced the power-dressing of most women I knew, and that she'd ditched the ubiquitous shoulder-pads gracing even everyday outfits.

She waved to her aunt and, after pecking me on the cheek in a disappointingly friendly fashion, settled herself in my Alfa. I took the road behind Asolo on route to the village of Monfumo, where I'd booked a table in the small restaurant overlooking the square. We sat on the balcony, the sinking sun casting a rosy glow over the surrounding hills. Peach and pear orchards hugged their crests, and farmhouses nestled in the dips between them, half barn and half living accommodation topped by terracotta roof tiles. The night air was warm, almost too warm, and perspiration beaded my upper lip. I wiped it away with my napkin.

'There's something I'd like to ask you,' I said after we'd ordered a plate of *prosciutto* with melon and a half a carafe of the house red.

'Oh?' Her eyes met mine.

'Last night I had an argument with my sister,' I said. 'I can't get anywhere with her, and I don't think I'm ever likely to. She'll have to come to the realisation Federico is wrong for her on her own. Mother is going out of her mind with worry, however. She thinks you're a good role model and would be really grateful if you'd try and befriend Chiara.'

'Your mother did say something along those lines before.' Fern picked up a bread roll and broke off a piece. 'I forgot to tell you I met your sister and her boyfriend in Altivole the other day. Didn't like him much.' Her mouth twisted. 'He reminds me of someone I once knew. Not a nice person.' She paused. 'I'll do my best. What's your sister interested in?'

'Her horses and Federico, of course, not to mention her political ideas. Oh, and after a lot of persuasion on my part, they've agreed to take part in the re-enactment of Caterina Cornaro's court at the end of the month.' A sudden idea occurred to me and I said, 'Maybe you wouldn't mind joining in with our dance group? You should have no difficulty with the steps…'

Fern smiled. 'That's if I still remember them. How often do you rehearse?'

'Once a week for now. As we get closer to the re-enactment we'll meet more often. The next rehearsal is in three days' time.'

'Good. Auntie and I have decided to treat ourselves to the opera tomorrow, at the Fenice Theatre. We'll stay the night in Venice then come home after breakfast.'

'That will be fun,' I said, envious. 'Which opera?'

'*The Capulets and the Montagues*. I know it's not based on Romeo and Juliet, but on an earlier work that many believe inspired Shakespeare to write his play.'

'If you were staying in the Veneto longer, we could go to the arena in Verona. Opera there is an incredible experience…'

Our waiter had arrived to serve the main course— lasagne with wild boar ragù. Fern and I lifted our forks and started to eat, chatting about the different attractions of Italy until our plates were empty.

'Coffee?' I asked.

'I've had my quota of caffeine for the day, but you go ahead. Oh, and no argument, Luca. I insist on going Dutch tonight.'

I decided not to contradict her. To her way of thinking, our being "just friends" meant this wasn't a date, much as I'd have preferred otherwise.

'How about a nightcap at the Caffè Centrale?' I suggested, not ready yet for the evening to end.

Half an hour later, in Asolo, I ordered a grappa for myself and

Fern requested a *limoncello*. We were sitting at a table on the outside terrace facing the fountain, with the Queen's castle dominating the skyline in the background.

'Can you tell me about your family?' I leaned back in my chair and fixed her in my gaze. 'There might be something in your background that links you to Cecilia.'

Fern chewed her lip thoughtfully. 'I can't think of anything that could be relevant.'

Curiosity had me saying, 'You haven't told me about your parents.'

'They used to have a landscape gardening business.' She tucked a strand of hair behind her ear. 'They sold it and retired last year. They spend their time pottering about their own garden near Chepstow or playing bridge.'

'No siblings?'

She shook her head. 'I always wanted a brother or a sister, but Mum had a hysterectomy after having me because of complications giving birth.'

Our drinks arrived, and we clinked glasses.

'Are both your parents English?' I asked after taking a sip.

'Welsh,' she said firmly. 'We prefer to be called British.'

'Right,' I cocked a smile. 'I was just trying to find out if you had any family connections that would have made Cecilia chose you…'

Fern's eyes narrowed. 'She was a lady of Venice and I'm just an ordinary girl from Wales. The only thing that links us, as far as I'm aware, is our love of painting.'

I was about to broach the subject of her being careful in Venice when a familiar voice echoed behind me. My heart sank. What the hell was Francesca doing here?

My glamorous blonde ex-girlfriend sashayed up to our table, shoulder pads forward, and gave me a frosty look. '*Buonasera, Luca. Come stai?*'

'*Bene, grazie.*' I introduced her to Fern, who met Francesca's frozen glare with a wide smile.

Francesca draped her arm around the suave-looking silver-haired man she paraded before us like a trophy. '*Il mio fidanzato, Gabriele,*' she said, emphasising the fact that he was her fiancé. They declined my offer of a drink, saying they had to get back to Treviso, and, arm in arm, practically waltzed off the terrace in the direction of the parking lot.

'Who was she?' Fern asked, her brow creasing.

'My ex,' I said, not wanting to elaborate. I glanced at my Rolex. 'It's getting late. I'd better take you home.'

I left some change on the table to settle our bill, then held my hand out to Fern. She slipped her small palm into mine, and just the feel of her soft skin soothed the irritation Francesca had stirred up within me.

Driving toward Altivole, I kept Fern's face in the periphery of my vision. She wasn't conventionally beautiful but compared with Francesca's fake glamour and that of the other women I'd dated in the past, her naturalness was far more alluring.

I pulled up in front of her aunt's house and she leaned toward me. 'Good night, Luca,' she brushed both my cheeks with her warm lips.

'Be careful in Venice,' I warned. 'Make sure you are always somewhere safe in case you have another episode.'

'I'll be fine,' she said with a wave of her hand.

I watched her until she was safely through the front door.

In the middle of the night, I woke suddenly, sweaty sheets tangled around my legs. I disentangled myself and switched on my bedside light.

Flipping three am.

I'll never get back to sleep now.

The air was too hot for comfort, but that wasn't what had woken me.

What the hell was it? There'd been no noises that I could discern. The street below was silent, and I couldn't even hear the owl that sometimes hooted in the tree beneath my window.

I shut my eyes and tried to drop off.

A sinking sensation invaded my mind, and then a voice. Now I knew what had woken me. I'd had that damn recurring dream.

Too late!

Too late!

Too late!

CHAPTER 11

'The island of Murano used to be a succession of vegetable fields, vineyards and gardens,' Auntie read from her guidebook.

I was only half-focusing on her words, distracted by the sight of Venice across the lagoon. Hundreds of church spires, and the domes of St Mark's gleaming in the sunshine. I took my camera from my bag and framed a couple of shots.

The ferry had started to make its way down Murano's main waterway. Pale pink, cream and terracotta-coloured buildings lined the canal banks, where tourists thronged like ants at a picnic table.

Auntie, sitting next to me on the top deck, tucked a strand of her frizzy grey hair under an enormous sunhat and continued reading, 'Murano's reputation as a centre for glassmaking was born when the Venetian Republic, fearing fire and destruction to the city's mostly wood buildings, ordered the demolition of all the foundries within the city in 1291.' She nudged me. 'Are you listening?'

My heart had thudded at the words "fire and destruction".

'Please read on,' I said as calmly as I could.

'Though the Republic ordered the flattening of the foundries, it authorised and encouraged construction outside the city, and by the late thirteenth century, the glassmaking industry was centred in Murano.'

I nodded, and a distant memory of the elegant chalices used at the Barco came into my mind.

'The glassmakers were soon the island's most important citizens,' Auntie continued. 'By the fourteenth century, glassmakers were allowed to wear swords, enjoyed immunity from prosecution by the Venetian state, and found their daughters married into Venice's most affluent families.'

My eyes widened. 'Immunity from prosecution? How weird!'

'Of course, there was a catch: glassmakers were not allowed to leave. Many craftsmen took this risk, however, and set up glass furnaces in surrounding cities and even as far afield as England and the Netherlands, despite the danger of retaliation from the Council of Ten, who wanted Venice to have exclusivity.'

My ears pricked. 'The Council of Ten?' I'd heard of them before. Was it something I'd read? *No.* 'Who were they exactly?'

'The Doge and other members of the *Signoria*, the ruling class. Highly secretive,' Auntie said, grimacing.

The ferry's engines grumbled into reverse as it drew level with the pier and then shuddered to a halt. After grabbing hold of my bag, I stepped ashore with my aunt.

'Are you certain you don't want to come with me and visit the glassworks?' she asked, pulling down her baggy t-shirt over her ample stomach. 'It won't take long. We can have some lunch nearby.'

'If it's okay with you, I'd like to sketch something to turn into a painting when we get home. I'll stroll around and find a good spot.'

Auntie cocked her head to one side. 'How will I know where to find you?'

'Can I see your map?' She held it out and I felt my eyes being drawn to the wording, "Palazzo da Mula". *The name calls to me.* 'We can meet there,' I said, pointing. 'What does your guidebook say about it?'

Auntie flipped the pages, and then read, 'The summer residence of the nobility. The frontage features large Gothic windows and Veneto-Byzantine panels from the twelfth and thirteenth centuries. One of the few palaces which escaped restructuration of the island in the nineteenth century.' She peered at her watch. 'It's eleven now. Say one o'clock? I'm sure we'll find a restaurant nearby.'

'See you soon, Auntie,' I smiled. 'I'll sit on the opposite side of the canal, so I can get a good view.' I pecked her on the cheek, hefted my bag onto my shoulder, and set off. It was good to stretch my legs; we'd left home over three hours ago, driving to the station at Treviso then catching the train to Venice. I lengthened my stride.

At a newsvendor's, I purchased my own guidebook and map. After crossing the Longo bridge, I followed the Fondamenta Venier, trusting my sense of recognition would tell me when I'd arrived.

No such luck, yet the palazzo was obvious for its evident age, and stood out next to the smaller more modern buildings surrounding it. I snapped a couple of photos before sitting on the bank of the canal. I took out my sketchpad, and drew a few perspective lines, getting the basic structure right before starting on the detail.

The Gothic windows with their pointed arches would be tricky, but not impossible. A light shone in one of them. *Good, that will engage the viewer's eye*. My 2B pencil flew across the page, my focus intent. Using a graphite stick, I started shading the high-water mark and then added tone to the stonework.

A motor-boat chugged past, making the green water slap the edges of the canal, rippling the greyish reflections of the building's windows. The cinnamon-coloured palace ached with history, and was definitely familiar, except I couldn't feel Cecilia tugging at my mind. Maybe I'd been wrong about her story continuing here? Dorotea had categorically stated this was where they were due to go with the Queen. A *pranzo*, luncheon, at her Murano villa for the Marques of Mantova. Disappointment flooded my chest. I gazed around. Maybe it wasn't such a good idea, anyway. If I'd gone into one of my trances, I might have fallen into the canal.

As I carried on with my sketching, I thought about Luca. He'd been such a gentleman last night, and he'd given me a comforting feeling of safety in his company. I screwed up my forehead, torn between wanting more from him and being relieved he so obviously only considered me a "friend". What the hell did I expect, anyway? I wasn't his type, judging by the beautiful woman who'd been his ex.

The sound of sandals flapping on the stone interrupted my thoughts. Auntie was approaching, her face red with sweat. 'I've bought a set of wineglasses,' she puffed. 'Can't wait to show them to you. But let's have some lunch first. I'm starving.'

I shoved my pad into my rucksack and levered myself to my feet. At least I'd have a painting I could use for a commission, so the visit here hadn't been a complete waste of time. And I was looking forward to the opera this evening.

'Let's go, Auntie,' I said, looping my arm through hers. 'I'm hungry too.'

My aunt had booked us into a hotel in the San Cassiano district right on the Grand Canal. After picking up our overnight bags from the left-luggage counter at the station, we took a water-taxi. 'It's not far,' she said. 'It won't cost an arm and a leg.'

We checked into a luxurious room on the third floor, furnished with antiques, a glass chandelier and velvet curtains. The hair on the back of my neck prickled when Auntie mentioned the building dated from the fourteenth century, but I reminded myself that most of the palaces in this fabulous city were as old, if not older.

We ate a light meal of mozzarella and tomatoes, ordered from room service, then showered and changed into what Auntie called our "posh frocks". (Auntie into a flowery ankle-length polyester tent-like garment, and me into a simple short white linen dress nipped in at the waist with a belt, another of my work outfits, which I'd packed in case I might need it.) We sat at the front of the water bus from Rialto, the setting sun gilding the sky, washing the beautiful buildings along the canal in a honey glow.

'Do you know why it's called the Fenice?' Auntie said as we disembarked at Santa Maria del Giglio. Clearly expecting no reply, she continued, 'It means the phoenix, and the theatre was renamed after it had burnt down and was rebuilt.'

I gave a shudder. 'Hope it's fireproof now.'

'Sorry! I didn't think.' She patted my arm. 'I'm sure it's perfectly safe.'

I followed her into the theatre, and my jaw dropped— it was so over-the-top. Gold-leaf dripped from the walls, ceilings, lights and mirrors. Ornate, but I loved it. Our seats were in the centre stalls, and we squeezed our way past the disapproving knees of the fellow-occupants of row seventeen. Within minutes, the curtain rose, and I found myself transported to medieval Verona. The Bellini opera (weird how that name kept cropping up) touched me to the core. Juliet being forced into an unwanted marriage. Why had it brought tears to my eyes?

Auntie went to the restroom during the interval, but I stayed in my seat. I thought about Cecilia. The story of Romeo and Juliet was based on an ancient legend and possibly known to her. How disappointing not to have connected with her this afternoon. It seemed the onus was on Cecilia to connect with me. That put paid to Luca's theory. I couldn't be possessing Cecilia; the boot was almost certainly on the other foot...

Maybe there wouldn't be any more episodes? I chewed my lip. Could what had happened up to now have been my imagination running away with me?

All through the final part of the performance, I found my focus wandering away from the opera to settle on Cecilia and Zorzo. If I didn't find out what had happened between them, I'd be flipping disappointed.

After the last encore, Auntie and I left the theatre arm in arm to take the water bus back to Rialto and walk to our hotel. 'I'm exhausted,' Auntie said when we stepped into our room. 'Let's go straight to bed.' She went to clean her teeth and change, then emerged from the bathroom in a voluminous white cotton nightdress, her face slathered in cold cream. 'Your turn, Fern,' she said.

By the time I'd finished getting ready, Auntie was already snoring. *How am I going to sleep through that?* I rifled through my overnight case and pulled out the book on Caterina Cornaro that my aunt had loaned me. I'd already read the first part of the history, up until when the Queen had been "coerced" into abdicating her throne. Now I read on, absorbing the description of Caterina's arrival in Venice, where she was met by the Doge in his magnificent state barge, the *Bucintoro*. 'As compensation for renouncing the Cyprus throne in favour of Venice,' I read, 'the Doge granted her a full and absolute control over the lands of Asolo, where she arrived on October 11, 1489, followed by over 4000 people who flocked there from the surrounding region to greet her.

'Soon Caterina felt the need to own a palace worthy of her reputation: the perfect chosen location to build a "villa di delizie" (a villa of delights) was Altivole, at the foot of Asolo.' *Nothing new there.*

Auntie's snores settled into a soft rumble and I felt my eyelids drooping. Tiredness seeped through me, and I started thinking about Luca. The attraction was there; no doubt about it. But only on my side. He treated me in the same way he treated Chiara. Like a brother treats his sister. Why did it bother me? I didn't want to betray Harry. He'd died because of me, and I owed it to him to stay faithful to his memory.

My eyes brimmed. Harry and I were planning on visiting Auntie when she'd moved to Italy shortly after becoming a published author, but we hadn't got 'round to it. Such a lucky lady to have been signed to a major publisher. And how wonderful that a large advance had enabled her to take early retirement from teaching. Auntie's bodice-ripping romances had a huge following on both sides of the Atlantic, and well deserved too. Her own love-life had been cut short when her husband had run off with his secretary five years ago. She'd sworn off men at that point, saying she preferred the ones she created in her stories to those in real life.

Am I doing the same thing? Fantasising about a man who died five hundred years ago because the reality of losing Harry is too painful. Is that what all this is about?

I was drifting, my mind floating, and I could feel a tugging sensation and a longing like I'd never felt before.

I lie in my bed, too excited to sleep, moving my hands over my body, imagining they are the painter's warm palms. I touch my breasts and my nipples harden. I trace a line down to my cleft, that secret part of me I've never explored before. Why did it throb so much when Zorzo kissed me? I suck in a breath, then cup myself, spreading my fingers so that the one in the middle can slip inside. The tip rubs against a small button of flesh, sending a raw shiver through me. I exhale sharply and touch the spot again.

Heat spreads through my body. What have I uncovered? Is there some deformity down there? I take my hand away and feel bereft of the sensation. Tenderly I caress the downy hair between my legs. I can't help myself, I want to discover more.

Slipping two fingers inside, I search for what I know is called my maidenhead. Could it be that fleshy protuberance? It doesn't take me long to find the button again, and I hook my fingers around it, applying gentle pressure to see what will happen. It swells under my touch like a tiny man's "thing". I didn't know that women hid such wonder in their folds.

I feel a rush of intense pleasure and let out a breath. Again, I stroke the button. Again, the joy, rippling under my fingers again and again and again. I release a soft sigh, but it's over too quickly and I feel bereft once more, my legs weak and my soul empty. Shame rolls through me; pleasuring myself is a sin, of that I am sure.

I hear a shout. Holy Mary, Signor Zorzo is calling from below my window. 'Lady Cecilia, come, we mustn't tarry. You'll be missed before too long.'

I lift my fingers to my nose and inhale the citrus scent.

There's a washstand in the corner of the room; I pour water from the jug next to it and rinse my hand.

The artist has placed a curtained canopy over the centre of his boat, and I sit inside, mask in place, hidden from the world. My hair is loose under my cape; I haven't had time to dress it. I keep my head down as he hands me ashore, not fully understanding why I'm here.

In his studio, I see it; and then I do know. This is what I want: the skill to work such magic on canvas. He has painted a picture of himself, holding a lute and leaning his red-coated back against an oak tree, the dark green transcribed into blackish blue in the thickening darkness of approaching night. And he has placed me on the other side of the scene, propped up on my right elbow, my face turned toward him. My hair is caught in the beam of the half-moon, which is only just visible between two dark-grey clouds. There's a white space opposite the oak tree, and I point to it. 'What will go there?'

'Our task for this morning.'

'Our task?' I dare not hope.

'You'll help me. It is easy enough. I'll start, and you'll finish what I've started, copying my technique.'

'W… w… what if I make a mistake?'

'That's the beauty of oil paint. I'll go over anything that doesn't please me. And, in the meantime, you'll learn. Isn't that why you're here?' he says, winking.

Heat whooshes to my face. 'You're insufferable.'

'If I'm insufferable, then I'm afraid I can't teach you.' He beams a smile. 'A pupil must respect her master.'

'Oh, you're my master now, are you?' I curtsey then giggle, my disquiet forgotten. The light-hearted banter between us is easier to deal with than the tension last night that made the place between my legs throb.

He doesn't respond immediately; he's mixing his paints. 'See how thickly I've laid the colour on the crown of the oak tree? We must do the same on this side of the canvas,' he indicates the white space. 'There's a copse here, blackish-blue merging into light blackness to reflect the approaching night.'

Smiling, he spreads the paint with a small knife. 'You know I was a pupil of Giovanni Bellini. But it was my meeting with the great Leonardo da Vinci that changed the way I view art. His use of the *sfumato* technique was something I wanted to develop according to my own style.'

'*Sfumato?* What's that?'

'Where we blur or soften sharp outlines by subtle and gradual blending, some say feathering, of one tone into another, to create a smoke-like haziness.'

'Oh, yes, I can see how you've shown the arrival of the night that way. The painting seems to have a sense of movement about it.'

The artist takes my hand in his and transfers his brush into it. Holding my wrist with a delicate touch, he guides my hand across the canvas and my heart dances.

Although it's he who's doing the painting, my hand is learning from his. I want this to go on forever. Yet, in no time at all, it seems, he's telling me we need to depart. 'The daylight hours are better for this type of work,' he says. 'Can you escape from your duties to the Queen tomorrow?'

Doesn't he realise she's a mother hen, and she likes to keep her chicks, as she calls us, close to her? Perhaps I can feign my painful monthlies one more day? 'I'll try,' I say. 'Call for me at the same time as today.'

Back in San Cassiano, I creep into my room.

Maria Santissima, Dorotea is sitting on my mattress, a frown darkening her face. 'Where have you been?'

And so, I tell her. What else can I do? She's caught up in what she calls the romance of my assignation, although she warns me that no good will come of it. She doesn't understand about art. Dorotea can only think of the pleasures of the flesh. 'Have you done it with him?' she asks.

I smile and do not correct her assumption.

Let her believe what she likes.

The Court leaves for Murano, where the Queen will stay until tomorrow. Besides entertaining the Marques, she wants to buy glass. I have a day and a night ahead of me to spend as I please. Well, not quite as I please for there are servants here who'll spy on me. Dorotea has told me I should stuff pillows under my bedcovers so that it will seem as if I am sleeping. And that's what I do when Signor Zorzo calls.

He takes me by boat again to his studio, where my fingers shake as they hold the brush. How clumsy I am today. He covers my hand with his and my confidence soars. I can feel his breath against my ear, soft and warm. Turning to him, I run the tips of my fingers lightly down his cheek. I suck in a gasp and a quiver travels down to my core.

He moans, but he does not stop me when I move my hand down his body and encounter his arousal. His eyes hold mine and I feel as if I shall sink into them; liquid gold, they burn with desire. How different he is from Lodovico Gaspare. I don't like to think of the man from Ferrara and banish him from my mind.

My painter reaches down and unpins my hair (for today I have dressed it properly). He entwines his hands in my tresses and pulls me against him. 'Lady Cecilia, you will be the undoing of me.'

I lift my mouth to his and our lips meet. The softness makes my insides shiver. We stumble to the bed in the corner of the studio and lower ourselves onto it. Our tongues are dancing and my entire body is on fire. 'Are you sure, *dolcezza?*' he asks.

I nod, the decision made. The step I'm taking will alter the course of my life, yet I can't envisage any other destiny for myself than to become one with this man.

'You are a horsewoman,' he says, lifting his lips from mine. 'Your maidenhead will have been stretched. Even so, I shall enter you slowly, so you do not feel too much pain.'

For a second, I am perplexed. Our gaze locks and his eyes burn with such love that I know this can't be wrong. Whatever the church says, we aren't sinners. There's no need for us to speak the words. There will be time for that later. He lifts my gown and I let out a small cry as he pushes slowly into me, my sex resisting only momentarily. Simply a twinge and then we rock together, and I'm lost to the exquisiteness of the sensation.

Too soon, it's over. He shudders and withdraws from me, pulling a kerchief from his pocket and covering his manhood. 'You know how babes are made?' he says. 'I can't spill my seed inside you or we shall have a child. The next time we make love, you will know the pleasure I've experienced. Just give me some moments to regain my strength.'

He gets up from the bed and goes to the sideboard where there's a flagon of wine. We drink and nibble biscotti, then wash, then take our time over lovemaking. I had no idea that a man could make a woman writhe the way I'm doing. Have I no shame? I'm lying naked with my legs apart and my lover's hand is doing such things to me that my whole body is trembling.

On the brink of that joy, like the one I felt the other night, about to reach the end of a blissful journey that has built and built, Zorzo stops what he has been doing. 'I want to be inside you when you climax. It will be stronger for you.'

And he is right. Pleasuring myself can't be compared with what is happening now. He thrusts into me and I arch against him. Arching and rubbing myself against him until a spark inside me grows into a flame of such exquisiteness that I'm completely lost to it.

I stare into his eyes, and he gazes deep into mine, stroking the side of my face and whispering his love. Tired, I feel myself drowsing; before I know it I have fallen asleep and into the strangest dream.

I shuddered awake— my PJs hot against my skin.

Who am I?

Where am I?

What the hell just happened?

I swung my legs out of bed and staggered into the bathroom. I switched on the light and stared at my reflection in the mirror.

Christ, my skin was still flushed from that orgasm.

The most earth-shatteringly amazing orgasm.

My nipples had formed stiff peaks and my insides were quivering with after-shocks.

I took in a deep breath.

Jesus, Fern. You've been deflowered for the second time in your life. And by a sixteenth century Italian artist…

After splashing my face with cold water, I climbed back into bed and curled in on myself.

The guilt had returned. It rolled through me, tinging my light with darkness.

I turned my head.

Oh, my God!

There, on the bedside table.

Caught in a beam of moonlight.

The piece of burnt wood.

A voice whispered, *'Lorenza…'*

And I screamed.

CHAPTER 12

Her aunt had dropped Fern off at the Caffè Centrale, about half an hour before the rehearsal. She approached in one of her floaty hippy skirts and a cotton blouse, looking so damn beautiful I wanted to put my arms around her and kiss her bow-shaped lips. But I didn't. Instead, I pulled out a chair for her and asked what she'd like to drink.

'Just a glass of sparkling water, please,' she smiled. 'I need to keep my head clear for the dancing.'

I signalled the young waiter and ordered a bottle of San Pellegrino with two glasses.

'How did your visit to Venice go?' I asked.

She spoke about her trip to Murano, the opera, and her dream of Cecilia's visit to Zorzo. When she mentioned that the artist and his muse had been intimate, she flushed bright red. 'I'll spare you the details,' she said. Then she told me that she'd woken her aunt by screaming at the sight of the piece of burnt wood and upon hearing the ghostly whisper.

Holy shit! I fought to keep my mouth from falling open. 'What happened next?'

'Well, of course the wood disappeared. Auntie thinks I've completely lost my mind again and wants me to see a doctor.' Fern shook her head. 'I told her categorically that I wouldn't. Such a shock, though, to see it there in Venice. I thought the fire was associated with the Barco, but now I don't know what to think…'

I let out a breath. 'Parts of Venice were always going up in flames in the Middle Ages. Most of the houses and bridges were made of wood in those days.'

'I know that's why they moved the glassblowing furnaces out to Murano.' She stared across the tables toward the fountain in the centre of the square. 'Shame we can't find out more about Giorgione's life. For instance, if he married. That book I bought at the Accademia was mostly about his paintings.'

'There aren't any records of a marriage, as far as I know. Just rumours of him being a lover of women.'

Fern frowned. 'Oh.'

Was that a jealous "oh"? The green-eyed monster was nibbling at me too. Crazy to feel jealous of a long-dead rival. *Rival?* The notion was totally insane.

I glanced up and spotted my sister and Federico pushing their way between the tables.

Chiara lowered herself, a sulky expression on her face. 'I'm not in the mood for this. Renaissance dancing isn't really my thing.'

I quirked a brow. 'How will you know until you've tried it?'

'I'm sure it will be quite amusing,' Federico said. He'd sat next to Fern and was staring at her in a way that made my blood boil. 'Have we got time for a coffee?' he asked.

I signalled the waiter and ordered espressos for Federico and my sister. An awkward silence ensued. Chiara was staring at her feet. Her boyfriend was eying Fern as if she were a piece of cake he'd like to devour, and Fern was looking as if she wished the ground would swallow her up.

'Let me get these,' she said, reaching for her purse when Federico and Chiara had finished their coffees. Before I could say anything, she'd headed toward the bar.

'So, you let the lady pay,' Federico smirked.

I folded my arms. 'The lady insists. Times are changing.'

He let out a laugh. 'Quite right. Your sister pays for both of us when we go out. After all, she has more cash than I do.'

'Money that my mother has given her,' I said through gritted teeth.

'Hey! Stop talking about me as if I wasn't here,' Chiara's voice shrilled. 'That is between Mum and me, Luca. Just butt out!'

I was about to tell her I only had her best interests at heart, but Fern had come up to the table with a smile on her lovely face. 'I'm looking forward to the dancing,' she said brightly. And it was as if oil had been poured over stormy waters. The atmosphere changed and both Federico and Chiara smiled back at her.

'I'm looking forward to it too,' Federico said in a smarmy tone.

I bunched my fists, only barely restraining myself from punching the living daylights out of him.

A noisy group of people had congregated in the sunken area below the inner castle walls. The Mayor of Asolo, a tall young man with dark hair and bushy eyebrows, was speaking into a megaphone, barking out instructions about who should go where and do what. I held Fern's hand. She in turn held Federico's and he held Chiara's. *Her* hand was then taken by the Mayor as we joined in the circle of dancers.

The steps weren't difficult. One, two, three in one direction, a turn on the heel and one, two, three the opposite way. Let go hands, face out of the circle, and join hands again. Six steps, let go, and swivel to face inwards again. Lift upheld hands and come together in the centre, then move back out to full circle. Into the middle, and once there, drop hands, twirl around, make a wider circle. Steps to the right, steps to the left, more twirls. Smaller circle with right hand held inwards, to form something like the spokes of a wheel. Turn and do the same with left hand. And so on and so forth.

The moves appeared to come easily to Fern; she seemed as if she could have done the dance in her sleep. I also knew what I was doing, having been part of the re-enactment before, but Federico and Chiara were struggling, getting the sequence of steps wrong and bumping into people. Federico whispered something into Chiara's ear, and they left the circle, which performed much better without them.

When Fern and I had rehearsed the dance twice, we found Chiara and Federico sitting at the bar on the terrace. 'Beers all round?' I suggested.

'Count us out,' Chiara said, groaning. 'We're off. This is not our scene.' She glanced at Fern. 'Remember you promised to come for a ride with me?'

I gave Fern what I hoped was an encouraging look. She responded with a nod. 'When, Chiara?'

'How about tomorrow afternoon? Say four o'clock? You'll enjoy it, I promise.'

'Perfect,' Fern said. 'I'll be there. Thanks.'

I watched my sister and her boyfriend slide between the tables, their arms around each other. Then I shot a glance at Fern. 'Are you up for a bit of espionage?'

Her eyes widened. 'What do you mean?'

'We need to be quick or we'll lose them,' I said, taking her hand. 'Those beers will have to wait.'

I led Fern down the road to the parking lot. 'Federico's old Lancia is unmistakable for its colour. Bright green.' I pointed. 'Thankfully they're too absorbed in each other to notice us, and we'll have to keep well behind them or there'll be hell to pay.'

'Where do you think they're going?'

'God knows, but you can bet your bottom dollar it won't be somewhere they should be.'

The bright green Lancia left Asolo, taking the road past the hospital. I made sure there were at least two cars between us. At the T-junction, Federico turned right, then right again toward the hills. I kept my distance and, when the Lancia stopped at a sleepy hamlet up ahead, I pulled in at the side of the road. *Cristo!* Federico and Chiara had jumped out of their car and were daubing paint on a sign at the side of the road.

I whispered to Fern, 'This could be the start of a slippery slope for my sister.'

I felt a touch on my arm. Fern's face was a picture of sympathy and my heart melted. Literally melted. I wanted so desperately to take her in my arms. How to get through to her? *Jesus!* Her fiancé had died two years ago. Hadn't enough time had gone by for her to have recovered from his death?

With an inner sigh, I switched on the engine. Chiara and Federico had already taken off.

I pulled up by the road sign, which should have read, "Paderno". My sister and her boyfriend had daubed out the letter "o".

'Venetian dialect,' I said to Fern by way of explanation. 'We leave the vowels off the endings of most Italian words. But we also have our own words for things. For instance, the word for "money" is *denaro* in Italian, but *schèi* in Venetian.'

'Wow! I knew about dialect, but never imagined the words could be so different,' she said in evident amazement.

'Most people don't realise that Venetian is an extremely old language.' I informed her. 'In fact, Cecilia, like the majority of people in the Republic, would have spoken Venetian.'

'She did,' Fern nodded. 'I can understand and speak it when I'm in the past. But if you asked me to translate anything for you now, I wouldn't have a clue.'

'Our dialect has more history than the national language. It's closer to French and Spanish than to Italian.'

'Something has just occurred to me, Luca. As Cecilia, I've experienced a time when Tuscan was adopted as the language of literature. I suppose because of writers like Petrarch and Dante. And Cecilia met Pietro Bembo in Caterina Cornaro's court. I understand he used Tuscan in his writing. Were there any Venetian writers?'

'Oh, yes. Many. Goldoni followed the *Commedia dell'arte* tradition of having the common folk speak in Venetian. He's ranked among the top Italian theatrical authors of all time, and his plays are still performed today. They're really funny.' I paused. 'You've heard of Casanova?'

'Of course.'

'Well, he translated the *Illiad* into Venetian. So, we have a proud tradition of literature.'

'Can you explain the rationale behind what Chiara and Federico are doing?'

'A significant number of people in the Veneto want to break free of the rest of Italy and form a separate state.'

She angled her head toward me. 'Oh? Why?'

'Pride, I suppose. You know we were a republic for over a thousand years? And a leading world power in the fifteenth and sixteenth centuries?'

'Yes, but I don't know why the republic came to an end.'

'It happened in the late eighteenth century. After a long decline, Napoleon divided the Veneto up between the French and the Austrians. Finally, after Italian unification, we were annexed to Italy.' I exhaled slowly.

'Now we're one of the wealthiest regions, thanks to the economic boom of the last decade. And everyone here hates paying taxes to fund the massive bureaucracy in Rome. Much of the money is channelled into the South of Italy. Supposedly for development, but generally swallowed up in corruption.'

'Do you believe the Veneto will ever become independent again?' she inquired thoughtfully.

I shook my head. 'Not in the foreseeable future. Perhaps, one day, as part of an integrated Europe.'

'A little like Scotland and Wales in the UK, then, I suppose. It's strange how we humans like to belong to our own tribe. We haven't changed that much since we came out of our caves and populated the planet.'

'In evolutionary terms, we haven't been out of the caves for that long,' I chuckled. 'Thousands of years compared with millions as cavemen.'

'I hadn't thought of it like that. So, Chiara and Federico are simply behaving like their ancestors.' Fern laughed.

'I wish it were that simple.'

She touched my arm again, and my heartrate accelerated. 'Try not to worry too much about Chiara,' she said. 'Your sister is young and idealistic.'

'If it were just Chiara, I'd agree with you,' I groaned. 'Federico is part of the equation, and there's something about him that makes my flesh crawl.'

A frown creased Fern's brow. 'I can sense a darkness in him too. Does Chiara have any other friends? Someone you trust who can talk to her. I know I said I'd try, but wouldn't someone closer to her have more success?'

'We've gone down that route, believe me. My sister has a strong personality, and her friends have all failed to talk sense into her. They're at university and concentrating on their studies, like she should be.'

'All right, then. I'll do my best,' Fern said, leaning back in her seat.

I restarted the car and drove toward Altivole with the window open. The night air was redolent with the scent of the honeysuckle growing along the hedges by the side of the road. Worry pinched at me and I wished I could shake off the feeling of foreboding that had settled in my chest.

I stopped the car outside Susan Finch's house. Fern leaned in and kissed me on the cheek. I turned my head slightly, and her second kiss, aimed at my other cheek, caught me on the side of the mouth.

Blushing, she murmured, 'Sorry.'

'No need to apologise,' I said.

Her eyes locked with mine and then we were kissing properly. Her lips were so soft, her mouth so inviting. My hands buried themselves in her luxuriant curls. She let out a soft moan and pulled away. 'Good-night, Luca,' she said, her voice throaty.

'*Buonanotte*, Fern. *A domani*. See you tomorrow.'

Driving home to Asolo, I took a hand from the steering wheel and punched the air. 'Yes!' I was finally getting somewhere with her.

I hoped...

CHAPTER 13

*T*he next morning, I was having breakfast with Auntie as usual. 'What are your plans for today?' she asked, pouring tea into my mug.

'I'll do some painting this morning, then I'm going riding with Luca's sister this afternoon.' I told her.

'That's nice, love,' she patted my hand. 'I remember you used to ride a lot when you were a teenager.'

'Chiara said it's like being on a bicycle. Something you don't forget. Let's hope she's right.'

I rubbed my tired eyes. Last night, I'd scarcely slept for thinking about Luca. I touched my lips, remembering the kiss. Remembered how Luca's mouth had opened over mine and how I'd felt myself dissolve into him. Problem was, though, was that when I'd kissed him back, I'd felt Cecilia in my head— and it was as if I'd been kissing Zorzo.

Am I going mad? Can I only let myself fall for a man who's been dead for five hundred years?

I shook myself. Maybe I should take Auntie's advice and see a doctor? This whole situation was becoming weird beyond belief.

I went up to my bedroom and stared at the print of *The Tempest*, which I'd taped to the back of the door. The girl in the painting seemed to be staring right at me. There was a resemblance to Cecilia, and consequently to me. Her blonde hair was held back in a headdress, so it was hard to tell if it was like my own. The girl was voluptuously plump, unlike Cecilia, who, so far in the story, had shown herself to be of average build like me. *The Tempest* was a highly sensual work of art, though, and I absolutely loved it.

I flipped open the book I'd bought on Giorgione and stared at his self-portrait. So weird to find myself here in the twentieth century gazing at a picture of my sixteenth century lover.

No! Not your lover. Cecilia's.

After taking a shower, I spent the rest of the morning working on my painting of the palazzo I'd sketched in Murano. It was shaping up nicely. I'd had the photos I'd taken in Venice developed at a shop in Altivole, and I'd pinned them to a board in the corner of Auntie's kitchen, where I'd improvised my "studio". I was using acrylics, which worked well with the hard-edged flat image of the building I was depicting.

As I worked, and moved from highlighting the windows and balconies, I began to focus on the trees and sky, remembering Zorzo's ability to bring movement to the scene through *sfumato*. I wanted to show the arrival of the night, so I started blurring and softening the sharp outlines by gradually feathering the tones into each other, creating the smoke-like haziness I'd learned from him. *That Cecilia had learned from him*. Then, why not? A stormy sky.

I shivered with excitement.

This was going to be one of my best paintings ever.

Two hours later, I put down my brush, satisfied. I'd leave my work to dry by the window and have a cup of coffee.

I sat at the kitchen table and closed my eyes, thinking about my nemesis… as Luca called her. Who was Lorenza? I hadn't said anything to Luca yet, but something told me Lorenza was the key to the mystery of why Cecilia was possessing me.

I frowned, trying to remember the names of all the characters I'd met when I'd been in the past. There hadn't been anyone called Lorenza. Could she have been one of Giorgione's other models?

I thought about my visit to Venice. Cecilia was impetuous,

that was for sure. She was playing with fire. *Fire.* The word jangled in my mind like an alarm. I shut my eyes again, and the familiar buzzing sensation filled my head.

The dining hall in the Barco is decorated for the Christmas celebrations. The Queen is giving a banquet, and we shall feast until we're fit to burst. It's been months since I've seen the painter. He has a commission in Venice from the Council of Ten, to paint a picture for the Hall of the Audience in the Doge's Palace. A great honour, and I try not to be sad that we are kept apart by it. Although, if I were to be honest with myself, we'd have little chance to see each other there. It is difficult to get out from under the Queen's shadow.

Zorzo and I haven't lain together since that first time, and I find little consolation in seeking my own joy under the sheets while Dorotea is snoring. After a few fumbled attempts, I've given up on it, for the sensation can't be compared with what I experienced with my painter. As for my art, I do what I can, which is drawing only. How can I find the right materials to paint here in the middle of the countryside? And even if I could find them, I don't have the coin to buy them.

I take a sip of wine and glance around the assembled company. There'll be music and dancing after the meal, but my heart isn't in it. With my elbow on the table, I rest my chin on my hand. My neck prickles. Someone is staring at me. I turn my head and my gaze encounters Lodovico Gaspare's. *Gesù bambino!* He licks his thin lips and smiles. A sense of foreboding grips me, and the saliva drains from my mouth.

After the last course, we assemble for the dancing. I know the man from Ferrara will be waiting, and he is. 'Dance with me, Lady Cecilia,' he says, bowing.

I drop into a deep curtsey, as I should, and incline my head, as I should. For months I've tried to convince myself that I'll never see him again, but here he is now, standing far too close to me. Thank God his breath is no longer fishy, or it would spoil the scent of pine from the evergreen decorations around the hall. I force a smile, while my whole being shouts, *Run away from him!*

The musicians are tuning up and the court takes to the floor. How can I refuse to dance with him? I tell myself there's nothing he can do to me here in public and I swallow my disgust. I let him take my hand. At his touch, my stomach tightens... and a sick feeling swells my gullet. We join a circle, holding hands, moving to one side and then to the other. Lodovico leans toward me and whispers, 'I apologise for my behaviour the last time we met. You've bewitched me, Lady Cecilia. I didn't know what I was doing.'

My chest tightens, and I step back. His crooked white teeth flash, and his thin lips are moist with spittle.

Oh, blessed Mary, the Queen is signalling to me that she wishes to retire. Relief floods through me as I make my reverences to the man from Ferrara, whose brow wrinkles in a frown.

The next day, my sister visits. I haven't seen her since she gave birth to her child at the end of the summer.

'How is the babe?' I ask, linking arms with her and strolling toward the fountain.

'He thrives,' she says, smiling. 'I've decided to call him Tommaso after our father.'

'And your husband? Does he thrive too?'

'He's afflicted with boils at present.'

'Oh, poor man. Where on his body?'

Fiammetta peers at me sideways. 'On his buttocks.'

I put my hand over my mouth, trying to still my laughter. Impossible. I shake with mirth and my sister joins me. We clutch each other, and the tears run down our cheeks.

'Oh, how I've missed you, Cecilia. Everyone is so stuffy in Treviso,' she says. 'Rambaldo's family is pompous and disregards me for not bringing a dowry to our marriage.'

I stare at her. 'What about your beautiful villa? Surely they would consider it dowry enough?'

'Huh! They're wealthy, but greedy with their riches. They say it is too small.' She sighs. 'And what about you, sweet sister?' She lifts my chin and turns my face from side to side. 'Has any man shown an interest yet?'

I've never kept secrets from Fiammetta in the past; however, I know she'll not approve of my painter. 'No,' I lie, crossing my fingers behind my back. 'They all consider me a child still.'

Fiammetta stands back and looks me up and down. 'You've filled out since last I saw you. Those womanly curves will have men standing in line for you before too long.'

Footsteps sound on the pathway and I let out a gasp as Lodovico Gaspare approaches. *Maria Santissima*, will I ever be free of that man? We make our reverences and I introduce Fiammetta, taking care to stress her married name.

His eyes flick over her as if she were a juicy piece of meat. Last night, I'd escaped him for the Queen's desire to retire early. At least I'm in the company of my sister now. There's nothing Lodovico can do to me here. I glance at her and, *Madre di Dio*, she's fluttering her eyelashes at him and giving him one of "her" smiles. Of course, compared with Rambaldo, Lodovico Gaspare is a veritable Adonis.

We stroll past the fountain toward the bare trees in the fruit orchards, the grass crisp with frost beneath our feet. I wrap my cape around me; the cold of the day has turned into early evening's freeze.

Lodovico Gaspare leaves us, and my sister pinches my cheek. 'He will ask for your hand, mark my words, Cecilia. You've made a formidable conquest, and this will be a good match.'

My bowels turn to water. 'No. I'm sure you're wrong. He will try to make me his mistress, and I'll refuse him. That man disgusts me.'

Fiammetta takes my hand. 'Sweet sister, you have to think of the future. The Queen is ageing, despite her wish to believe the contrary. I've noticed a difference since my wedding. You know she isn't well.'

It is true. From the time of our return to the Barco from Venice, Domina has taken to her bed more and more often straight after supper. A tremor passes through me and I grab hold of Fiammetta's arm. 'What will happen to me if she should die?'

'You'll need a protector.' My sister's tone is practical. 'It is the way of world, my dear. I've heard speak of the man from Ferrara. His family is rich with lands and money. If he doesn't ask for your hand, you *should* become his mistress. Lodovico Gaspare will ply you with gifts and property to keep for your old age.'

'I'm not a courtesan,' I say, shocked.

'Of course, you aren't. This is different. He would be the only man to whom you'd give yourself.'

Unable to tell my sister what I truly think, I distract her from this topic of conversation by asking about Tommaso. Fiammetta then gives me a blow by blow account of the first three months of her baby boy's life. I wonder how she could leave him with his wet nurse so much does she dote on him. All the while she prattles on, encouraged by the occasional nod from me, I worry about the man from Ferrara...

Baby Jesus, spare me, I beg of you!

Our circuit of the gardens over, Fiammetta and I return to the Queen's chamber to help her prepare for lunch. My sister will stay tonight and go back to Treviso tomorrow in time for Christmas. I hope Lodovico Gaspare's visit to the court will be just as short.

After we've eaten, the Queen retires for an afternoon rest. With time to myself, I take my sketches from the chest in the corner of the room that I share with Dorotea, and where Fiammetta will also join us tonight. I unroll the parchment and stare at the drawing I made of Zorzo. Bending down, I kiss his charcoal lips. A feeling of such longing passes through me. I stifle a sob.

'*Dolcezza,*' comes a whisper.

I turn around, my head spinning.

· · ·

'Are you asleep?' a voice echoed. I'd been dreaming. Of a man I couldn't have. Of an impossible love. Zorzo in Venice and me, penniless, dependent on the ailing Queen.

'Fern?' the voice repeated. 'Wake up!'

I opened my eyes, and my soul cried out in pain. I didn't want to be in the twentieth century. I wanted to be back in the room Cecilia shared with Dorotea. To find out if that whispered, *dolcezza*, had been real or not. I rubbed my throbbing forehead.

'Oh, it's you, Auntie,' I said, peering at the woman who was touching my arm in concern.

Auntie knitted her brows. 'Have you had another funny turn?'

'Just a strange dream.' I shook my fuzzy head. 'What time is it?'

'One o'clock.'

I got to my feet. A pile of potatoes was stacked by the sink. 'Let me peel those for you, Auntie.'

'Thanks, love. I'll grill us some chops for our lunch.'

'Remember I'm going riding this afternoon,' I reminded her as I picked up the peeler.

'I'm sure you'll have a lovely time.'

Chiara was right. It *was* like getting back on a bicycle. Magic's back was broad, though, and my jeans chafed against my thighs. I'd borrowed a pair of boots and a hat from Vanessa, who wore the same size as me, but borrowing breeches hadn't been an option. Both she and Chiara were much taller.

Side by side, Chiara and I took the path that meandered between the cornfields, our horses trotting down the dirt track, the late afternoon sun warming our backs. A cuckoo was making desperate calls in the cherry tree to our right, and soon came the bubbling reply of his mate.

'I can see you know what you're doing,' Chiara said. 'Let's have a canter.' She was riding a much livelier mount than mine. 'Pegasus can't wait much longer.'

'Pegasus?' I repeated, stunned.

'Not very original, is it?' Chiara laughed then surged ahead. Her back straight, she seemed practically glued to the saddle.

'Come on, Magic!' I gathered in my reins and urged him forward. I'd always loved cantering and relaxed into the movement, my bottom taut. It was just a coincidence that Chiara's horse should have the same name as Cecilia's, I told myself. It was a common enough name. But, even so, the hairs on my arms tingled. I stared ahead, keeping Chiara in sight.

I hope she waits for me.

She'd disappeared in a cloud of dust, but Magic's pace, even though he was doing his best, was much slower.

Where is she?

I can't be on my own.

Not doing something that Cecilia loved.

I'll have a flash-back and fall off.

The path turned at the end of the field and there was Chiara, who'd dismounted and was examining Pegasus' right foreleg. 'He's gone a little lame,' she said. 'I'm sorry, but I'll have to walk him back.'

'No problem.' I dismounted and fell into step beside her. 'I don't mind walking.'

'Are you sure?' She shot me a glance. 'Not much fun for you. Why don't you ride back the way we came? You can't miss the villa if you follow the track.'

'No way.' I said firmly. 'A walk will do me good and we can have a chat.'

Chiara regarded me suspiciously. 'Oh? What about?'

'Nothing special.' I pretended nonchalance. 'I'll tell you about my painting, if you like.'

A spark of interest flashed in Chiara's eyes. 'What do you paint?'

'Mostly landscapes, although I've tried my hand at portraiture.'

'Is that your work? I mean, are you an artist?'

'No. My day job is with a bank.' I wouldn't tell Chiara about my ambition. How it had driven me. How it had almost destroyed me. It was a part of my life I'd buried. I'd asked for a demotion when I'd returned from sick leave after Harry's death, and these days kept strictly to what was required of me, leaving the other "bright young things", the yuppies, to fight and outdo each other on their way to the top. 'I'd give anything to earn enough from my art to devote myself to it full-time,' I said.

'Why don't you chuck in your job and give it a go? What's holding you back?'

'Fear of failure, I suppose. Also, I've got a big mortgage...'

Harry hadn't made a will, even though we'd been engaged to be married. The proceeds from the sale of his flat and all his investments had gone to his parents. They hadn't offered me any of it, and I'd been too distraught and too proud to ask.

'I can see my brother likes you a lot,' Chiara said, changing the subject. 'I've never seen him so besotted.'

I frowned. 'We're just friends. Nothing more. Nothing less.'

'When people say they're "just friends" it usually means the complete opposite, in my experience,' Chiara smirked.

I let out an embarrassed laugh. 'Not in our case.' I tilted my head. 'However, I did wonder why he hasn't married yet...'

'He used to be a bit of a playboy and always said he hadn't met the right person.' Chiara gave me a searching look. 'Something tells me he's done that now. He doesn't regard you as a friend, believe me. How do you feel about him?'

'Well, you don't pull any punches,' I laughed again. 'I like him. I like him a lot. But there are issues in my life I need to sort out...' *My turn to change the subject.* 'Tell me about Federico. How did you meet him?'

'At a rally organised by the Veneto Freedom Party. Some friends of mine from the university took me along.' Chiara's face had assumed a dreamy expression. 'When I talked with him, I just knew he was the right guy for me.'

'Oh? How's that?'

'He's so passionate. About politics, about life, about everything.' Chiara's smile would have lit up the world. 'Don't you think he's wonderful?'

I cleared my throat. 'Well, he's certainly different.'

'Yeah. He's nothing like the boys I grew up with. All *mammoni*.'

'*Mammoni?*'

'Mamma's boys. Luca and I are lucky our mother's English, otherwise we'd suffer from the same oppressiveness as the rest of this matriarchal society.'

I lifted a brow. 'The one you're fighting so hard to preserve?'

'Ha,' Chiara shrugged off my sarcasm. 'Actually, recently we've thought about joining the Anarchist Party.'

'Wow!' I clamped my jaw to stop it from dropping. 'Isn't that a little extreme?'

'We decided against it,' Chiara said in a serious tone. 'Too Tuscan. We feel the influence of Florence and Rome, especially Rome, is bad for the Veneto. And we're not really Communists.'

'I don't know much about it. But I do know there are far too many political parties in Italy.'

'You're right there. The sooner the Veneto can become independent of the frenzy of corruption and argument that rules in Rome the better.'

Chiara sounded as if she were quoting a dogma, but I didn't want to go down the route of political discussion. I didn't know enough about Italian politics, nor did I want to. 'Tell me more about Federico,' I said. 'Does he have a job?'

'He's an undergraduate still. At least that's his "cover".' Chiara glanced from left to right and I had to bite my lip to stop myself from laughing. *Student pranks, that's all.* How could Luca and his mother be so concerned? Then I remembered the bad vibes I'd felt radiating from Federico, the way he'd tried to come on to me, and I shuddered.

'We're nearly there,' Chiara said. Within minutes we were unsaddling our horses. 'You go ahead. I need to bandage Pegasus' leg. Luca will be back from work soon, and Mum will no doubt want to find out what I've said to you.' She grinned. 'I'm not stupid, you know. But I like you and really enjoyed our ride, what there was of it, and I liked talking with you.'

'I did too.' I returned Chiara's grin.

'Let's do it again, then. When Pegusus' leg is better. I'll take you farther afield next time. There's an old Roman road to an ancient chapel hidden in a valley near the mountains. We could take a picnic lunch there. I go to the farmhouse nearby sometimes with Federico. It belongs to my family and it's the ideal place for him and me to be alone.'

'Sounds wonderful,' I said.

I left her at the stables and went back into the villa.

Vanessa got up from her chair in the living room as I came through the door. The two Labradors, lazing by her feet, lifted their heads then went back to sleep. 'How did you get on?' she asked.

'Fine,' I said. This was so difficult. What did Luca and his mother expect of me? Best to come clean, I supposed. 'Look, Vanessa. I'm happy to befriend Chiara. She's a lovely girl. The thing is, she's realised that you set us up. If I'm to gain her confidence, I can't be a "spy" … if you know what I mean.'

'I understand,' Vanessa smiled. 'Enough said. Pop along to the cloakroom and freshen up while I get us some Prosecco.'

I changed into my sandals, used the facilities, and washed my hands. I checked my hair was as tidy as it could be, then made my way back to Luca's mother.

I could hear voices as I approached.

Luca's and Vanessa's voices.

I paused in the corridor, not wanting to intrude.

'I've fallen for Fern,' he was saying to his mother. 'All these years I've been searching for someone, not knowing who that "someone" was. Everyone thought I was playing around. It wasn't a deliberate choice, believe me. Every woman I met felt wrong. That's not the case with Fern. For the first time, I've met someone who feels right. Only she doesn't seem to want to know.'

Mortified, I spun on my heel and returned to the bathroom. Then I slammed the door hard, so they'd think I'd just come out from there.

Luca has fallen for me?
How had I not seen this coming?
And how the hell am I going to deal with it?
My heart skittered in my chest, but I ignored it.
I was not going to let myself fall for him in return.

CHAPTER 14

I was putting the finishing touches to my painting of the Barco– not a representation of today's ruined villa, but how it had appeared at the time of Caterina Cornaro. Auntie had given me a strange look when I'd shown her the work but hadn't said anything. I'd been on the point of making another attempt to share Cecilia's story with her, but I'd stopped myself. Auntie's disbelief seemed insurmountable. Weird, really, considering she was a writer and must have considerable powers of imagination.

I lifted my gaze from my palette, and found my attention distracted by Gucci Cat. His leg in the air, he was cleaning between his toes as he lay on the floor by my easel. With a sigh, I let my thoughts wander. Last night, when I'd got home, I'd been so emotionally drained that I'd gone straight to bed and had slept dreamlessly. Now, however, I couldn't stop thinking about what Luca had said to his mother.

After coming out of the bathroom, I'd gone up to him, too flustered to do more than mumble, '*Buonasera,*' before sipping from my glass of Prosecco. Now my heart skittered. I couldn't deny it any longer; I liked being with him too much for him to be considered "just a friend". That kiss, when I'd kidded myself that my response had been Cecilia kissing Zorzo. I'd known damn well what I was doing when I'd opened my mouth under Luca's.

I'd sat next to him on the sofa and had looked at his hands, imagining how it would feel to have them explore my body. But it wasn't right. I had to put a stop to it straight away.

Before he found out.

Before he knew.

Before the truth turned him against me.

The terrible truth about how I'd caused Harry's death.

Luca had asked me if I was all right last night when I'd pleaded a headache and declined his dinner invitation. 'Just tired,' I'd said.

Coward! You should have broken things off with him there and then. Told him you couldn't help with his sister. Thanked him for everything he'd done for you. Said you'd prefer to spend the rest of your vacation painting and living quietly at Auntie's as you were still suffering from stress.

No more Renaissance dancing.

No more trips to Venice.

And definitely no more kissing.

My lower lip trembled, but I stiffened it; I wouldn't give in to indulgent self-pity. What's done is done, and can't be undone, Mum always said. I straightened my shoulders and wiped my paintbrush. Standing back, I scrutinised my work. *At least that's coming along well.* I'd need to pay for excess luggage on the plane when I took everything back to London. Hopefully, it'd be worth it. If I could set up an exhibition, I might be able to sell my paintings instead of relying on commissions from greetings card companies. The work I'd accomplished so far in the Veneto was the best I'd ever produced, and I couldn't help loving it.

I put my brush back down on the small table Auntie had provided for me.

My hand touched something rough, and I knew, I just knew without looking, what it was.

The odour of burnt wood assailed my nostrils and my pulse leapt to my throat.

I steeled myself as Gucci Cat ran from the room.

When it came, it seemed to come from nowhere. *'Lorenza,'* a caress against my cheek, cold and filled with misery.

'Cecilia? What happened? Who is Lorenza?'

Of course, there was no answer.

Heart pounding, I pulled out a chair and sat down.

'*Dolcezza.*'

I turn and he's there behind me in the room I share with Dorotea. He holds out a small canvas. 'I've darkened your hair and made your face rounder so no one will recognise you.'

I feel as if I'll burst with happiness at the sight of him. 'How are you?'

'Well,' he replies softly, his gaze fixed on mine. 'And you?'

'The same.'

A sudden shyness has seized me, and I blush as I stare at my portrait. He has painted me showing my naked breast and I have a grave, thoughtful expression on my face. I'm holding open the fur collar of my red robe to expose a pink nipple. What can this mean? Did he draw my bosom while I was resting in his studio? My white skin is delicately shaded, and my breast is like a small hillock. Perhaps he remembered it like that? In the painting, I'm not looking at anything in particular; it's as if I have a secret that I'm keeping to myself. I stare closely at the canvas and notice a small part of the background is unfinished.

'I've brought you a gift.' Zorzo hands me a cloth-wrapped parcel.

With trembling hands, I untie it to reveal a set of brushes and glass bottles of pre-mixed paint. It must have cost a fortune. Throwing my arms around him, I lift my face to receive his kiss.

'Time for another lesson,' he says, after kissing me so thoroughly my knees started to swim away. He picks up a brush and holds it out.

'Are you sure?' I ask.

'See that space there? I've left it for you to complete.' He places the canvas on the table, reaches into his sack, and takes out a palette. Then he mixes the colours, so dark they're almost black.

Excitement and trepidation swirl through me. I take the brush from his hand and can no longer tell if my dizziness is a result of the nearness of the painter or the challenge of the painting. Yet when the lustrous colour slides off the brush onto the canvas my nerves settle, and my wrist flicks backwards and forwards, filling the blank space with iridescence. When I encounter the laurel leaves forming a crown around the woman– me– I'm careful and precise. Exhilaration grips me as the scent of linseed oil fills my nostrils, and I feel as if I could go on forever.

We work in silence, Zorzo mixing the paint for me. Eventually my fingers grow numb and I stop. 'There,' I say. 'It is done.' I look at him, my breath catching. 'Will you stay long?'

He frowns. 'I must go away this night. I've been working on a commission in my hometown, an altarpiece for Tuzio Costanzo. Just a few finishing touches. I have an urge to bestow your sweet lips on the Madonna's face. And there's a fresco in the house next door I have to complete.'

His arms enfold me, and desire wells up like a hot spring between us as we kiss again.

Jesu Cristo!

A sudden sound of female voices interrupts us.

The door bursts open. Fiammetta and Dorotea erupt into the room, laughing together; they stop in their tracks.

I jump back from my painter, who grabs the canvas.

Too late.

Fiammetta sidles up to him and stares at the painting. 'Is that you, sister?' she asks, pointing.

'Of course not. It is not my hair you see, is it?'

'Has a look of you. Only I have not seen your exposed breast, so who am I to judge?' She turns to Zorzo. 'What, pray sir, are you doing in our room?'

'He's brought me some paints and he's been teaching me,' I say in a steady voice.

Fiammetta gives me a quick glance before saying to Zorzo, 'I think it is time for you to leave us. It is not seemly for you to be here.'

We make our reverences, and I catch the wink in his eye as he departs.

Dorotea collapses in a fit of giggles. 'Oh, Cecilia! You are a one. Hiding your secrets from Fiammetta. She should know what you get up to at night in Venice.'

I grab Dorotea's shoulder. 'You promised not to say anything.'

'That was before. It is better she knows.'

I cross my arms. 'There's nothing for you to know, Fiammetta. Dorotea has been imagining things.'

'Me? Imagining? What about the time you sneaked out to visit him? And the day when you pretended your monthly pains to get out of going to Murano?'

'It was only the once. I haven't had the chance to be with him since.'

Fiammetta frowns. 'So, you admit to being with him? Thank God you're not with child, Cecilia! Whatever have you been thinking of, my dear? Clearly, you haven't been thinking at all. Your painter can't afford marriage or even a mistress. I warrant he can barely afford to keep himself. Artists like him are penniless. You'd be much better off with Lodovico Gaspare.'

I curl my lips. 'I will not go with that man. He disgusts me.'

'You're behaving like a child,' my sister says.

I practically growl at her. 'Enough of this talk. We must go now to help the Queen dress.'

And that is what we do. Later, after dinner, I have the excuse to miss the revelries when Domina retires early. I'm pleased not to have to dance with Lodovico Gaspare, but I've caught him staring at me throughout the meal, licking his thin lips as if he would devour me.

The night is cold, and at bedtime I snuggle together with my sister and Dorotea in the large bed. Soon Dorotea and Fiammetta are snoring softly. I puff out a breath and it steams the freezing air. Sleep comes slowly for I am worried. What will tomorrow bring?

Directly after we break our fast the next day, the Queen sends for me. 'I have some wonderful news for you, sweet girl. Lodovico Gaspare wishes to marry you.'

My heart sinks. This is what I've been dreading and, when the Queen looks at me with her kind eyes and nods encouragement, I haven't the nerve to say what I really think. I gulp like one of her golden carp and croak, 'Oh? When?'

'Something for you and him to decide,' she smiles. 'Just know that I give my blessing. And, of course, I shall provide you with a bridal chest of linen. I had a villa built for your sister, Rambaldo insisted upon it. Lodovico Gaspare requires nothing, but I will give you a gold necklace anyway.'

I drop into a deep curtsey, before explaining that Fiammetta is leaving for Treviso at any minute. 'Might I bid farewell to my sister?'

The Queen waves me off and I manage to hold back my tears until I arrive at my quarters. Fiammetta is alone, folding away her nightdress. 'Whatever is the matter?' she asks when she sees my face. I explain, and she throws her arms around me. 'I knew it. Didn't I tell you?'

'But I don't love him. I love Zorzo.'

'*Per l'amor di Dio*, Cecilia. And does he love you? Has he made any such declaration?'

'He doesn't need to,' my voice catches on a sob. 'I can tell it from the way he looks at me.'

'That painter looks at you with lust, not love. I wasn't going to say anything, but you need to know. He has a string of women visiting him in that studio of his. It is a well-known fact. You aren't the only one.'

My breath is sucked from me as I collapse onto the bed. Every bone in my body is shaking. 'Surely not?'

'This marriage is a wonderful opportunity for you, Cecilia. It is highly unlikely that any other man of such repute and wealth will make an offer for you. You need to be more cautious. Your purity mustn't be questioned.' She pauses, appearing to consider what to say next. 'Lodovico Gaspare is an honourable man and he seems to be smitten with you. Once your betrothal is announced, his family and friends will criticise his choice, mark my words, for you have no dowry. The only thing you can offer is your reputation. If that is sullied, then he will throw you away like a dirty rag. Don't think me cruel, dearest sister. Believe me, I know what I'm talking about. Did the Queen promise you any kind of settlement?'

I'm still reeling from her revelation about Zorzo, and struggle to understand what she's asking. Then I remember the Queen's reference to Lodovico declaring he requires nothing, and I tell Fiammetta about that and about the necklace Domina will give me.

'As our guardian after the death of Mother and Father, she is generous toward us for their loyalty to her,' Fiammetta smiles.

I sniff back my tears and get up from the bed. 'You will have to explain what to do when the doctors examine me and find I'm no longer a maid.'

Her face is a picture of confusion and I blow out a laugh. 'Perhaps I should tell the Queen about Signor Zorzo. But first, I'll confront the artist and find out the truth.' My voice is firm, yet my insides are quivering. 'He's gone to Castelfranco, so it is too late for me to see him now.'

'What about your answer to Lodovico Gaspare?'

'I'll think of a way to delay things,' I say with more confidence than I feel. I place my hands on Fiammetta's shoulders and kiss both her cheeks.

A strange ringing sound echoes in my ears and I dart my gaze from left to right. The chime jangles relentlessly, louder and louder, until buzzing fills my head and my vision blurs. I rub my temples, then reach for my sister. But all I encounter is thin air, and I crumple to the floor.

I found myself sprawled on the tiles, the ringing still echoing in my ears. Shakily I got to my feet. *The damn telephone.* The realisation sent me spiralling through the centuries, and, as ever, I had to choke back the nausea in my throat. *Why doesn't Auntie answer it?*

The ringing continued. Whoever it was had no intention of

hanging up. I lurched across the room and picked up the receiver. '*Pronto.* Hello?'

'Is that Fern? It's Luca. I was wondering if you'd like to go to Castelfranco tomorrow. I've a client I need to visit and thought you might like to see the Giorgione Madonna.'

I caught my lip between my teeth.

Castelfranco?

Oh, my God!

My heart was almost beating out of my chest at the coincidence.

What about my resolution not to see Luca again? Just hearing his voice made my heart hammer. 'Th... th... that would be lovely. What time?'

'I'll call for you at nine. And you can take me to lunch, if you like.'

With a smirk, I agreed.

After I'd hung up, a sudden chill prickled my arms.

The air in the kitchen shifted.

'*Lorenza!*' the ghostly voice whispered.

And I yelped.

CHAPTER 15

'*I* went to the library in Treviso yesterday,' Luca said, starting the engine of his Alfa as I settled myself into the passenger seat the following morning. 'I tried to find out more about Giorgione. The art historian, Giorgio Vasari, who wrote in the mid sixteenth century, claimed Zorzo was only thirty-three years old when he died.'

'Yes, I know that from the book I bought at the Accademia. So young.' I stared down at my hands. 'It's really sad. He was the same age as Harry...'

'And me,' Luca said with a frown. 'Giorgione died of the plague, apparently. There's a letter dated October 1510 that's survived, written by Isabella d'Este, the Marques of Mantova. She asks a Venetian friend to buy a painting by him for her collection. The letter shows her awareness that he was already deceased.'

'Ah, that's interesting,' I twisted my fingers together. 'Did she get the painting?'

'No. There's a reply saying it wasn't to be had at any price.'

I gave Luca a quick glance. 'Have you found any reference to Cecilia anywhere?'

'None at all. No one wrote letters about her and she clearly wasn't a letter-writer herself. Most of our knowledge of life in the distant past comes from correspondence, you know.' He paused. 'Have you had any more episodes?'

'Yes,' I said, and went on to tell him about Zorzo's visit to Cecilia's room, followed by the offer of marriage from Lodovico and all that it entailed. 'I feel so sorry for her. She's caught between a rock and a hard place.'

'I expect her sister was right about his women. He would have met several before and after Cecilia appeared on the scene. Not all of the paintings look like her...'

I wondered again if Lorenza could have been one of those women and I clenched my jaw to stop myself for making a sneering remark about them.

How ridiculous to feel jealous on Cecilia's behalf... or my own, to be honest.

Luca and I lapsed into silence for a few minutes, and then I said, 'I'm really grateful to you for being here for me. Don't know what I'd do otherwise.'

He took his hand from the wheel and squeezed mine briefly. Heat flushed through me. I was intensely aware of him, his long, lean thighs and his broad shoulders. To distract myself, I stared out of the window at the passing countryside, the villages with their church spires, ice-cream shops and cafés, interspersed with cornfields, fruit orchards and vineyards. There was an assortment of factories, too, in tastefully-built modern buildings, testament to the wealth based on manufacturing of this industrious part of Italy.

Such an amazing place.

Luca found a place to park in the main square of Castelfranco, just outside the moated old part of the town, or *centro storico*. We sat on the terrace of a café opposite a grassy piece of ground, where a statue of Giorgione had been placed. A pigeon fluttered down and perched on the statue's head.

I laughed. 'It's not much like him. They've made him too "pretty". Zorzo wasn't a "pretty boy".'

Luca's smile crinkled the corners of his deep blue eyes. 'I've seen a photo of his self-portrait. In my Giorgione book. Yours too, I presume?'

I glanced away. I wouldn't mention the effect that photo had on me, how I'd fingered the sensuous mouth and been captivated by Zorzo's brooding expression. I gave myself a shake. 'When's your business meeting, Luca?'

'Just before lunch. Shall we visit the cathedral and take a look at the maestro's masterpiece?' he said, putting change on the table to pay for our coffees.

'Lead the way!'

He took my hand, and I loved how he made me feel; I was a woman enjoying the company of an attractive man.

A very attractive man.

I leaned into him as we walked under the archway below the clock tower then followed the cobbled street to the cathedral.

The altar piece towered over the vaults in the Costanzo chapel, to the right of the nave. A soldier in shining armour graced the left of the canvas, and a monk in Franciscan garb stood on the right. The Virgin sat enthroned on a high pedestal in the centre.

My shoulders drooped as sudden sadness washed through me.

'I'm not sure I like this painting,' I said.

'Oh? Why's that?'

'They're all so unhappy, they're practically crying.'

'I expect Zorzo wanted to show the family's sorrow.'

'Even the baby seems miserable. He's not even looking at his mother. Not like the babe in *The Tempest*, who could win a competition he's so adorable.'

A feeling of longing overcame me, and my body quivered.

Longing for what?

I turned my gaze away from the altarpiece.

'*The Tempest* celebrates life,' Luca said, taking hold of my hand again and giving it a squeeze. 'This painting is the opposite. They're mourning the death of young Matteo, who was taken in the flower of his youth. He was the son of Tuzio, Caterina Cornaro's general in Cyprus.'

'I know. Just find it depressing, that's all.' I shivered. 'Is it time for your meeting?'

'Yes. You can go next door and have a look at the frieze Giorgione painted, if you like. Then why don't you wait for me in the café opposite? I shan't be too long.'

'Good plan,' I smiled.

The fresco on the east wall of the Casa Marta-Pellizzari was sixteen metres long, according to the leaflet I'd picked up at the entrance to the house, and the work measured about a quarter of a metre high. It consisted of scenes of a series of musical instruments, cameos, books and utensils used by an astronomer/astrologer (apparently the two were the same in Giorgione's time). Everything about the work struck me as being dark. It resonated with the sadness I'd felt in the chapel.

Nausea suddenly swirled up from my stomach.

Get some fresh air!

I made my way out of the house. There was a stone bench at the side of the building, and I lowered myself onto it.

I knew this place.

It was as familiar to me as if I'd only been here yesterday.

I closed my eyes and let Cecilia in.

I approach Castelfranco at mid-morning, having set out on Pegaso at dawn's light. After a night of tossing and turning, the idea came to me that this was the only thing to do. The stable boy, bribed with the silver comb Queen Caterina gave me for my last birthday, found me a man's doublet and hose. My hair is bundled up under a hat, and I've swathed myself in a cloak against the winter cold. No one wears masks outside of Venice, which is a pity for one of them would complete my disguise.

It doesn't take me long to find the house next door to the Costanzo chapel; it is the only church within the moated part of the town. I dismount, tie Pegaso to the railings outside, push open the door, and glance around. No one here, so I go up to the first floor.

I stand in the doorway and feast my eyes on my painter, who is standing on a scaffold running the length of the wall. I watch him, enthralled by how focused he is on his work.

There's someone else in the room with him, and I take a step back to observe. A young man, younger than Zorzo. My age, probably. And he's grinding the paint powder with a pestle and mortar. A shout from above echoes as Zorzo calls out to him; the young man comes up to me and bows. 'Zorzone asks your purpose here.'

'Tell him I've come from the Barco. If he's busy, I can wait.'

The young man goes to the foot of the scaffold and relays my message. Zorzo puts down his brush, and his apprentice, for that's who I imagine the young man to be, takes his place. I stand and stare as my painter vaults down from the scaffold. Of course, only men can do such things, for how could a woman cope in voluminous skirts? My hopes of becoming an artist are only foolish; I have but one destiny, I know that now.

Zorzo approaches, anger at being interrupted marking his stride. However, when he gets closer, he stops in his tracks. 'Lady Cecilia! What are you doing here?'

'The Queen has received an offer of marriage for me.' I cross my arms. 'I thought you should know.'

'From whom?' His brows crease.

'Lodovico Gaspare of Ferrara.'

'And the Queen has accepted?' Zorzo seems unconcerned, and I'm so shocked I can scarcely hold myself upright.

'Yes. But she does not know I'm no longer intact,' I say in a miserable tone.

'*Dolcezza*, that won't be a problem for someone with your resourcefulness,' he smiles. 'Ask to wear a veil during the examination to protect your modesty. It shouldn't be difficult for you to find a maid to take your place.'

'You don't mind if I marry?' I ask in desperation.

He holds my hand. 'Of course, I'd like to marry you myself. I said you held my heart, didn't I?' His eyes are fixed on mine. 'But that would be impossible. You're used to a life of luxury. With me, you'd have to cook and clean and make do with all manner of things of which you have no conception. Better that you wed a rich man, for then you'll have freedom. We can still see each other, of course.'

Part of me knows that what he says is true. The other part is screaming a silent *no!*

'And what of your *other women*?' The question has slipped out of my mouth before I've even thought about it.

'Simply dalliances. And, from the time I met you there's been no one else. I swear on my mother's life.' He pauses, his finger tapping his nose. 'I wonder why the man from Ferrara asks for your hand instead of taking you as his mistress.'

My chin rises. 'You think me not worthy of marriage?'

'You're too good for him, but I wonder about his motives for other reasons.'

My chest tightens. 'What reasons?'

'Nothing to worry about now.' His gaze holds mine and he squeezes my hand. 'You're extremely fetching in that outfit, but you would fool no one. I can't let you ride back to the Barco alone.'

'You'll accompany me?' My heart races. 'What about your work?'

'A few hours won't make much difference. First, let's take some refreshment in my quarters. I'll wager you've yet to break your fast.' He chuckles. 'The owners of this house are away. We're alone except for Tiziano upstairs, and he knows better than to interrupt us.'

'Is he your apprentice?'

'My friend, more like,' Zorzo says warmly.

He leads me back down the stairs to a room on the ground floor. There's a bed in the corner, from which I keep my eyes averted. A table at the side has a tray on it with wine, bread and a pot of honey. He pours me a goblet and hands it to me before pouring one for himself. We drink, and our eyes meet. Then he breaks off a piece of the bread, dips it into the honey, and gives it to me. I bite into the sweetness and chew. Our eyes meet again, and now I'm finding it hard to swallow. *Maria Santissima*, this man does such things to me.

I take a gulp of my wine, and cough. A splutter of liquid wets my chin. Zorzo leans in and kisses me, licking the liquor from my lips. I can feel every nerve in my body tingle, I need him so. Then, his hands are on my buttocks, and his breath is coming in short, sharp rasps. This can't be wrong, what we're doing, and I want it so much my legs begin to give way.

We fall onto the bed together. Within seconds, he has removed my leggings and unbuttoned my doublet. My breasts spring free of the binding with which I've strapped them. Zorzo cups my right bosom with one hand and slips the other hand between my legs. 'Ah, *dolcezza*, you're ready for me.'

I pull off his shirt, then caress his chest, running my fingers over his muscles. I help him out of his hose and we're both naked. Feeling his hard body against my soft curves excites me even more, and I'm desperate for him.

'Let's savour this,' he says. 'For we might not be able to lie together for some time.'

His tongue circles my nipple, making it stand proud of my bosom and sending waves of pleasure through me. Zorzo sucks like a greedy babe, and I let out a moan. He takes my hand and places it on his manhood. I don't know what to do, except some instinct within me takes over and I stroke him up and down, feeling him grow so big I wonder if I'll be able to take all of him inside me.

He parts my legs and kisses the silkiness between them, his mouth is where his fingers were before and I'm gasping as my joy approaches. He stops suddenly, leaving me weak with longing. But only for a couple of seconds before he thrusts into me, and we become one. He moves with gentle care, building me back up and there it is: my joy, that rippling pleasure only he can give me.

'I love you, Zorzo.'

He groans, 'And I you.'

He withdraws from me and shoots his seed into his kerchief.

We kiss, deep and lingeringly, before he wets a cloth from the hot water pail on the stove and gives it to me to wipe myself.

Shivering now in the sudden chill, we hurriedly pull on our clothes.

'What shall we tell them at the Barco?' he asks. 'How do we explain your absence all morning?'

For the life of me, I can't come up with any excuse whatsoever. My impetuous nature has got the better of me again. I close my eyes to the world around me, and a strange man's voice speaking a language I don't understand, fills my ear.

'Are you all right?' the voice came from right next to me. A familiar voice. Who? Where was I? Then I remembered. I was in Castelfranco. I stared at the man who'd sat himself down next to me. *Luca.*

'I'm fine,' I breathed. 'Just give me a moment to collect my thoughts.'

'Have you been in the past?' He sounded concerned.

'Yes.'

He helped me to my feet, and my body felt languidly relaxed.

The tension I'd experienced earlier had dissipated, and I was able to hold his hand without wanting him to make love to me.

I'd been desperate for sex, I realised that now. A sudden sense of unreality assailed me. *You're completely nuts, Fern. Lusting after Luca then making love with Zorzo.*

'Come on, let me buy you lunch,' I said, squeezing his fingers. 'I'm starving. And then I'd like to find a gift for Auntie. A handbag, I think. Her old one is practically falling apart...'

CHAPTER 16

*I*t happened as Zorzo suggested, and I bribed a kitchen maid, who is the same build as me, to wear my clothes and the veil I negotiated to spare my modesty. The maid was pronounced intact; I could go to my wedding "pure".

A month after my return from Castelfranco, when my painter accompanied me as far as the gates of the Barco and let me go in on my own, to sneak into the stables and quickly change into my own clothing, I realised my courses were late. Yes, I am with child, and I go to my nuptials carrying Zorzo's baby. He must have spilled some of his seed inside me when I went to see him in Castelfranco.

The thought of our child makes me tremble and at the same time lightens my spirits. No one knows. Not my sister. Not Dorotea. Not the babe's father. Lodovico will think the child is his and has arrived early, I hope. He was delighted when I accepted his offer of marriage, and even more so when I asked that we wed immediately, using the excuse that it will soon be Lent.

Tomorrow is the day when we'll make our vows in the Asolo church of Santa Caterina. I have been given leave by the Queen to rest tonight, in preparation. So far, the only sign of my pregnancy is the lateness of my monthly bleed and a tenderness in my breasts. No sickness, unlike Fiammetta, who told me she'd been nauseated for months.

I'm working on a painting, using the oils Zorzo gave me, a representation of Pegaso, and I work without thinking, for I can't bare to think too much. The future will be what it will be, and I'm tossed like a leaf in the winds of destiny.

Lodovico has been the epitome of a gentle knight these past weeks, praise God, and I've allowed myself to believe that all will be well. I've learnt not to shudder away from him when he approaches; I've learnt not to long for my painter during the long, cold, winter evenings when the Queen has kept me close to her while she suffers from her stomach colic; and I've learnt not to wish I could be marrying Zorzo.

I won't let myself think about my true love's burning glances that make my skin flame, and how his touch sends my sex into a quiver. Such thoughts aren't seemly in a maid about to be married to another man. I won't dwell on how Zorzo makes my heart sing and how, when I paint with him, I feel as if I have some value in this world. And I won't give in to the misery that bubbles beneath the surface of my bravado.

There's a lot for which I can be thankful. Lodovico has bought a house in Asolo. His family in Ferrara are so against our marriage he won't subject me to the scheming and gossip of his people. Part of me can't help but feel he won't subject *himself*. Instead, we shall live in the shadow of the Queen's castle and she has promised we'll always be welcome at her court.

I put down my paintbrush and survey my work. It isn't a masterpiece, that's for certain. There's still much I need to learn…

Later, after supper taken with Domina in her rooms, I prepare myself for bed. I've been given quarters on my own this night, so that I can rest. I unpin my hair and shake it loose before brushing it. Then I slip off my clothes and put on my nightgown. The bed is cold, and I wriggle around to get warm. How can I sleep with the thoughts no amount of denial can keep out of my head? I shut my eyes and I must have slept, for when I open them morning has come.

· · ·

My wedding day passes in a blur and before I know it, Lodovico and I are married, the banquet is over, and it is time for the dancing to start. We're at his Asolo house, having walked in a procession up the hill from Santa Caterina, the whole town on the streets to watch us in our finery. Now we're in the dining hall; Lodovico's servants have pushed the tables to one side and the musicians are preparing their instruments: lutes, pipes and tambourines. We are to dance a *saltarello*, and I sense the excitement of the guests as they form a line.

My husband *my husband!* bows and I drop into a deep curtsey. His thin lips flash a white-toothed smile as he takes my hand and leads me into the intricate hops and leaps of the dance. I can feel my face set in a mask, the mask of a happy bride. I don't need a *Bauta* from Venice; my bravado is "mask" enough. There's a lump in my throat and a great heaviness in my chest. But I won't give in to self-pity. I won't let anyone see that I'm unhappy. I have my child to think of. He or she will be born into a home with wealth. Lodovico must never know the baby isn't his. Tonight, he'll believe I'm his virgin bride. I've ground some nutmeg into a powder, which I've pushed up inside me; Dorotea has assured me it will serve its purpose.

We've eaten a feast that would grace the Queen's table, and did so in fact, for she was our guest of honour. Antipasto of salads followed by lasagne, risotto and ravioli. Then roast pheasant, veal, turbot and carp, as well as capons and suckling pig. I watched Lodovico gobbling everything with his bony mouth, but I ate little myself.

When I'd dreamt of marriage to a handsome suitor—- *was it only a year and a half ago?* — I never imagined what my wedding feast has been like today. The noise, and the richness of the food, and the clattering of the dishes. I've kept my "mask" in place throughout, smiling and nodding and smiling and nodding and chewing food that tasted as I imagine sawdust would taste.

My stomach suddenly heaves, and I swallow down vomit.

Of all times to have sickness from the babe…

Dorotea was envious when she helped me to dress earlier. 'I told you he wanted you,' she said. 'Right from the first moment.

Thank God you've seen sense about the painter. Let's hope the nutmeg powder works.' She carried on pinning up my hair. 'Signor Lodovico thinks the world of you, Cecilia. You mustn't let him down. Then he'll provide well for you.'

And for my child, I'd said to myself.

Now I'm dancing with him, my hand in his. I sail through the air in a leap of the dance's *posture*. My "mask" is firmly in place as Lodovico and I hop apart, and I'm smiling and nodding and smiling and nodding again. Within me, however, dread has made its abode. Dread of what is to come this night. Will I get away with it? For if Lodovico finds me not a virgin, it will be his right to send me from his bed, from this house, from this town. And I shall be but a beggar-maid or worse.

I leap in the dance, heat creeping into my face, my hair flowing behind me, encased in a long net. A prickle of sadness invades me as I remember Zorzo running his fingers through my tresses and lifting them to his lips. How he insisted I leave my curls free when he painted me. Why am I thinking of him? *Put your mask back on, Cecilia.* So, I nod and smile and nod and smile.

Lodovico smiles back and whispers, 'It is time for us to go to our room.'

I dip a curtsey and turn away. I walk across the hall feeling numb. Dorotea falls into step beside me and we make our reverences to the Queen. 'Bless you, my girls,' she says. 'Sweet Cecilia, you've done me proud today. I wish you every happiness.'

Dorotea leaves me at the door to the bedroom that overlooks the valley below, and the maid Lodovico has employed to take care of me – *imagine! I have a maid of my own* – helps me undress. Marta, a peasant woman with garlicky breath, unclasps the gold necklace (the wedding gift from Domina), and places it on the chest in the corner. Then she helps me into my nightdress and braids my hair.

When she leaves, I'm alone and can remove my invisible mask. My mouth droops as I get into the large bed to wait. I hear voices outside the door, Lodovico's friends making ribald jokes, so I put my "mask" on again and it's so rigid I fear my smile will crack the pretence.

My husband comes into the room. He stops and rubs his hands together. 'Ah,' he says, and my belly quakes. He goes to the chest and takes off his doublet, eyes glinting in the candle-light as he sizes me up like a prize horse he has bought.

I can hear our guests, laughing and drinking and dancing now that they've seen us to our chamber, and I want to crawl under the covers and never come out again. *Act your age, Cecilia. You're not a child anymore.* I sit up in the bed and the sheet falls from me.

Without warning, my husband is upon me, pinning me down under his weight, and thrusting into me under my nightdress without so much as a kiss or a touch. My sex is dry from the ground nutmeg and it hurts.

It really hurts.

It hurts so much that I cry out.

'Shh,' he says. 'It is only your maidenhead. Lie still and let me finish.' Relief fills me momentarily, but then he ruts into me, making the bed ropes creak and the headboard thump against the wall. I lie there and stare up at the ceiling until he groans and collapses on top of me.

'Not bad, for a first time. It will improve. Ah, my wife, I've waited so long for this day. I knew I'd have to marry you to bed you.' He withdraws his "thing" from me and, without so much as a *goodnight*, turns over and falls asleep. I put my hand between my legs, and when I remove it, Holy Mary Mother of God, there's blood on my fingers.

I let out a cry of fear for my baby.

OH God, oh God, oh God, I've lost the baby. Not again. I can't bare it. I jerked awake, tears streaming down my face. I lifted my hand. No blood. I rolled over in the bed and stared at the sheet. White.

I hadn't been pregnant; that had been Cecilia. It had brought it all back to me, though, the shame of what I'd done.

And the terrible, agonising guilt.

When I'd found out that Harry and I had conceived a child,

I'd been in denial. I hadn't looked after myself. I'd worked all the hours God had sent and, when I'd come down with the 'flu, I hadn't gone to the doctor. The infection and the raging temperature were what had caused my miscarriage. I'd been glad at first; I hadn't wanted a baby. It was too soon, we weren't married yet, and I needed to get my career established before taking a break to have children.

I remembered being so angry with Harry for not using a condom that one time. It had been after a party, and we'd gone back to his place a bit tipsy. Maybe I should have kept the contraceptive coil I'd had put in after we'd started sleeping together. But it had made me bleed constantly, which was why I'd had it removed. Then, when I'd missed that first period, I'd barely noticed I'd been so busy at work.

After my period hadn't appeared for the second time, and I'd started the most terrible morning sickness, I'd bought myself a pregnancy test kit. When the result had shown positive, I'd cried hot tears of despair and had kept my pregnancy to myself for a week. Then I'd told Harry and he'd been over the moon, suggesting we bring our wedding date forward. I'd argued against that. After all, the church and the reception venue had been booked for the following summer. The baby would have been born by then.

In the meantime, we'd decided not to tell anyone. We'd wait until my bump was showing. I'd insisted on it, saying I didn't want to jeopardise my chances at work.

How selfish of me!

It was the sight of a mother with her new-born baby at the supermarket that had brought on the guilt. That tiny scrap of human life had seemed so vulnerable, but at the same time so vibrant. I'd wanted to cradle the other woman's child in my arms and whisper, sorry, as if it had been my own baby.

Harry had been distraught at the loss of our child. He hadn't come out and blamed me outright, but I was sure, deep down, that he held it against me. It was the way he'd started being less affectionate toward me, hardly touching me anymore. So, I'd buried myself in my work again, thinking he'd eventually get over it.

Within me, the guilt festered like a wound that wouldn't heal. When Harry had died, I was sure it was some form of punishment for what I'd done. Even when the sensible voice in my head had told me not to be silly, divine retribution didn't exist, I couldn't help myself.

I knew I wasn't worthy of being loved by any man. I was tainted. Harry had been waiting for me on the concourse at King's Cross Underground and I'd been late. If I hadn't cared so much about my damn career, we'd both have left the station before the fire started.

I'll pay the price for my selfishness for the rest of my life.

A keening sound escaped from deep within me as I sat up in my bed at Auntie's house, tears streaming down my face. A knock sounded at the door, and she poked her head into the room. 'Whatever's the matter, love?'

'She… she… she's lost her baby.'

'Who's lost her baby?'

'Cecilia.'

Auntie put her arms around me and rocked me. 'Shush! You've had another nightmare. There, there. You'll be fine now.'

I wasn't fine, but I wouldn't say anything to her. That part of myself I'd keep hidden forever. That hard, ambitious woman wasn't who I was today. But the festering guilt would always be with me.

And now Cecilia has lost her baby too…

I can't go back there into the past anymore. The pain would be too much to bare.

'Auntie,' I said. 'I know you think I'm still suffering from stress and don't believe I could be slipping back in time. Maybe you're right. Whatever the case, I can't stop it of my own accord.'

'Then I think you should get medical help,' she said, stroking my arm.

'No, not that. Luca's mother mentioned we could ask the local priest to bless this house. What do you think?'

'Hmm. Not sure about all that mumbo-jumbo,' she shrugged. 'But if it would make you feel better, of course.'

'Thank you,' I said, pecking her on the cheek.

'How about a nice cup of camomile tea and a chocolate chip cookie?' Auntie got to her feet. 'It would help you get back to sleep again.'

I followed her down the stairs but stopped halfway.

There was that smell again, the odour of burnt wood, so strong, it almost made me puke.

I rubbed my nose on the back of my hand and was hit by a chill that raised the hairs on my arms.

'Lorenza,' the voice whispered right by my ear.

I flinched and my heart hammered against my ribs.

uca

I put the phone down and ran my fingers through my hair. Fern had caught me just as I was setting off for work. Something had definitely spooked her, but what good would a priest do? Cecilia didn't just come to her at Susan's place. And why the sudden change of mind on Fern's part?

After promising her I'd ask my mother's advice, I'd tried to elicit more information from Fern, but she was reticent. 'I'll explain everything when I see you,' she'd promised. 'Please call me as soon as you've spoken to Vanessa.'

I left for the office, where I spent the day trying not to worry about Fern. Then I stopped off at the villa on my way home.

'House blessing is a common enough ritual,' Mother said matter-of-factly when I'd explained Fern's dilemma. 'You'd know if you'd continued in the faith into which you were baptised.' She bumped my shoulder with a smile. 'I'll see what I can arrange. The priest will advise a full exorcism if he senses an evil spirit or demon. But I don't think we're dealing with that, somehow.'

I snorted out a wry laugh— I couldn't believe I was discussing demonology with my mother. We were in her small study at the back of the villa, her genealogical research spread out on her desk. 'How are you getting on with the detective work?' I asked.

'Well, it would help if the family still had any of its *palazzi* in Venice. The archives from the sixteenth and seventeenth centuries seem to have been lost.'

'Shame about that,' I said. Whenever any of my ancestors had suffered financial difficulty over the years, they'd sold off their Venetian properties one by one and today there were none left. Granted, several were still standing bearing the Goredan name, but the family had no rights to them, and hadn't for at least two centuries. All we had was this villa, and the old farmhouse on a hillside below Monte Grappa.

'I really should go to Venice and visit the library in San Marco,' Mother continued. 'They have records of births and deaths going back hundreds of years there.'

I made strong eye contact with her. 'Why don't you let me handle that for you?'

'You could take Fern,' she said enthusiastically. 'To see Venice again before she returns to London. A romantic interlude...'

My mother's words cut deep. Fern would leave Italy in about a fortnight, and I'd pushed the imminence of her departure from my mind. 'I'm getting nowhere on the romance front.' I exhaled a long slow breath. 'It's impossible to compete with rivals who're both dead.'

Mother put her arm around me. 'Do you think Fern is doing the right thing?'

I quirked a brow. 'What do you mean?'

'Trying to block Cecilia. That woman seems to be a very determined spirit. She'll find a way to get through, I'm sure she will.'

'Fern's adamant she wants nothing more to do with her. She wouldn't tell me why, except it seems to be connected with the fact that Cecilia has had to marry someone she didn't love.'

'It was common enough in her day. I'd have thought Cecilia

would have been quite accepting. Especially if it meant financial security...'

'She was deeply in love with the painter. But he couldn't support her in the style to which she was accustomed, as they say, although I'm convinced Giorgione was a womaniser and liked to play the field. Cecilia seems to have accepted this alternative arrangement readily enough, from what Fern told me. I don't know why Fern should find that so upsetting...'

'My darling boy.' Mother gave me a hug. 'I can see how much you love her. It breaks my heart she doesn't love you back.'

'Mine too,' I said. 'Mine too...'

The next day, I drove to Altivole as I'd arranged. The local priest was standing at Susan's door. He introduced himself as Don Mario and was about ten years older than me, with wavy dark hair which gave him a charismatic look.

'*Buongiorno*,' I said before thanking him for giving up his time and coming to the house so quickly.

Susan ushered us into the kitchen, where Fern was waiting, her forehead creased with worry.

'Can I get you a coffee?' Susan asked.

Don Mario and I thanked her but declined, and the priest unzipped his rucksack.

'I'll leave you to it,' Susan said stiffly. 'I've got to go out and do a little grocery shopping.' She picked up the handbag Fern had bought her in Castelfranco, a *Fendi* no less, and went to the door.

I shrugged to myself... Fern had told me about her aunt's disbelief.

The blessing was a simple enough process, it seemed. Don Mario took a bottle of holy water and a crucifix from his bag, and we progressed from the kitchen to Susan's bedroom and study upstairs, the priest raising his crucifix, and sprinkling the water in every corner, while he blessed the house in Christ's name and that of His angels.

When we reached Fern's room, however, her eyes assumed that "rabbit in the headlights" expression. 'I feel sick,' she whispered. 'How much longer is this going to take?'

I took her hand; her fingers felt cold and clammy. 'Almost done now, I think.'

White-faced, Fern took her hand from mine and spun around. 'Please ask him to stop.' Her voice trembled. 'I've changed my mind.'

I shivered.

The warmth of the morning had turned into a sharp chill.

'Lorenza!'

I'd heard it.

Jesus, I'd actually heard that voice.

Incredible.

Heart thudding, I glanced at the priest, but Don Mario, apparently oblivious, was intoning, *'Visita, Signore, te ne preghiamo, questa abitazione e creatura tua, respingi via da lei tutte le insidie del nemico; in essa abitino i tuoi santi angeli, Michele, Gabriele e Raffaele, che la custodiscano in pace dagli spiriti immondi.'*

'What's he saying?' Fern whispered.

'He's asking the Lord to visit you and your room, to banish all signs of the Devil and he's intoning the Holy angels Michael, Gabriel and Raphael to take up residence here so that you can be at peace from unclean spirits.'

The cold was eating into my bones. Fern's face had turned rigid and her eyes expressionless. Was she about to go into one of her trances? I put my arm around her and felt her body shaking. 'I think I'm going to throw up,' she said.

Electricity crackled through the air.

Couldn't Don Mario sense it?

'La tua benedizione sia sempre sopra di noi. Per Cristo nostro Signore. Amen,' the priest said as he lifted his crucifix. *'Ho finito.* I have finished.'

'Oh, thank God, thank God, thank God.' Fern held her head in her hands. 'I thought my brain was about to explode. Cecilia's voice was in my head, repeating, *Lorenza,* over and over. I couldn't bare it.'

'I heard it,' I said.

She stared at me, her mouth falling open.

Don Mario made the sign of the cross on my forehead, asking the blessing of the Father, Son and Holy Spirit. However, when the priest lifted his hand to bless Fern, she ducked away, and muttered something about needing the bathroom.

I thanked Don Mario and gave him fifty thousand Lira for the church. As I saw him to the door, he said, 'Peace be with you, and with the signorina. I hope my prayers today will be enough to keep the restless spirit away from her.'

'*Spero anch'io*. I hope so too.' So, Don Mario *had* sensed Cecilia's presence.

Of course, he had.

He was a priest.

Dealt with the supernatural all the time…

'Thanks for helping,' Fern said when I'd returned to the kitchen. She'd sat herself down at the table, but she still looked terrible– her face pale and her eyes stricken. 'I wasn't up to it.'

'No. I can see that. Maybe this wasn't such a good idea…'

'I could feel Cecilia's misery, you know, more sharply than ever before.'

I took Fern's hand. 'Can you tell me why, all of a sudden, you decided you wanted nothing more to do with her?'

Her brow furrowed, and she pulled back her hand. 'I can't tell you. Not yet. I will, though,' she said haltingly. 'Soon.'

'Is the smell of burnt wood still here?' I asked.

'No. Do you think the priest has managed to send Cecilia away? Part of me wants that, and another part of me, the part that empathises with her and wants to know what happened, is worried she's gone for good.'

'Then why did you ask for the priest?'

'I can't tell you.' She had the grace to look flustered and gave my hand a squeeze. 'You're a lovely man, Luca, and I really like you.'

'I know you do,' I said, my arms enfolding her. *But you don't love me.*

She lifted her chin and kissed me.

Oh, God, how I kissed her back, long and hard, loving her so much I felt as if my heart would break.

My hands found their way to her hair, then cupped her face and then her firm breasts and then they were around her luscious buttocks, pulling her body against mine.

I pressed my nose into her luxuriant hair and inhaled her fresh scent.

We clung to each other, breathless.

I brought my mouth down and kissed her again, claiming her.

She nipped at my lips and I tilted my pelvis to accommodate my hard-on.

Her eyes fixed on mine, she stood back and slipped off her t-shirt.

The sight of her stole my breath— her smooth fair skin, the dip to her waist.

She reached behind to unclasp her bra, her gaze still holding mine.

As if in a trance, she stepped out of her jeans and all that was left were her panties.

I stood still as a statue, not wanting to spook her. She was so goddamn beautiful.

Silently, she took a step forward and started unbuckling my jeans.

Then she ran her hands up inside my dress shirt over my chest. *Oh God.* A quick kiss and she was undoing the buttons.

We became frantic, lips on mouths, throats, behind the ears, then mouths again. Together, we pulled off our underwear and I lifted her onto my erection.

She wrapped her legs around me as I leaned against the table, pushing myself up into her, my soul rejoicing.

With a throaty moan, she rolled her hips to take more of me, demanding that I bury myself deeper inside her, and I did.

I held back until she let out a gasp and her body convulsed, then I lost myself inside her. I kissed her and lowered her legs to the floor. With a half-smile, she looked up at me, her hair swinging forward to cover her breasts.

She stared at me and I stared back at her, trying to discern her thoughts.

'Luca, I'm so confused,' she said softly.

'What do you mean?' I tried to keep the anxiety from my tone.

She bent to retrieve our clothes. Handing me my shirt, jeans and briefs, she said, 'I don't want you to get the wrong idea.'

My heart sank. 'What idea would that be?'

'That we can be together. There're things you don't know about me, and those are things I don't want you to know. Not now. Not yet. Something's blocking me, you see.' She paused. 'Maybe when I've got to the bottom of the mystery of Cecilia.' She sighed. 'I just don't know…'

'*Dolcezza*. We can take this as slowly as you like.' I bent and kissed her cheek. 'One thing I want you to know, I'm in it for the long-term.'

'What did you just say?' she bit out the question.

'That I'm prepared to wait.'

She shook her head. 'What did you just call me?'

'*Dolcezza*. Italian for sweetheart.'

'Please don't call me that,' she said, her tone brittle.

It was like a slap in the face. My heart in pieces, I dressed quickly and said nothing, keeping my eyes cast down.

She touched my arm. 'Sorry. I didn't mean to be so blunt. You must think I'm such a bitch.' She blew out a breath. 'It's what Zorzo called Cecilia, you see.'

'Oh, that's all right then,' I said unable to keep the sarcasm from my voice. 'Your long dead lover can call you sweetheart, but I can't.'

She stood back and raked her eyes over me. 'He's not my lover. He's Cecilia's.'

'Of course. How stupid of me. Please take that back,' I said through gritted teeth.

'Please, Luca.' She took a step toward me. 'Don't take it the wrong way. I care about you. But I can't handle getting serious right now.'

I kissed her on the forehead. 'I'd better get to work,' I said, neither accepting nor rejecting her apology. 'Remember there's a rehearsal for the re-enactment this evening.' I paused for a beat. 'Oh, and I'm off to a conference in Vienna for five days from tomorrow. A last-minute arrangement. Someone in the office was supposed to go but has come down with 'flu. Before I set off, though, would you show me your latest painting?'

She led me to the corner of the kitchen, and I stood in front of her watercolour of the Barco. My skin prickled at how realistic it was. Realistic and incredibly good. 'It's brilliant,' I said, and I meant it.

'Thanks, Luca,' she smiled.

She saw me to my car, and I watched her go back into the house.

I sat for a moment, yearning for her so much it was if I was being wrenched in two.

With a groan, I banged my head three times on the steering wheel.

I was well and truly screwed.

CHAPTER 18

I kept myself focused by painting and by doing some local sightseeing. Cecilia stayed away from me. The house blessing must have worked. I visited the city of Treviso, where I strolled under the porticoes of streets echoing to the sound of exuberant university graduates, celebrating their *laureate* with crowns of laurels and singing raunchy songs in the wine bars.

Giving them a wide berth, I headed for one of the many canals, to take photos and do some sketching. Treviso wasn't known as "little Venice" for nothing, and I found it charming. I was behaving like an everyday tourist, interested in the past, but not reliving it. Yet my heart ached for Cecilia and I was regretting banishing her from my life.

The next morning, I went to Marostica, in the nearby province of Vicenza. There, I gazed up at the ancient walls encircling the fortress at the top of the hill; it seemed as if the fort was reaching its arms down and hugging the town below.

I strolled to the main square, dominated by the lower castle, where every other year, in September, they played a "live" game of chess with human chess pieces. In a café facing the distant mountains, I sat and thought about Luca. At the rehearsal the other night he'd been distant toward me. I knew I'd upset him. When he'd made love to me, I'd wanted him so damn badly.

154

Sighing, I thought about the strength of his body, the way his hands had touched me, the feel of his lips. I remembered the sensation of flesh on flesh, skin on skin and felt a warm tingle between my thighs.

Luca wasn't a typical, debonair, suave Italian, one of those Mills & Boons stereotypes that didn't exist in Italy from what I'd seen. (Federico's leering sprung to mind.) Luca was good-looking, granted, but he wasn't big-headed with it. There was a sensitivity to him and a kindness that touched me deeply. Chiara had said he'd been a playboy, and Luca had admitted to his mother that he'd played around in the past. But I couldn't imagine him being like Zorzo. Cecilia's artist was using her as his muse and for sex; that much was obvious.

Why couldn't I open my heart to Luca? It was as if there was a lump of stone in my chest. And now he'd gone to Vienna, I was missing him.

I scrubbed a hand over my face then reached for my handbag. Feet dragging, I went to pay for my drink and then made my way home.

After lunch, I went riding with Chiara. We rode as far as Asolo, on the unpaved tracks winding between the farms and vineyards. Back at the villa, I stopped for a cup of tea with Vanessa. We talked about her genealogical research. The Goredan family was descended from the Doge of Venice at the time of Caterina Cornaro, she told me, elected as usual by the aristocracy of the city.

Chiara had made herself scarce, but Vanessa was true to her word and didn't ask me to tell her about what we'd discussed during our ride. There wouldn't have been anything to divulge in any case; there hadn't been the opportunity for a chat as Chiara had taken the lead and galloped ahead of me when dark clouds started gathering above the mountains.

In the evening, I ate supper back at my aunt's house. While we were clearing away the dishes, a crack of thunder made my ears ring. 'Grab the candles,' Auntie called out. 'The lights will go out at any minute.'

Lightning zigzagged through the open windows. I helped her close all the shutters, clear the dishes and then wash up.

I took a candle and wished her goodnight. I was tired and there wasn't enough light to read. My period had arrived and with it unusually fierce dragging pain. I stretched out on my bed and closed my eyes. One crack of thunder followed another. Fireworks, launched to break up the hailstones, competed with the cacophony. Would I ever get to sleep? But I did. Soon I'd fallen into a dream so real I was crying out in agony.

'Make it stop,' I scream. Another wave of pain hits me and I twist my body. I'm sitting on a birthing chair, the wood hard against my buttocks, with a hole in the middle to allow the midwife's fingers to poke about inside me. My labour has been going on since dawn and it is now evening. I can't take any more. Between each bolt of torture, I've sunk into near oblivion as exhaustion has claimed me, but then the torment has built again and again, each time closer to the last, wrenching me back into screaming wakefulness. To make it even worse, there's a thunderstorm going on outside, a veritable tempest.

I arch my body as the next spasm hits me, and blood squirts onto the straw below the stool. I'm going to die. I'm sure of it. Gripping my robe, I let out a yell then breathe in the sickly-sweet smell of the almond oil the midwife has rubbed on my nether parts. 'To reduce the tearing,' she says.

Fiammetta and Dorotea are both here to help. They don't know I've been carrying the painter's child and believe I've just started my labouring early. Thankfully, my belly has been small, and no one suspects. Another bolt of pain rips through me as lightning streaks the sky outside. I scream, 'Help me!'

Fiammetta wipes my brow, 'Sweet sister, you must be brave and tolerate the discomfort. Baby will come soon enough, and you'll hold him in your arms, and all will be well.'

'This is not discomfort. This is what Hell must feel like,' I mutter staring at Dorotea; she's wringing her hands and bleating helplessly... about as much help as a wet rag in this thunderstorm.

My sister wipes my brow again while agony knifes through me. I feel as if I'm passing a boulder, a boulder that stretches and tears me apart. Then an irresistible urge to push grabs hold of me and I push, and push and push until the "boulder" slithers out of me, letting out a thin wail.

There's bustling and the movement of skirts. The glint of a knife as the midwife cuts the cord. 'A girl,' Dorotea says. 'Very small.'

'Please, can I see her?'

They place her on my stomach, and she's sticky with blood and wax, her face red and angry-looking at being expelled from the warmth of my womb. In an instant I forget the pain, as love for my daughter *my daughter!* rushes through me with such force that I'm left breathless. 'She's beautiful,' I say. And so, she is. Her eyes are blue-black and fringed with dark lashes; her nose is tiny and her mouth like a rosebud.

Fiammetta asks, 'What will you call her?'

I haven't thought of a girl's name. Lodovico had been adamant the child would be a boy. He wanted to name him Federico after his father. For some unfathomable reason, the name was abhorrent to me, and I'm relieved to have a daughter instead. The months of waiting are finally over. My fear at losing the baby on my wedding night was short-lived, thank the Holy Virgin, for my bleeding was but momentary. I endured my husband's rough love-making for the first weeks, until I could use the excuse of my pregnancy for him to stop sticking his "thing" into me. He's away in Ferrara this night, praise the saints; I won't have to face his disappointment yet. Instead, I can revel in my new motherhood without his disfavour.

I look down at the child's wrinkled face and screw up my own as I try to bring forth a name. A name for someone who'll be wise and practical and with an appreciation of beauty. A name for a girl who'll grow up strong and independent. A name for a woman who'll find the fulfilment in life I have yet to attain. The name hovers at the edge of my consciousness like the puff of a breeze and there, I have it. 'Lorenza.' I kiss her downy head. 'Her name is Lorenza.' A crash of thunder rents the air and my vision blurs.

Damn storm still going full-tilt. It might upset the babe. I bent to kiss Lorenza's head again, but my arms were empty. Panic flooded through me. Who had taken my baby?

A scream rose in my throat. Then the stench of burning filled my nostrils, making me retch.

I struggled to bring myself under control, taking deep breaths until my pounding heartbeats stilled.

A flash of lightning, and I saw the piece of burnt wood on my bedside table.

Heart thudding, I fumbled for the box of matches and lit the candle.

I wasn't Cecilia; I was Fern.

With a groan, I lay back on my bed, my arms aching to hold the baby, my body battered and bruised.

Tears trickled down my cheeks and I cried out for the child; a part of me had gone.

My breasts were hurting, and I crossed my arms. *Oh my God!* There was a cold wetness on the front of my cami.

I ran to the bathroom, where I pulled off my top and let it fall to the floor. My breasts had grown huge and laced with blue veins. A drop of watery-white liquid seeped from my left nipple, and I gasped.

I stumbled back to bed, grief overwhelming me. I coiled in on myself, and wept for Cecilia, for Lorenza, and for my own lost baby. Then I rubbed at my tears; I hated the loss of self-control. Even when Harry had died, I'd bottled up my emotions.

Restless, I drifted in and out of sleep. Morning came and the storm abated. After showering, I dressed and stuffed Kleenex into my bra. I caught sight of my print of *The Tempest* on the wall and my legs turned to jelly.

The child in the painting was Lorenza.

No doubt about it.

I toppled onto my bedcovers, shock wheeling through me.

'Lorenza!'

How I longed to hold her in my arms. I closed my eyes and waited…

I'm made to rest in my bed. Fiammetta is back in Treviso and Lodovico has returned from Ferrara with his brother, Giovanni. My husband isn't pleased that I've produced a girl-child. I smile sweetly. 'We can have more.' It pains me to say this, but I need to keep my baby safe and the only way to do so is within the confines of this marriage.

Lodovico grunts and his thin lips curve in such a way that my skin tightens. He'll have to wait until I'm churched before he can have knowledge of me like I know that he wants. His rough treatment will resume. If only I could be with Zorzo. I haven't seen him since we conceived our baby, and my entire being longs for him.

I hold Lorenza. She sucks greedily at my breast, my milk coming in so quickly it dribbles down her chin. Standing next to me, Lodovico gives a shudder. 'We should get a wet nurse. It is unseemly that you should suckle the babe yourself.'

'I've asked around, but there's no one available,' I lie. I'll not have anyone else feed Lorenza. She's mine. The only person who is mine to love, and, *Maria Santissima*, I'll keep her with me.

The following day, the Queen visits with Dorotea. She picks Lorenza up. 'She's like you. A real beauty.' She kisses my baby on the forehead and hands her back to me. 'I shall be her godmother.'

'I'm honoured, Domina,' I say. My sister will be Lorenza's other godmother, and Lodovico's brother has agreed to be her godfather. The baptism will take place in Asolo's main church tomorrow.

My maid brings refreshments – sweet wine and cakes. As ever, the Queen nibbles daintily, but I'm hungry and so is Dorotea. Soon the carafe is empty and there are only crumbs on the plate. Domina kisses me on both cheeks and chucks Lorenza under the chin. My daughter seems to know that she should not cry and regards her Queen with a solemn expression.

Alone, at last, I revel in my baby. I stroke her soft cheek and she looks into my eyes and I feel as if my heart will swell out of my chest, I love her so much. Her little hand clasps my finger.

I would do anything for her.

Anything.

I'm tired, but dare not fall asleep, for if I sleep who will check that Lorenza is breathing? I lay her in the cradle beside my bed and watch her small chest rise and fall, rise and fall.

The next day we set off at midday, and I enjoy leaving the house and getting some fresh air. I inhale the scents of Asolo as we walk up the hill. Roses grow on the wall of the baker's, their heady fragrance mixing with the aroma of newly baked bread. We pass the blacksmith's and the sour stench of molten iron tickles my nostrils. Then, there's the pong of horse manure and I need to move to one side to avoid stepping in dung. I think of Pegaso. He's remained at the Queen's stables the past eight months since I was wed. How I long to ride him again…

I steal a glance at Lodovico, who's carrying Lorenza. He walks stiffly, unaccustomed to holding such a precious burden. His brother strides on the other side of him; they're so alike they could be twins: short, thin, with almost-black hair. The only thing different about Giovanni is that his face doesn't have a scar on the cheek like Lodovico's. My husband told me he received it in a sword-fight while he was training for the Duke's cavalry. I wish he would go back there and leave me in peace. We walk quickly, for there's a chill in the air. My babe is warmly wrapped in woollen blankets and is fast asleep.

Inside the church, the atmosphere is bright with candlelight. Sunlight filters through the windows and I catch the fragrance of incense. The Queen is here, and Dorotea and Fiammetta. After Mass is said, we gather at the font, a gift from Queen Caterina to the people of Asolo, and the priest, a stout man clearly fond of pasta, intones as he pours the Holy water on Lorenza's forehead, and signs the cross, *'Lorenza, ego te baptizo in nomine Patris, et Filii, et Spiritus Sancti.'*

The words echo in my head as if I'm hearing them for the first time and my baby, in Fiammetta's arms, lets out a hearty cry. 'It is the Devil leaving her,' the Queen pronounces, and I laugh before saying, 'Amen.'

We progress to the castle, where Domina has ordered a meal to be prepared for us. I feel blessed as we make our way up the steps from the church to the square. No one suspects that Lorenza is not Lodovico's, much less my husband himself. If only her real father could know her; yet that knowledge might risk her safety, for how could he fail to love her and want to be with her?

My breasts engorge with milk and wetness trickles down my chemise. Lorenza will be hungry and I'm eager to feed her, to rock her gently as she suckles, and to kiss her sweet head. My fingers itch to take her from Lodovico and hold her in my arms. We pass the blacksmith's again and my stride falters as a feeling of dread overcomes me. The heat from the forge wafts toward me and the hairs on my arms stand up on end. Horror engulfs me, and I lose my footing, stumbling on the cobbles. Bitter fumes make my eyes water and the breath is sucked from my lungs. I gasp and retch and start to sway.

'Cecilia!' My sister's face is pinched with worry. 'Whatever ails you? Are you ill?' She links arms and the affection she has for me banishes the demon, for that's what was plaguing me I'm sure. I shouldn't have laughed at the Devil back there in the church.

'I'm recovered,' I say. 'It was only the heat from the forge.'

I fall into step beside my husband, and my breath falters. He's looking at me, his eyes appraising me. The feeling of dread returns and the world around me shimmers.

I gave a start. Sunlight came through the window; it was still morning. *I'm Fern again, of course.* So much happened when I was in the past, days would go by, that when I came back to the twentieth century it was as if I'd been jarred, the sense of displacement was so great. It reminded me of my one and only ride on a roller-coaster. The mad race along the tracks, the plummeting down the loops and the final grinding halt, jolting me backward and leaving me feeling disorientated and nauseous. I'd not ridden one since, nor did I want to.

A burning in my breasts alerted me to the fact that I was leaking again, and the ache to hold Lorenza felt unbearable. I prodded the piece of burnt wood on the bedside table. No point in throwing it away; it would vanish of its own ghostly accord.

I shuddered, then stuffed my bra with more Kleenex. After putting on a pair of jeans and a t-shirt, I went downstairs to the phone. I picked up the receiver and dialled Vanessa's number. 'Is it all right if I come and see you?' I asked.

CHAPTER 19

'Spontaneous lactation is unusual,' Vanessa said, pouring a glass of Prosecco and handing it to me. 'But not unheard of. I read an article about a mother who'd adopted a baby and then started producing milk. Only what you're suffering from is extremely rare, I think.'

'My breasts are really sore. Isn't there some kind of medication I can take?' I asked before taking a sip of my drink.

'Only Paracetamol. You'll stop lactating in a day or two, as you're clearly not breastfeeding. I'm so sorry for you, my dear.' Vanessa leaned across the table and patted my hand. 'What a disturbing thing to happen!'

An urge to unburden myself took hold of me. Slowly, haltingly, and then more firmly, I told Vanessa about my pregnancy nearly three years ago. How I'd tried to ignore it, and how I'd lost my baby. 'And now I feel as if I've lost her again,' I said, unable to stop the hot tears trickling down my cheeks.

Vanessa got up from her chair and held me. 'I'm so sorry, Fern.'

'When I thought Cecilia had miscarried,' I said, wiping snot from my nose, 'I didn't want to go back into the past anymore.'

'That's why you asked for the priest?'

I nodded. 'And now I can't wait to return to Cecilia and see Lorenza again. It feels as if she's my baby too.'

'Only natural, I suppose.' Vanessa gave me a sympathetic look. 'You went through the birth with her.'

I nodded. 'I'm scared, though. Cecilia had a premonition of fire. I'm more and more convinced that's how she died, and I couldn't bare it if Lorenza died with her. It would be like losing my own baby all over again.'

'I can understand your concern.' Vanessa shook her head. 'It's a case of damned if you do and damned if you don't.'

'What do you advise?' I asked in desperation. 'Should I go back to London earlier than I'd planned?'

'I'm afraid I can't tell you, my dear. It's your decision. Perhaps you should come and stay here for a couple of days? It might give you some respite from Cecilia, and also a chance to reflect. You say she only comes to you in places associated with her...'

'That's right. It's very kind of you,' I said. 'Are you sure I won't be a bother?'

'Not at all. I'd be delighted. You can repay me with one of your watercolours. Luca told me how good they are.'

And so, it was decided. I went back to Auntie's to collect an overnight case. She was happy enough for me to stay with the Contessa. 'As long as you're back in a couple of days,' she said. 'Otherwise I'll feel like you're abandoning me.'

Trust Auntie to be so forthright!

'Luca's mother wants me to paint her a watercolour of the villa,' I said. It was a good excuse. 'It shouldn't take me long.'

I ran upstairs to pack my things, deliberately leaving my print of *The Tempest* behind in my room.

It took the three days I'd been staying with Vanessa for my breasts to more or less return to normal. I spent the time helping Luca's mother organise her genealogical research, taking the dogs for walks, riding with Chiara, and painting.

The Goredan family tree had so many branches, my head spun as I helped sort through myriad shoeboxes full of notes.

Chiara rode with me in the mornings, but after lunch she would leave to spend the rest of the day with Federico, only returning in the early hours of the next day. Vanessa had given up insisting her daughter be home by midnight but was firm about her coming back to sleep. 'As long as I'm paying for your upkeep,' she said. 'You have to follow my rules.'

In bed, at night, while I lay waiting to drop off to sleep, I could hear the ghost of the lute-player strumming a centuries-old tune. And, just like Vanessa had told me the first time I'd met her at the Cipriani Hotel, the sound wasn't frightening. I found it quite soothing, in fact.

Luca was still at his architectural conference, and I was glad of that. He was an added complication I could do without. If he should catch sight of the occasional wetness on my blouses, I'd die of embarrassment. Thankfully, the leakages occurred mostly in the evenings when Chiara was out; I would have found them impossible to explain. Gradually, I'd needed to replace the sodden Kleenex less often and now I was almost dry.

Whenever thoughts of Lorenza came into my head, I made myself think of something else, just like I'd done when I'd lost my own baby.

The mind was a powerful instrument…

Finally, on my last evening at the villa, Luca returned from Vienna. 'Let me see the painting you've been working on,' he said, after he'd greeted his mother. The excuse for my visit had been given to him as well. He followed me to the covered part of the patio, where I'd improvised my studio. My watercolour was on an easel in the corner. I'd concentrated on depicting the central part of Luca's ancestral home, suggestive of a Roman temple with its Ionic columns. 'What do you think?' I asked him, suddenly nervous.

What if he hates it?

But his face reflected his admiration, and he stood back in obvious awe. 'It's amazing. I don't know why you want to go back to working in a bank. You have a great talent, Fern. You should focus on your art.'

'Wish I could,' I chuckled. 'But I have a mortgage to pay.'

'Rent your flat out and use the income to live off here. You know it makes sense. London rentals are much higher than Asolo ones.' His deep blue eyes burned into mine. 'You'd probably cover your mortgage and have enough left over to live on while you get established.'

'Hmm, tempting.' The idea *was* tempting, but now wasn't the right time to go into it. 'How was Vienna?' I asked, deliberately changing the subject.

'Beautiful. We must go there together someday.' He stopped as he caught sight of my frown. 'I've done it again, haven't I?'

'I know you mean well, Luca.' I touched my hand to his arm. 'But you *are* a bit of a caveman...'

He smiled. 'Evolution hasn't caught up with modern society. Remember our discussion?'

'About tribal instincts. Yes.' I laced my fingers through his. 'I've missed you.'

'Well, that's a relief because I've missed you too.'

I glanced around the patio. We were alone. So, I wrapped my arms around his waist and lifted my chin. When his mouth came down on mine, I knew what I was going to say next. 'Can I take you out for dinner tomorrow night? There's something I need to tell you.'

I would finally come clean with him about my past, I decided.

I only hoped it wouldn't make him hate me...

The dining room of the Cipriani Hotel hummed with the low buzz of conversation. We were sitting at a table next to the picture window overlooking what had to be one of the most beautiful views in the world. The ancient buildings of Asolo marched along the crest of the hill in the foreground, toward an imposing villa which seemed as if it was perched on stilts, the loggia on the ground floor, and cypress trees standing sentinel at its sides. Sunset had caught the clouds, tinging them with pink, and the distant mountains rose up like guardian angels, spreading their wings over the landscape below.

Luca handed me the menu. 'I hesitate to make any suggestions, or you'll accuse me of being a caveman again.'

'Suggest away,' I gave him a smile. 'You know this restaurant.'

'The spaghetti with ham is excellent, as is the fish. We could have the pasta to start then grilled sole. And a bottle of Pinot Grigio.'

'Perfect,' I said, glancing down at my breasts. Thankfully, everything seemed to be all right in that department.

The waiter arrived and poured us a Bellini each before taking our order. I let out a sigh. 'I'm going to miss all this so much when I go back to London.'

'Then stay.' His mouth twisted.

I shot him a warning glance and he held up his hands. 'Sorry!'

While we ate, Luca filled me in with more details about the conference (boring) and the city of Vienna (fascinating). Butterflies fluttered in my chest. Maybe I wouldn't tell Luca about losing my baby after all; I couldn't bear it if it made him hate me. I finished my glass of wine and our waiter jumped to refill it.

'*Dolce?*' Luca asked when we'd finished our main course. 'The Tiramisù here is delicious.'

'Why not?' I said, knocking back another gulp of wine.

The dessert *was* delicious, but at the same time too rich and now I was feeling queasy. 'I can't eat or drink another mouthful.'

'Shall we go for a stroll in the garden? We can have our coffee on the terrace. Then you can tell me about what's been worrying you so much… you've had ants in your pants all evening…'

I linked my arm through his; I was feeling more than a little light-headed. He guided me to a chair next to the low wall protecting guests from the drop into the valley below. 'I'll fetch you some sparkling water, Fern.'

'Sorry,' I said, embarrassed. 'Didn't realise how much I was drinking.'

I watched Luca striding across the garden, then, heart thudding, swivelled my gaze toward the castle.

The plaintive cry filled my head.

'Lorenza!'

I sit in the Queen's Asolo orchard, watching my daughter crawl toward me. Happiness fills all my empty spaces. She's a sunny child, with dark eyes like her real father's as well as her supposed one's. It is good fortune they both have the same colouring. Her nature is like mine, however; she's impetuous and always into mischief. Only yesterday, she grabbed one of my brushes, dipped it into my ultramarine blue, and daubed the canvas I was working on, a painting I was doing of her. Lorenza's first birthday will be next week, and I've drawn and painted each stage of her development. Finally, I've been able to study a naked body, albeit that of a babe; I've learned much from observing then sketching my daughter.

Today, I've brought Lorenza to visit the Queen. I needed to get her out of Lodovico's way. His brother is visiting, and neither he nor Giovanni have any patience with my little girl. How can they fail to love her? Everyone else dotes on her… from the Queen, to Dorotea, to my sister. And I'm besotted with her too; to me, she's perfection. I open my arms and she comes into them, giggling as I hug her to me. Lorenza's soft cheek is like a peach and I give her a resounding kiss. She nuzzles at my chest; she's thirsty.

The court is taking an afternoon rest; I glance around to check we're alone. I unlace my kirtle and pull off my chemise, which I drape around my shoulders. Lorenza still suckles from my breast, once or twice a day. I place her next to me, on the other side of my raised leg, and her mouth latches onto my nipple. A tickling sensation arrives as my milk lets down, and then my daughter begins to suck greedily.

'Dolcezza,' comes a voice from behind the cherry tree.

I give a jump and my pulse quickens. 'Zorzo! What are you doing here?'

'Searching for you,' he smiles his beautiful smile, the corners of his lips rising. 'Your maid told me you were here.'

I make a move to cover my nakedness.

'Don't,' he says. 'Your babe will not thank you if you stop the feed.' He delves into his bag and takes out a rolled-up parchment and a stick of charcoal. Then he removes a board and ties the parchment to it. With quick strokes he starts to draw. 'I've a commission for a painting from a wealthy Venetian nobleman and have been searching for the right Madonna for it. Should have realised I didn't need to look far.'

My heart is jubilant at the sight of him; it has been far too long. His theory that I'd have had more freedom as a married woman has come to nothing because of my pregnancy and motherhood. Nevertheless, I don't regret Lorenza, not for one minute, she's everything to me.

I gaze at him while he works. My body has filled out since last he saw me; I'm no longer a nubile girl but a woman who bears the signs of childbirth. I try to pull my chemise around my nether parts, but Zorzo tells me to leave them uncovered.

'*Dolcezza*,' he says, his eyes drinking me in and his voice approving. 'I would have come to Asolo sooner, except work has kept me busy. Your Zorzo is much in demand of late.'

My Zorzo!

'The babe is delightful,' he adds. 'Hidden behind your leg, no one will realise she isn't a boy. A cherubic *Gesù bambino*.'

After a while I need to change Lorenza over to my other breast, but by then Zorzo has finished sketching her and has moved on to roughing out a drawing of my face and body. 'I don't need to spend much time on your countenance. For it is in my heart and soul.'

When my babe has drunk her fill, she sits back and regards her father. Neither she nor he will ever know of the relationship, I've sworn to myself, yet seeing them together makes me feel proud of them both. I hand her to him to hold while I dress, and he lifts her in the air. 'Look at you! The reflection of your mother.'

He whirls her above his head, making her unleash a stream of giggles.

'I think she's more like her father,' I say, smiling to myself.

Zorzo frowns. 'Does he treat you well?'

'Well enough.' I will not tell him of Lodovico's rough handling of me in bed, of the many bruises I've had to endure. Fortunately, of late, he scarcely bothers to visit me at night. I think he must have a woman in Ferrara. He goes there, supposedly on the Duke's business, more and more often. 'Although I do wonder why he wanted to marry me,' I say. 'There's no love in him.'

'Granted, you're the most beautiful woman at the Queen's court, but I have my suspicions about where Ferrara stands with respect to the Pope's alliance with the Hapsburg Emperor.'

I remember the brief visit of Maximilian at the banquet, when I was first introduced to Lodovico. 'He looks at the Venetian territories with envy,' the Queen said at that time. My husband has never made any secret of the fact that he's a man from Ferrara first and foremost. Could he have married me for my closeness to Caterina Cornaro? She doesn't involve herself in the highs and lows of politics, but her brother, Giorgio, is in charge of the Venetian Army.

My heart thuds and I close my eyes to dispel the disquiet invading my mind.

I blinked my eyes open and glanced around for Zorzo, but he'd vanished along with the child. My head spun, and I felt sick. A man was approaching with a glass and a bottle of something in his hand; I'd seen that man before.

'This should help.' The man froze and stared at the outline of my breasts. 'Fern! The front of your dress is damp.'

I felt the cold wetness seeping through my chemise. Only it wasn't my chemise; it was my work dress, the white one I'd worn to the opera with Auntie, that I'd put on especially for my dinner with Luca. *Dammit!* Cecilia wasn't supposed to come to me here. This villa hadn't been around in her time.

I glanced down at myself; Luca deserved an explanation. 'Cecilia has given birth,' I whispered. 'And my body thinks I have too.' I took in a deep breath and let it out again slowly. 'I know who Lorenza is.' I paused. 'She's Cecilia's daughter…'

Luca's eyes widened. 'Wow!'

I decided to go all in. 'I was pregnant once.'

'Oh?' His jaw literally dropped.

'I lost the baby,' I blurted out.

Luca looked deep into my eyes. 'I'm so sorry, Fern.'

'All my fault,' I said, rocking in my seat.

'How could it have been your fault?' His tone was gentle.

And then, I told him. About my so-called wonderful career, about my ambivalence toward my pregnancy, about my refusal to take care of myself. In a quiet voice, I told him about the guilt. The dreadful, unrelenting guilt. And how Harry's death was my punishment.

'You're being far too hard on yourself,' he said, putting his arm around me.

'No, no. Don't you see?' I clutched at my hands. 'It's why Cecilia chose me. She didn't miscarry, but she lost Lorenza all the same. I think she's searching for her.' My mouth trembled. 'I've decided I'll have to follow her story to the end. I need to find out what happened to Lorenza...' I shivered.

He took my hands and rubbed them. 'It's getting a bit chilly out here. Why don't we go back to my place for that coffee?'

I shot him a look and he smiled. 'No strings.'

'That's all right, then.'

The words had come out of my mouth before I'd even thought about them.

CHAPTER 20

*L*uca's flat was only a couple of minutes' walk from the Cipriani, at the top of an old palazzo. The views from the roof terrace stretched as far as the Dolomite mountains to the north and the Venetian plain to the south. 'It's stunning,' I said, gazing at the panorama. 'Have you lived here long?'

'About a year. I moved in just after I split up with Francesca.'

I met his eye and risked asking, 'Why did you break off with her?'

'The chemistry wasn't right. Something stopped me from introducing her to the family, so they never knew about her. In any case, we weren't together long.' He shrugged. 'Are you ready for that coffee?'

'Have you got any herbal tea?' I gave him a smile. 'I've had my caffeine allowance for the day.'

'Let's go through to the kitchen,' he said, taking my hand and leading me inside.

I watched him fill the kettle, his long lean hands grasping the handle. I remembered how those hands had touched my body and how they'd unravelled me. Don't think about that, I told myself, but I couldn't help it.

Luca reached up to the cupboard for two mugs, his shirt rising to expose his flat belly. Designer jeans, Armani, tight against his buttocks. I swallowed hard and made myself glance away.

'Sugar?'

'No thanks,' I croaked.

He trapped me in his deep blue gaze. 'Are you all right?'

'Fine.' But I wasn't fine; I was burning with the need to press my lips to his, to run my hands down his chest, and for him to do the same to me.

And, and…

I sipped my drink in silence and he did the same. We put our mugs down, and I fought the urge to go up to him and rest my head on his chest. He seemed to be keeping his distance from me, and I suddenly felt a tad shy.

'Regarding Cecilia,' I said, trying to keep my voice steady. 'I read in the book Auntie loaned me about Caterina Cornaro, that the Queen was in Venice when the Barco was destroyed.'

He nodded. 'That's correct.'

'The book doesn't give much information about the whys and wherefores.'

'I'll try and find out for you.'

'I'm interested in knowing where Ferrara stood. I mean, if the Duke supported Venice or the Emperor.'

'More likely the Pope. And *he* had a hatred of the Venetian Republic.'

I crinkled my brows. 'Oh? Why?'

'Because the Serenissima had taken control of several of the Papal States.'

'The Serenissima?'

'The Most Serene Republic. Venice.'

'And the Pope wanted the Papal States returned?'

'Got it in one,' Luca said.

'Zorzo told Cecilia that the Pope had formed an alliance with the Emperor Maximilian.' I remembered.

'He wasn't called the Holy Roman Emperor for nothing.'

'I thought the Roman Empire was long gone by then?'

'These emperors were German but liked to think they held supreme power inherited from the emperors of Rome.'

173

'Why the "Holy"?'

'Because from the tenth to the sixteenth centuries the Holy Roman Emperors were crowned by the Pope.'

'I'm beginning to see a connection here.'

'Yep,' Luca said.

'Although, of course, I won't be able to warn Cecilia.'

'One thing's for sure. We can't change the past,' he said wryly.

'Not like *Back to the Future*, then?' I gave a nervous laugh.

'Ha!' He glanced at his watch. 'Time to get you home, I think.' He jangled his car keys.

Disappointment flooded through me.

Don't be such an idiot, Fern. You gave Luca the brush-off after you had sex with him. He has his pride. He won't make a move on you again.

When he took my hand as he led me to where his car was parked in the basement of the building, heat spread up from my core. Luca was goddamn sexy, and I wanted him so badly. If he'd made that move, I would have fallen into his arms.

Sitting next to him in the Alfa while he drove me home, I thought about his reaction when I'd told him about losing my baby and my guilt. Maybe that's what had put him off?

No. Couldn't be. He'd said you were being too hard on yourself.

And I was; I knew I was. But I was unable to do anything about that. It was part of my personality. All my life I'd been told to lighten up...

'Penny for them?' Luca asked, as he brought the car to a halt outside Auntie's house.

'Sorry?'

'Your thoughts. Penny for your thoughts. One of Mother's favourite expressions. You've been so quiet.'

'Are you sure you don't hate me?'

He stared at me. 'Why would you think that?'

'Maybe because I hate myself a lot of the time.' There, I'd said it. Given voice to the darkness within.

He stroked my cheek and looked deep into my eyes. A sob rose up from my throat. He kissed my tears and enfolded me in his arms. 'Darling Fern,' he said between kisses. 'I love you so much and I'd give anything for you to love me in return. But you can't do that, can you?'

'I wish I could. I really do…'

'You need to love Fern first. Don't you see that?'

'What do you mean?'

'Accept yourself for who you are. The good, the bad, and everything in between.'

I nuzzled against him. Why hadn't my therapist picked up on this? Then I remembered that I hadn't told my therapist about losing the baby.

'One step at a time, Fern,' Luca said. 'You've taken that first step tonight, I think.'

'I hope so.' I kissed his cheek, catching the scent of his spicy aftershave. 'Will I see you tomorrow?'

'There's a rehearsal, don't forget.'

'Of course.'

Standing at the front door, I watched him drive off. Already, I felt bereft. How was I going to feel when I went back to London?

I went inside. The house was quiet; Auntie must have already gone to bed. I cleaned my teeth and put on my PJs. Then I slipped between the cool sheets, closed my eyes and waited for Cecilia to reveal herself.

I study my husband eating, his jaws chomping like a lizard's while he chews his meat. 'I received a letter from the Duke today,' he says, taking a swig of wine. 'He wishes me to purchase a painting by Zorzone.'

Hearing my true love's name spoken by Lodovico cuts me to the core, and my hands tremble with the effort of not showing any reaction. Zorzo is a part of me I have learned to keep hidden from the world, however. I haven't seen him these past five months, since he came upon me at the castle. Whenever I think about him, these days, I find it hard to reconcile myself with the carefree girl who threw herself at him without a thought for the consequences. I have grown up since and would not be so reckless now.

'Oh.' I keep my voice nonchalant. 'How interesting. Which painting?'

'There's a rumour of an un-commissioned work in his studio. A lute-player serenading a woman as night falls.'

Fear grips me. If Lodovico should see the painting, he'll recognise me. 'Will you go to Venice, then?'

'Momentarily.'

We finish our meal in silence, as usual. Conversation between us has always been sparse. Hard to believe we've been man and wife almost two years. Years filled with sorrow at being apart from Zorzo and, at the same time, the happiness of my Lorenza.

Lodovico gets to his feet. 'I shall visit you tonight, Cecilia. Be ready for me!'

I drop into a curtsey to hide my consternation. What has brought this on? Perhaps he no longer has a woman in Ferrara? It has been months since he and I lay together. As if reading my thoughts, Lodovico says, 'Time you gave me a son, wife.'

When he comes to my bed later, I lie still with my legs apart as he lowers himself on top of me. I turn my face away from his slobbering. He grabs my arms so hard I'm sure he leaves bruises.

He thrusts into me; I'm dry and it hurts. He finishes quickly and gets up from the bed. 'It's like fucking a wooden doll. Have you no passion, Cecilia?'

Not for you, husband. 'It is not in my nature,' I lie.

He leaves me, and I wash my nether parts in the bowl of water I keep by the bed. I must get rid of his seed. A child by him would be an abomination.

I go to check on Lorenza, who sleeps with her nursemaid in the room next to mine. She's lying on her side, with her thumb in her mouth. I stroke her soft cheek, and whisper, 'Heart of my heart. I'll do anything for you, to keep you safe. Sleep well, *bambina mia*, and in the morning we'll visit the Queen.'

Lorenza's nursemaid lets out a snore while I tiptoe out of the room. My daughter is weaned now, and so lively Lodovico has insisted we take on a woman to look after her. Granted, I'm able to spend more time painting, yet I wish I could keep my child with me every hour of the day.

The next morning, I feel battered and sore. This is the last time I'll put up with Lodovico's brutish advances, I swear to myself. I have some dried valerian herbs in my medicine chest, given to me by Fiammetta. 'I use them with Rambaldo,' she said. 'If I don't feel in the mood for "you know what", I stir them into his night-time wine, and he sleeps until midday.' She'd handed them to me with a knowing look.

After breaking my fast, I take Lorenza to see Domina, who is visiting Asolo. We discover huge excitement in the Queen's castle; the servants are scurrying around, packing coffers. Dorotea grabs my daughter from me and gives her a kiss. 'We are to go to Venice. You and your husband too. The Queen insists.'

'Why?'

'There's been a battle. Domina's brother has defeated the Emperor Maximilian. And her brother, Giorgio Cornaro, has also taken Pordenone and Gorizia for the Republic. Hurry home and pack your travelling chests! We depart tomorrow.'

My heart sings at the thought of going to the city of my birth and where Zorzo lives; he'll be part of the celebrations, I'm sure. Yet, also, my belly constricts with worry. If Lodovico finds the painting he seeks for the Duke of Ferrara, all will surely be lost. And how will I manage without Lorenza? The Queen doesn't allow children to travel with the court to Venice. It will be impossible to take her with us. 'Where is Queen Caterina?' I ask, thinking I might request a special permission.

Dorotea hands my daughter back to me. 'She is the Domina of Asolo, isn't she? There's famine in the countryside and she has imported grain from Cyprus. She always puts her people first and is distributing flour to them.'

'There's no one as dutiful and kind as our queen,' I say before taking my leave of Dorotea and hurrying home.

I find Lodovico pacing up and down the hallway. He scowls when he catches sight of me. 'We are commanded to go to Venice.'

'Does that not please you?' I dip a curtsey.

'Humph. The Emperor has been humiliated.'

'A good thing, don't you think?' I hand Lorenza to her nurse-maid and remember my suspicions about my husband. If Lodovico isn't on the side of the Republic, what are his purposes at the Queen's court?

I stare at him, but my vision blurs. Then, it is as if I'm gazing down on myself from a great height. A feeling of dread over-comes me and, *Maria Santissima*, I start to swoon. My legs buckle from beneath me and I crumple to the floor.

I opened my eyes. It was morning already. My mind felt fuzzy from an unremembered dream. What the hell had it been about? My mouth felt dry. *Must get a glass of water.* I swung my legs from the bed. What Cecilia called my "nether parts" were feeling really sore.

In the kitchen, Auntie glanced up from her manuscript, a red pen in one hand and a cup of tea in the other, Gucci Cat curled up on the rug by her feet. 'Sleep well?'

'Very deeply. I feel a bit woozy now, though.' I grabbed a glass from the draining board and filled it from the tap.

'Sit down, love. You look pale. Have you had another funny turn?'

'No, I don't think so. Although I did dream about something. Can't remember what, to be honest.'

'There's a packet of *brioches* in the cupboard.'

'Thanks.' I poured myself a mug of tea, added milk then placed a *brioche* on a plate.

'Any plans for today?'

My heart suddenly lurched and I put down my mug, the tea souring in my mouth. It was as if a video had started to play in my head. *Poor Cecilia!* I shifted in my seat to ease the discomfort between my legs. I could remember the feel of Lodovico's weight on top of me, his slavering tongue, his vice-like grip.

A sudden thought occurred to me.

There's somewhere I need to go.

178

'I think I'll visit Venice again. I'd like to stroll around on my own and do a few sketches,' I said to my aunt.

'Fine by me.' She settled her glasses on her nose. 'But I thought you had a rehearsal with Luca tonight? Will you be back in time?'

'Oh no! I'd forgotten...'

'Why don't you give him a call? I'm sure he won't mind if you cancel.'

I went to the phone and dialled Luca's number. Before I had a chance to mention the rehearsal, he said, 'I'm so worried about Chiara.' His voice came out strained. 'She's taken a fall from her horse and has badly broken her leg. It's being operated on now.'

My stomach clenched. 'Oh my God!'

'Mother's with her and I'm about to go to the hospital. Can we meet up later?'

'Of course. I was going to visit Venice.... I'll put it on hold.'

'Has Cecilia gone there?'

'To celebrate the Venetian victory over Maximilian's army.'

'I think you should go,' he said firmly. 'Just be careful to find somewhere safe. Please come to my apartment as soon as you get back. I could do with your company tonight.'

'I'll be there.' Nothing would keep me away. 'So sorry this has happened.'

'The doctors reckon she'll be all right.'

'Give your mother and sister a hug from me,' I said before disconnecting.

'What a shame,' Auntie responded when I'd told her about Chiara. 'But go to Venice, Fern. It might be your last chance before you return to London.'

I nodded. I couldn't tell her how conflicted I felt about my developing feelings for Luca, my need to find out what had happened to Cecilia, and my dread of returning to my old life.

CHAPTER 21

I caught the vaporetto water bus to Rialto, then, holding the map I'd bought at the station, made my way to Campo San Polo. I'd read in the book I'd borrowed from Auntie that Giorgio Cornaro, the Queen's brother, once had a palazzo here.

The square (more oblong than square in shape) was hot and dusty. Almost as large as Saint Mark's, but not as touristy. I strolled toward a café on the right-hand side, keeping out of the way of a group of boys kicking a football. A man and a woman crossed in front of me, taking their small dogs for a walk. I found an empty table shaded by an umbrella and pulled out a chair.

The waiter arrived, and I ordered a cappuccino. Where was the Cornaro palazzo? I opened my guidebook and read that it had burnt down in 1535. *Another fire.* I shuddered. A new structure had been built in its place, the side entrance in the corner of the *campo*, its façade facing a small canal. I was in the right area.

Was I being reckless coming here and opening myself up to Cecilia? No, the blaze in which Cecilia had died was at the Barco; I was sure of it now. That piece of burnt wood had appeared in Venice, admittedly, and fires were commonplace in the sixteenth Century, but I hadn't got to the end of Cecilia's story yet.

The waiter brought my coffee. I stirred it, sipped, and then waited. Would this work? The last time I'd deliberately tried to contact Cecilia here my attempt had failed. I'd been in Murano, though, which had turned out to be the wrong place. Hopefully, this time I'd got it right.

I sat and waited and before too long, that familiar buzzing sensation came into my head.

So many guests have been invited; the celebration has spilled over into the *campo*. The Queen's brother is giving a masquerade ball, not only to celebrate the victory, but also because it is the season of *Carnevale*. Iron braziers, their flames licking the wood, stand at regular intervals to warm us in the cold February night air. There are lanterns strung above us and groups of musicians wander in between us, serenading us with their lutes and viols. Domina's dwarf, Zantos, runs between the different groups, animating their songs.

I'm wearing a silver *Volto* full-faced mask, decorated with a half-moon in the centre and stars sprinkled around the edges. Lodovico has become a peacock, and, *Maria Santissima*, he's strutting around like that pompous bird in all his finery. We're dressed in our best attire; my husband spares no expense in keeping up appearances.

A sleeveless shimmering blue satin gown, laced at the front, covers my mother-of-pearl sleeved kirtle. My hair has been plaited into a *Coazzone*, with topaz and diamonds tied into my braids. Anticipation blooms in my chest; I'm sure I'll see Zorzo soon.

All around us circle the masked faces of the other guests. No one on this occasion wears the plain white *Bauta*. Instead, people have become cats, jesters, lions, tigers and columbines. *'Dolcezza,'* a voice whispers in my ear.

I turn and glance from left to right.

Where is he?

Vanished.

I spin around.

He's behind me, in a black doublet and wearing a gold *Volto*. 'Are you well?' He bows.

I nod, my mouth dry, and I drop into a curtsey. 'How did you know me?'

'Your beautiful tresses, even more lovely when they're tied with jewels.'

I blush beneath my mask and try to think of a suitable response. My husband is approaching, however, so I say nothing.

Two rows of people gather on the other side of the *campo*, and Lodovico claims me for a dance. '*La Moresca*.' He hands me a set of bells he's picked up from a basket being handed around, and I tie them to my wrists.

I catch sight of Zorzo bowing to another woman, and jealousy rears up within me. The woman isn't wearing a mask, which means she's a courtesan. Courtesans are forbidden to wear masks. I've heard rumours of Zorzo consorting with them but have ignored the gossip until now.

Out of the corner of my eye, I watch my painter. Is he watching me?

Foolish, Cecilia. You can't expect him to have kept his codpiece laced up all this time…

Lodovico and I join a chain of dancers, zigging and zagging, hands raised above our heads, as we shake our bells. I'm facing Zorzo now and we link arms in the dance. 'Will you come to me tomorrow, *dolcezza*?'

My heart beats faster. 'When?'

'In the early hours. Can you escape from your husband?'

'I've brought valerian herbs. I'll give them to him, and he'll sleep late. Wait for me here at first light.' We twirl away from each other and join the circle.

Supper is served on long tables down the side of the *campo*. There are sugar models of the cities of Gorizia and Pordenone. The emblem of the Cornaro family is depicted on myriad cakes. 'The Republic is drunk with success,' my husband says. 'Don't forget that pride comes before a fall.'

What is this dread that twists my belly? I think back to the feeling of foreboding I'd experienced after Lorenza's baptism. I tell myself not to be silly. The Serenissima has endured for over seven hundred years; nothing will ever destroy it.

After eating, we watch a theatrical performance, Plato's *Menecmi*. A stage has been erected on the far side of the square and has been covered in green velvet. There are over one hundred actors dressed in the classical style, wearing tunics of fine silk with threads of gold. I find it hard to concentrate on the performance; my thoughts are filled with anticipation of my visit to Zorzo.

When the time comes to retire, Lodovico and I go to the chamber allocated to us, a small room (much to my husband's chagrin) at the back of the palazzo. 'There are far more important guests than us,' I remind him as I pour his bedtime wine. Surreptitiously, I slip ground valerian into the goblet, stir it, and hand it to him. 'Your health, husband.'

He quaffs the drink in one gulp and starts to undress. 'Come, wife!'

I slip into the bed next to him, dreading his touch. What will I do if the herbs don't work? Lodovico places his hand on my breast and gives my nipple a rough squeeze. Then, praise the Holy Virgin, he's suddenly snoring under the blankets. I dare not risk sleep, for I might not wake in time. So, I get out of bed, put my dress back on, and sit on the ledge by the window. Picking at the skin around my fingernails, I wait for dawn's light.

After about an hour, Lodovico clambers out of bed and lets out a grunt. My heart drops; I'll never get away now. He goes to the chamber pot and pisses, letting out a fart at the same time, and the bitter stench of urine and bodily odours assails my nostrils. Then, after giving me a bleary glance and asking me why I'm fully dressed and sitting by the window, to which I reply that I'm feeling unwell, he's snoring in bed again and I pray to all the saints that he'll stay there.

Will the sky never lighten? I yawn and stretch. Perhaps I can sleep awhile? Shutting my eyes, I feel myself drifting off. *No, Cecilia. Stay awake!* I get up from my seat and pace the floor, my soft-soled shoes quiet on the stone flagging. Finally, weak sunlight filters through the panes and I grab my *Bauta*, cloak, and hood.

In the square, Zorzo is wearing a mask as well. 'It's only a short way,' he says, taking my hand. Walking beside him, I'm aware of how tall and broad he is compared with me. I practically run to match his stride. He notices and apologises. 'I don't wish to waste a moment of our time together.'

I free myself of my disguise when we arrive at his studio, and I walk toward the canvas placed on an easel in the corner. I can see my likeness, suckling Lorenza in the middle of the most forbidding landscape. There's another figure, a woman, who's also naked, watching me. She looks just like me, but her eyes are green. Between us, in the centre of the painting, are two broken pillars. I know what they signify: death. A shiver passes through me.

The background shows a town, above which a storm is gathering. The use of the greens and blues in the brooding sky projects an ominous feeling. Lightning streaks the clouds and, even though shivers pass through my body, at the same time I'm filled with admiration at Zorzo's skill.

There's a small white bird on the roof of the building on the right-hand side. I peer at it: a heron, warning of fire. My skin shivers with fear, but I tell myself not to be fanciful, and admire instead the wondrously detailed landscape of trees, bushes, flowers and a stream. The palette of soft greens, subdued blues and silver emphasises the mood of the gathering tempest above the bridge and the tranquillity below it, where I'm suckling Lorenza watched by a woman with green eyes.

'Who is she?' I ask, pointing to the lady watching me, although I know that I have seen her before.

The woman is sad and fearful of the love of a good man who is besotted with her. She should give him a chance, or she will lose him.

'The woman came to me in a dream,' Zorzo says. 'I saw her hover around you, *dolcezza*. But I shall have to paint her out. The man who commissioned the painting has requested a male figure, so I shall drop myself into the canvas instead.'

'I do believe this is your masterpiece, *amore mio*. There's a feeling of menace, though. What does it mean?'

'Did you know that the Republic has resisted the demands of the Pope for the restitution of the Papal lands?'

'N... n... no,' I stutter.

'Maximilian was rebuffed by the Council of Ten when he proposed an alliance against France.' Zorzo goes to his sideboard and pours two goblets of wine. 'That's why he attacked the Republic. Now he's been routed and forced to sign a truce.'

'What will happen?' I blurt out.

'The Emperor will fall in with the Pope and the French king, I suspect. He'll not take this humiliation from the Serenissima lying down.'

'So, there will be more battles,' I murmur, anxiety for my daughter's wellbeing uppermost in my mind.

'You will be safe enough in Asolo,' Zorzo says as if reading my thoughts. He hands me a goblet. 'The Emperor's quarrel is with Venice not the Queen. In any case, Maximillian will need time to recoup his losses. There might not be further trouble for a while.'

'I do hope you're right.' I take a sip and meet his gaze.

'It seems you find yourself in my quarters at the time of breaking your fast, once more, *dolcezza*. However, I've asked you here to pose for me again.'

What did I expect? It always was his purpose. Everything else comes at that price, I realise, and I'm not unhappy with the prospect for I can turn it to my advantage. 'Provided you will teach me too,' I say. His love for me is physical, I know. Our time together has been too short for it to reach his soul.

'I need you to be completely nude.'

'Then I require the same of you. When I draw *you*.'

Zorzo's eyes twinkle and he nods. 'I shall build up the fire so you're not cold,' he says, and proceeds to do so while I undress.

He piles up cushions on his bed and tells me to stretch out with my right arm above my head, and my hand tucked behind it. 'Place your left hand on your mons, *dolcezza*, for modesty. I want this work to be a hymn to the beauty of the female form, which you epitomise, not something that would entice men to leer.'

My maid plucked me of all my body hair just two days ago, something she does for me on a weekly basis, as is the custom. I bathed last night before the ball, and I thank the Holy Virgin that I still smell sweet as I stretch out on the bed. It's warm in here and I feel comfortable. Before I know it, I'm asleep.

How long have I been dreaming? My dreams are of the strange woman. She's dressed as a man and looks like me but has the freedom to wonder through the city in broad daylight without a mask. Why does the woman Zorzo painted watch Lorenza and me? I feel a shadowy connection to her, but, for the life of me, I cannot fathom why that should be…

'*Dolcezza*, wake up, I've finished,' I hear his voice. 'The outline is done, and I can do the rest from memory.'

I open my eyes and stretch, feeling refreshed. 'What hour is it?' I ask, getting up and reaching for my clothes.

'Still time for me to pose for you,' he says, stripping off his doublet and hose. 'No, don't dress! Come to me first, *dolcezza*.'

And then we are kissing, and his hard body is against mine, and all thoughts of drawing him vanish from my head as his hand reaches down and caresses me between the thighs. Oh, dear Lord, how I've missed this.

A knock sounds at the door, and we stop kissing. Who can it be? Our eyes lock as we hold our breaths. Another knock. Then my husband's voice echoes through the morning air. 'Signor Zorzo? I've come to see you about a painting.'

And I fall into a faint.

My head had slumped onto a table. What was I doing back in the *campo*? There was a cup in front of me, full of a bitter-smelling frothy-brown liquid. I tasted it, and the coffee jolted me back to the twentieth century. *Damn! What a time to leave Cecilia!*

Hopefully, my nemesis had managed to hide from Lodovico and give some explanation later for her absence. *I know Cecilia almost as well as I know myself. I expect she was up to the challenge.* Poor girl, not getting her wicked way with Zorzo. Almost certainly, she'd engineered him stripping off for her with that in mind.

I smiled to myself, remembering making love with Luca. *Luca!* How I longed to see him. Had it been worth it coming all the way to Venice to learn that Cecilia was the muse for Giorgione's *Sleeping Venus*? I'd deduced that myself from looking at the picture of the painting in my book on the artist. The work was no longer in Venice, I recalled, but I couldn't remember exactly where. Germany? I shrugged.

How weird that both Zorzo and Cecilia had been aware of me. My one claim to fame: the mysterious woman whom he'd painted over in *The Tempest*. Not that I would ever tell anyone... except Luca, maybe.

There was a pay-phone on the other side of the square. I left some change on the table for my coffee and strode over to it. Then I dialled Auntie's number.

'How's the sketching?' she asked.

'Terrible,' I sighed. 'I'm really not in the mood for it, so I'll pack it in and catch an earlier train. I promised to go and see Luca. I'll ring you from his flat.'

I can't wait for him to hold me in his arms again.

A memory stirred of my time as Cecilia and the advice that I should give the man who was besotted with me a chance. How weird that she should know about me and my situation. But, maybe not so weird, come to think of it; our minds became one when I was her.

$\mathcal{T}$he train was crowded with university students who commuted to Ca' Foscari from nearby towns and villages. I sat squashed next to a chubby woman, who was eating a salami *panino*. The greasy smell slid down my throat and made me feel sick. With a shudder, I took Auntie's latest novel from my bag; I was almost at the end and had finished reading it by the time I arrived in Treviso. I fetched Auntie's car from the parking lot, and, an hour later, I was ringing Luca's doorbell.

'Fern,' he said, opening his arms.

I went straight into them, enjoying the feel of his rock-hard chest against my cheek as I breathed him in. 'How's Chiara?' I asked, pulling back and meeting his gaze.

'Still in hospital.' He kissed me briefly on the lips. 'Mother's with her. The operation was a success, thank God. Her leg will be fine. They're allowing her to come home tomorrow at lunchtime.'

'What happened, exactly?'

'Apparently, she broke up with Federico.' He paused. 'They used to meet up at an old farmhouse we own in the foothills of Monte Grappa.'

'Yes, she told me about it. We were going to ride there and take a picnic.'

'Well, she'd started to suspect Federico was seeing another girl, so she decided to play a trick on him.'

'Oh?'

'She said she wasn't feeling well and wouldn't meet him yesterday. Then she went to the farmhouse and found him there *in flagrante*.'

I narrowed my eyes. 'What a pig!'

'Yep. This morning, she went for a mad gallop to get it out of her system. Pegasus spooked as a crow flew into his path and that's when she took a tumble.'

My heart jumped. 'I've just remembered something... something beyond amazing.'

'What?'

'The first time Cecilia took over my mind, she fell off her horse, Pegaso, which is Italian for Pegasus, isn't it?'

'It is. What a coincidence!'

'More than a coincidence. It's like an echo of the past.' My hands were shaking. 'And it's scaring me.'

'Would you like to stay here with me tonight?' he asked. 'As a friend, of course.'

I smiled, relieved I wouldn't be on my own; I needed his soothing presence... I needed *him*. 'That would be wonderful,' I said. 'I'll phone my aunt.'

∼

Luca made *spaghetti alla carbonara* and, after we'd eaten, he switched on the television. 'If you don't mind, I'd like to watch the news, then we can enjoy a video...'

The broadcast was taken up with the repercussions of the Tiananmen Square massacre in China. 'So many dead,' Luca said after translating for me. I nodded, and a feeling of deep sadness spread through me. *Man's inhumanity to man.* I remembered the well-worn phrase, *So much pain and suffering.* When viewed collectively, the huge number of dead people in Beijing was hard to envisage. However, each person came from a family, and that family would be in mourning.

I thought about Harry. The terrible circumstances of his death and a life cut short in its prime. I would miss him for the rest of my own life, of course, and I knew I should accept what had happened, and also the fact that it hadn't been my fault. No one could predict what was around the corner in life; it was best to take each day as it came and live it to the full.

Not easy, though.

Luca held up the video. 'Guess what?'

I laughed. *Back to the Future* would make a welcome distraction.

We sat through the movie, holding hands and sipping Prosecco.

Afterwards Luca said, 'It's getting late. I'll take the sofa and you can sleep in my bed.'

'You don't have to,' I said, looking directly into his eyes. I blushed. 'I'd like you to make love to me, Luca. That's if you want to, of course…'

He enfolded me in his arms, and, when I lifted my mouth to his, he kissed me. It was like drinking sweet wine as I kissed him back, opening myself up to him, my tongue on his. When we stopped, it was a wrench and we immediately started kissing again.

He took me to his room. We faced each other, and I lifted my fingers to his face, tracing the outline of his features, holding his gaze. Then, slowly, he unbuttoned my blouse and slipped off my jeans, placing them on the chair by his bed. He pulled off his t-shirt and unzipped his own jeans, throwing them onto the same chair. With a groan, he cupped my face and kissed the tip of my nose, the corners of my mouth, the pulse at the base of my neck. It felt perfect, as if this was what was missing from my life.

I unclipped my bra and let it fall to the floor. With a sigh of longing, I wrapped my arms around his waist, then pressed myself against him and kissed his chest.

'It's all right,' I said, thinking that, although this was our second time together, I should reassure him. 'My doctor put me on the pill because I had irregular periods.' I let out an embarrassed laugh. 'Don't worry. I haven't been with anyone since Harry.'

'I'm not worried and you can be sure I'm clean,' he said, embracing me again before lifting me in his arms and taking me to his bed.

We made love slowly, savouring each moment, our kisses long and deep, our coupling unhurried. By unspoken agreement, it seemed, we drew out the solace of our lovemaking, to arrive at our climax together.

Luca fell asleep quickly, but I found it difficult to drop off. The night was warm, and a mosquito buzzed by my left ear. *Better put on some repellent.* I got out of bed and went to the bathroom. *There's bound to be some here.*

I stared at my reflection.

A sudden drop in temperature, and the mirror wavered before my eyes.

'*Lorenza…*'

Cecilia was standing right behind me.

A sick feeling in my stomach, I watched as she lifted her hand and pointed at me.

Then the mirror wavered again, and my head spun.

I returned to Asolo six months ago, my heart torn between my daughter and my painter. I'm greedy for the feel of Zorzo's lips on mine, yet Lorenza's sticky kisses (after she's eaten a zabaglione) are those I'm enjoying this morning. That time away from her, only five days, seemed like a year, and I counted the hours during the long, dusty journey from Venice to get back here. Lodovico has not let me out of his sight since my brief escape from him after the Cornaro celebration. I give an inward smile, remembering.

Zorzo shouted through the door that he was busy and told my husband to come back in an hour. I could hardly believe my own audacity as I pulled my painter toward me. We fell onto the bed; our lovemaking was quick yet satisfying. I reached my joy within moments and he did too. Zorzo did not withdraw from me, and I hope for another babe from him. A dark-eyed son would suit me perfectly. 'Do not sell my husband that painting you did of us,' I begged. 'Or let him see the canvases with my likeness.'

'Fear not, *dolcezza*,' Zorzo said, putting on his hose and doublet. He went to *The Tempest* and wrapped it in white cloth. 'This one is already accounted for, and the lute-player and his true love I shall not part with at any price. I'll let Signor Lodovico into my quarters after you are gone, but I'll tell him the Duke of Ferrara is out of luck.'

And so, he did. When Lodovico returned to the Cornaro palace, I was back in our room. 'Where have you been?' he asked, his voice sharp.

'Out taking the morning air. I needed to clear my head.'

'And did your maid go with you?'

'Of course,' I lied, thinking I had to remember to bribe her.

I've put up with Lodovico's advances every night since our return to Asolo, lying back and thinking of Zorzo. What else can I do? I'm not with child yet, and, much as it is abhorrent to me, I need to let my husband rut into me, his fingers bruising my body. Tonight, we are to attend a banquet at the Barco for the Queen's brother, who is visiting. There's to be a joust before we dine, and then the usual dance. My breath catches with excitement; I know Zorzo will be there.

In the early afternoon, Lodovico and I set off for Altivole. Again, I'm to be away from my babe. Except, she's no longer a babe but a little girl of two. And she's learning to paint. Even at such a young age, she's quite a prodigy and has an innate understanding of colours. I'll persuade Lodovico to let me find a teacher for her when the time is right. It is my heartfelt wish that Lorenza will become the artist I can never be.

Cloud hangs low over Monte Grappa and mist hugs the valleys in between the Asolo hills and the Venetian plain. The Queen's villa of delights is nearly completed now, and it is wondrous to behold. Frescoes adorn most of the outer walls, the gardens are fully stocked, the game park bursting with life, and the air perfumed with the scent of late-flowering roses.

Afternoon sunlight catches the tops of the cypress trees near the gates of the Barco as our carriage pulls up outside. Autumn has come early this year, the year of our Lord 1508, and the days are drawing in. We go to our quarters, servants bringing our chest of clothes. I leave my maid to unpack my gowns and set off with Lodovico to the jousting green.

The Queen has spared no expense for the tournament in honour of her brother. There's cloth of gold everywhere, from the banners, to the curtains, to the tapestries draping her tent. Even the plates and goblets from which refreshments will be served are gold. 'A great occasion to celebrate the Republic,' she says.

Lodovico and I make our reverences. I drop into the deepest, most elegant curtsey, and my husband bows low. 'We're honoured to be your guests, Domina,' he says.

'Your brother is already here.' She smiles. 'Somewhere.'

'I shall go and find him,' Lodovico responds with another bow.

The Queen rises to her feet and claps her hands when a knight bearing her colours of silver and red gallops into the yard on a fine black destrier. The banners of the last crusader state of Cyprus, her late husband's. Her champion's opponent wears Giorgio Cornaro's orange and blue. It is only a friendly joust, but I do not like to watch, for I abhor any form of violence. I decide to slip away and go for a walk in the orchard. Coming around the hedge, I hear voices. Lodovico's and his brother's. I have no wish to greet Giovanni yet, so I wait behind the hedge.

'Any news for me to report to the Duke?' Giovanni says to my husband.

'The Venetian army is still in Brescia,' Lodovico mutters. 'Is the Duke over his disappointment that I couldn't procure a Giorgione painting for him?'

'Already forgotten. It was to be a gift for the Duchess. He's busy making cannons for the war to come. The first time in history that Venice has so many enemies at once.' Giovanni lets out a laugh. 'The Republic is far too complacent.'

'The Doge deems Emperor Maximilian too short of money to finance an army.'

'Ha,' Giovanni says. 'I shall relay that information to the Duke.'

Gesù bambino!

Zorzo was right.

My heart thumps wildly against my ribs, and, turning on my heel, I tiptoe away.

The tournament is still going strong; the cheers of the courtiers ring in my ears. Should I say something to the Queen? Yes, I should. But, when? She sits so calm and smiles so sweetly at all in her court. How can I break the trust she has in us? Domina has been through so much. She was married at the age of eighteen to a man she barely knew. Everyone says she did love him, and he loved her back. How terrible that he died when they'd been wed only nine months. My chest tightens as I remember her second heartache. The death of her infant son at the age of one. She must have been devastated. I know how I would feel if my Lorenza were to leave me. How could the Queen have borne the pain of her loss?

The plots and conspiracies to take her throne must have seemed paltry in comparison, yet she held onto Cyprus for fifteen years, and was well-loved by her people. No surprise there, for we all love her. Her loyalty to the Serenissima has always been unswerving, and she will be distraught that Lodovico has been using his position in her court to spy on her.

I sit through the jousts, looking away each time a knight is unhorsed, and I listen to Dorotea chatter excitedly. 'Domina has an admirer,' she says.

'Who?' I ask feeling pleased for the Queen. She has been without love too long.

'Pandolfo Malatesta, Lord of Rimini. A great knight and *condottiero*. He's in the service of Venice so there shouldn't be any obstacles. Except, her pride at having been the wife of a king has stopped her from taking things further.'

'She deserves to find happiness again. If only there was someone for her.'

Dorotea sighs. 'And me. I'm fast becoming an old maid.'

She huffs and frowns, but I don't feel sorry for her. A string of lovers has wound its way through her life, and her reputation is sullied. She'll be lucky to find a protector and become his mistress before her young flesh withers. Perhaps I'm being too hard, and should wish for her to find happiness, if not with a man then by having her own child like I have. 'There's time,' I say gently, patting her arm.

I wish Fiammetta were here, but she's had another baby, a girl. It was a difficult birth and she's not yet recovered. Fiammetta would give me good advice about how to carry on being married to a traitor.

Lodovico takes his seat next to me, looking as innocent as the day he was born (although I doubt even then he was innocent). If I were of a violent disposition and had a dagger, I would stick it into his heart.

Soon the jousting is over, and we go to our quarters to rest before the banquet. When Lodovico starts snoring on our bed I creep out, and within minutes I'm in the Queen's chamber. 'Please, Domina, I beg a moment in private.'

'Yes, my dear, what is it?' she asks, waving her ladies off to the far side of the room.

I quickly recount what I'd heard in the orchard. 'Such treachery,' I say.

She gives her tinkling laugh. 'Sweet Cecilia. Do not worry! My brother has the Venetian Army well-trained and the Emperor's forces are no match for us. If Maximilian dares attack again, he'll be routed once more. As for your husband, I've had my suspicions for some time. I'm sorry to have had them confirmed.'

'What shall I do?'

'Can you watch over him? Report back to me if you hear anything of importance. Two can play at the same game, you know.'

'Yes, Domina.'

I go to change into my evening gown: a deep rich, red, silk brocade. Lodovico asks me where I've been, and I tell him the truth. 'To see Queen Caterina.' He leaves me to the attentions of Marta, my maid, who disentangles my hair and places a garland on my head to hold my tresses back from my face. I fasten my gold necklace and pinch my cheeks to give them some colour.

'Very beautiful, signora,' Marta says, dropping into a curtsey. I slip a couple of coins into her hand then leave her to tidy the room. Marta is my best ally, although I'm no fool and ensure her loyalty by greasing her palm on a regular basis.

Zorzo is at the banquet. I spot him immediately and study him from the corner of my eye. He's seated at the far end of the room, dressed in a purple velvet doublet, so tall and handsome; he catches my glance, making my heart skip a beat.

I'm seated on my husband's right at the meal, which seems interminable: course after course after course. My stomach is too jittery to eat much and, finally, we lever ourselves from the table and progress to the hall, where the musicians are already tuning up.

The Queen and her brother take to the floor, and I suggest to Lodovico that he should invite Dorotea to dance. He doesn't need much urging. She's been fluttering her lashes at him all evening, and his eyes have only left her pillow-like breasts when he's helped himself to food and eaten it.

I watch them join the dancers and, within seconds, Zorzo is at my side. He bows low, '*Dolcezza*.'

We commence the hesitating march of the *pavana*, and I catch the scent of linseed oil from his hands, and the manly odour of his sweat. 'How are you?'

'Well enough,' he says. 'And you?'

I tell him of my discovery this afternoon as he turns me slowly to the music of the viol.

'As I feared, then.'

'The Queen does not make much of it. She simply wants me to keep a watch on Lodovico. I shall spy on him spying on her.'

'Take care, *dolcezza*. There's trouble on the way.'

'Are you sure?'

'The Republic thinks that by using diplomacy, it can divide allies like the French King and the Hapsburg Emperor. It won't work.'

'Haven't they been mistrustful of each other for years?'

'Their hatred of the Serenissima is far greater than their mistrust of each other.'

The dance comes to an end. As we make our reverences, he whispers, 'When can I see you alone?'

'It will not be easy. I'm watched by my husband. Are you here long?'

'A week. There's a final fresco I need to complete in the chapel.'

'Lodovico and I return to Asolo tomorrow, after the hunt.'

My husband approaches. He bows to Zorzo, who salutes him. Then Zorzo walks away and Lodovico says, 'I don't like that fellow. Or the way he looks at you.'

I supress a laugh for has he not been doing the same with Dorotea, the woman he's often referred to as being so loose that she "opens her quiver to every arrow"? We go to our quarters and Lodovico watches me undress. I catch the gleam in his eyes. 'I'm tired. Do we have to?' I say.

'Do we have to?' he repeats in a mocking tone. 'Tiredness is of no import. All you do is lie there while I do all the work.' His voice rises. 'If you were with child, I wouldn't bother.'

'No.' I shake my head, my mind made up.

'Yes,' he contradicts me. 'This is my right as your husband and you must do your duty to me, wife.' He grabs my shoulders and pushes me down on the bed.

'Leave me alone!'

'How dare you tell me what to do,' his voice has become even louder. I wish someone would hear him and come to us, yet, at the same time, I know that won't happen. I'm Lodovico's woman for him to treat as he wishes, for he has "paid" for me, housing, clothing and feeding me.

Lodovico pushes my legs apart and thrusts into me. '*Madre di Dio!* Get with child quick, Cecilia. I can't be doing with this much longer.'

Nor I.

He rolls over and lets out a fart. The stench of foul gases makes me retch. I wait, then, as soon as he's asleep, I creep out of bed and go to my chest, where I've hidden a flask of vinegar. I soak a cloth with the liquid and rub my sex. It stings, and I have to stop myself from crying out. But better this soreness than the pain of bearing Lodovico Gaspare's child.

I turn to go back to bed and catch my reflection in the glass above the washstand. Only it isn't just my likeness I see, but that of the strange woman who haunts my dreams. Her green eyes widen in surprise as she catches me standing behind her. I lift my finger and point, and then the glass ripples. The lady in the mirror disappears and it's only my refection staring back at me.

My mind is playing tricks on me, I decide, as I slip under the blankets next to the snoring Lodovico. Shutting my eyes, I curl in on myself and, before I know it, I'm asleep.

After we've broken our fast the next morning, Giovanni sidles up to my husband. 'A messenger has arrived from the Duke. We're both needed in Ferrara.'

I cannot believe my luck. Freedom, of a sort, so rare and so longed-for, will be mine for a few days at least. I go to the hunt without my husband, and the pleasure of riding Pegaso again far outweighs the discomfort I feel from Lodovico's rough treatment last night.

Zorzo is galloping next to me. 'I know a place where we can be alone,' he shouts above the sound of hoofbeats. 'Slow your horse and fall behind! We can pretend he's thrown a shoe and I'll say that we'll return to the Barco.'

It happens as he suggested. I dismount and walk beside him. 'There's an old Roman road to an ancient chapel hidden in a valley,' he says. 'No one goes there anymore, but I've visited it many times to sketch the landscape.'

As soon as the hunt has moved on, we remount and follow the road up behind the hill. The air is heavy with humidity and a falcon soars overhead. Crows caw from the tops of the trees beside us as we trot past. 'Come, Cecilia!' Zorzo urges his horse into a canter. 'We don't have much time.'

In the churchyard, we dismount and fall into each other's arms. When I say "fall", I mean that literally, for we do exactly that, becoming one within seconds so great is our passion. No need for decorum, for we are the only people in this secluded part of the countryside. If anyone is watching us, it's only the spirits of the Romans who were here before, guarding the entrance to the valley.

We don't even bother to undress. Zorzo unlaces his codpiece and lifts my skirts, hoisting me onto him as he leans against the wall of the building. I'm ready for him, my legs wrap themselves around him, my lips on his, my sex sucking him in greedily, and oh it feels so, so wonderful and I say to him as we reach our joy, 'Give me another babe, Zorzo!'

I spun away from the mirror, my dizziness and sense of dislocation mixing with something else. I'd heard mention of the church where Cecilia had been with Zorzo, I was sure of it.

I returned to Luca's bed, slipped between the sheets, and rolled over onto my side, my body languid. Weird how I'd experienced Zorzo's lovemaking along with Cecilia. Beyond weird, in fact. Just like I'd gone through giving birth to Lorenza and the pain of separation from her.

God, Fern, you've made love to two men tonight. I took in the sight of Luca sleeping next to me. I mustn't confuse him with Zorzo. The way his mouth turned up at the corners was like the painter's. But that was the only similarity, except for the way they both made love. Cecilia's last encounter with Zorzo had mirrored my own with Luca the other week. *Another echo of the past.*

What about that ancient church? I'd heard an ancient church being mentioned before. Who'd told me about it? Vanessa? No. Not Vanessa. *Chiara!* It had been Chiara. That time when I'd gone riding with her and Chiara had suggested we take a picnic to the Goredan family's farmhouse. Poor Chiara. How terrible for her to have found Federico there with his other woman.

In the morning, I told Luca about Lodovico's treachery and Cecilia and Zorzo's tryst. 'Cecilia let slip to Zorzo that Lorenza is his,' I said.

'That must have set the cat among the pigeons.'

'I expect so. I returned to the present without finding out.'

'I'm worried about you, Fern.' He kissed me. 'Cecilia won't leave you in peace. You're getting to the end of her story. And I think you'll agree we know what happened. The piece of burnt wood is a warning, I think.'

'Yes, I know, but there's nothing I can do about it.' I thought for a moment. 'Do you have to go in to work today?'

'No. I've got the day off to help Mother take Chiara home from the hospital. Why?'

'I'd like to visit your farmhouse and compare the area with the one where Cecilia and Zorzo went. I'd like to see if it's the same church. Just to set my mind at rest, if that's okay with you.'

His blue eyes shone. 'I'm not due at the hospital until midday.'

I smiled. 'I'll phone Auntie and tell her when to expect me.'

An hour later, I was standing next to Luca in front of the farmhouse, which was set halfway up the hill behind an old chapel. 'The view is amazing,' I said.

'Look over to the right.' He pointed toward the distant hills on the horizon. 'Those are behind the city of Padova an hour's drive away.'

'And that's the back of Asolo.' I indicated the closer chain of knolls on the left, seven of them, undulating like a Chinese dragon's back, separated by wooded valleys, the Rocca topping the second crest to the last on the right. In between the two ranges stretched the Venetian plain, dotted with towns and villages, their church steeples reaching to the sky.

I gazed down toward the chapel, nestled at the foot of the hill. *Another echo.* 'It didn't have a steeple in Cecilia's day, nor those cypress trees, but I recognise the building.'

'There was a Roman guardhouse there, apparently, two thousand or so years ago. Protecting the pass into the valley.'

I thought about the house on the River Wye in Wales where I'd grown up. It had been a refuge after Harry's death. I'd had to leave London when neighbours had called the police after I'd woken them repeatedly screaming from my nightmares of fire and death. It was then that I'd been signed off work. Home was where I'd embarked on art therapy, where I'd been comforted, where I'd felt secure.

Maybe I should cut my losses and go there now for the last few days of my vacation? It would be the safest option. I should get away from those echoes of a past I couldn't change. I stared at the ancient church.

'Lorenza!'

The voice resounded in my head imploringly.

I straightened my shoulders; I had to find out what had happened to the child.

And the only way to do that was to carry on until I reached Cecilia's final moments.

But I wouldn't do that now.

Focus on something else!

It was such a clear day that I was sure I could spot Venice on the southern horizon. The Republic of olden times. A long history of war and conquest. I *was* scared, but I was also intrigued. And there was so little time left before I had to leave. My job, my life as I'd known it up until a few weeks ago, my future, all waiting for me in London.

What about Luca, then?

Did I love him?

All I knew was that I'd miss him terribly when I left Italy…

'Please have supper with us tonight, Luca. Auntie told me on the phone that she was making one of her Welsh stews.'

'My mouth's watering already.'

I laughed and he laughed with me.

I should take Cecilia's advice and let myself love him. He's such a lovable man…

CHAPTER 23

I watched Auntie puff herself up with pride as Luca requested a third helping. She piled his plate high and matched him by having another helping herself.

'What about you, Fern?' she asked.

'It's yummy, but I'm full. Thanks.' I rubbed my belly.

I sat back and studied Luca as he chatted with Auntie, informing her that Chiara was home from the hospital but confined to bed for a few days and under sedation for the pain. Federico had been on the phone to the villa, but Vanessa had told him point-blank not to call again.

Luca went on to talk about lightning conductors. *Lightning conductors!* 'They're essential,' he said. 'If lightning were to strike this house during a storm, it would be conducted into the rod, and pass through a wire to the ground.'

'Sounds like a good idea,' Auntie said. 'Can you get one for me? Although the chances of being struck by lightning seem small, best to be safe than sorry.'

'Of course,' Luca said, mopping up the last of his stew with a piece of bread. 'Thank you for this amazing meal.'

I got up from my chair. 'We'll do the washing up, Auntie,' I said.

She made her way over to the television set and switched it on to watch an episode of *Knots Landing*, dubbed into Italian.

Luca took a plate from me and put it into the dishwasher. 'I've been thinking about how to keep you safe,' he said.

I shot him a look and he held up his hands. 'Don't accuse me of being a caveman, but is there any way I can persuade you not to go through with this?'

'I haven't got much option. If I'm anywhere associated with Cecilia, she almost always finds me. I managed to block her from my mind this morning when I was at the farmhouse, though. Perhaps I'm getting stronger?'

'Or Cecilia's getting weaker…'

'So, what do you propose I do?'

'I don't think you should be left alone. If you're with Cecilia when she dies, you might find it impossible to return to the twentieth century.'

My heart missed a beat. 'That's crazy.'

'Is it? As crazy as burnt wood appearing and disappearing?' He shook his head. 'As crazy as feeling the labour pains of a girl long dead?'

'Point taken. What about when I'm asleep? She comes to me in my dreams sometimes.'

'Well, I think you should stay at the villa. The only time you had a vision of Cecilia there was when she was out with the hunt. I've discussed it with my mother, and she agrees it would be a good idea if you spent a few days with us.'

'Are you sure?'

'Of course. And you can lend a hand with Chiara.'

'I still want to learn what happened to Lorenza,' I said in a determined tone.

'You can come to my apartment for that, and I'll keep an eye on you. Make sure nothing untoward happens.'

I opened then closed my mouth, weighing the pros and cons in my head. Luca only had my best interests at heart.

'You know it makes sense,' he confirmed.

'All right. Thanks. I'll tell my aunt then I'll go and pack a bag and my art things.'

I went to Luca's room in the villa after everyone had gone to bed. Our lovemaking was as tender as before. I was getting used to this. The long, languorous kisses, the feel of his hard chest against my breasts. The way he ran his fingers through my hair, the way he cupped my buttocks, the way he brought me to orgasm so slowly that when I reached my climax, I thought I would explode with pleasure.

I spent the night with him and when we woke, Luca reminded me it was our final rehearsal this evening for the re-enactment, which would be tomorrow. I kissed him. 'Can we go back to your flat after the practice?'

'If you insist,' he groaned, knowing full well what I intended.

Despite my misgivings, I was adamant I wanted to find out what had happened to Lorenza. It was the only way I'd find peace.

'Thank you, Luca,' I said.

'It's very kind of you to come and give us a hand,' Vanessa said at breakfast. 'And I think Luca's right. You're probably much safer here. Would you mind keeping Chiara company while I go to the pharmacy and pick up some prescriptions?'

'I wouldn't mind at all. She can watch me paint. People tend to find it quite soothing. I know I did when I first started art therapy.'

Chiara's room overlooked the vineyards at the side of the villa. There was a small church in the foreground, and gentle hills dotted with woodland behind. A perfect landscape for a watercolour artist. I'd done more painting over the past few weeks than I'd done in months in London, I realised. And I felt proud of the work I'd produced. Having Cecilia in my head and watching Zorzo must have improved my technique. I couldn't wait to show my art to an agent.

Chiara was asleep, her leg raised up on cushions. I tiptoed across the room, set up my portable easel, dipped my brush in the glass of water I'd brought with me, and proceeded to wet the paper. I mixed a jade green tint and set to work. I almost jumped out of my skin when I heard Chiara say, 'Can I have a look?'

I unclipped my painting and took it over to the bed.

'Very nice,' Chiara said, scrunching up the sheets to her chest. She frowned. 'I hate Federico for what he did, you know. He's made a complete fool of me. I'll never forgive him.' She burst into great, heaving sobs.

I put my arms around her. 'Cry it out, sweetie. Cry out your pain. Cry out your frustration.' As I said it, my own bottling-up gave way, and I found myself sobbing with Chiara, crying for Harry, for my lost baby, for the future we'd never have. And, as I cried, I felt my guilt being washed away by my tears.

After a couple of minutes, Chiara said, 'You're right.' She sighed. 'I do feel a lot better. But I'm still very tired. I think I'll go back to sleep now.'

She closed her eyes. I gazed at her; she appeared so young, lying there, her long dark brown hair spread over the pillow. I waited until she was breathing regularly then slipped from the room.

Vanessa had returned from the *farmacia* and was nursing a cup of coffee in the sitting room. She smiled as I approached. 'How's Chiara?'

'We had a good cry together. My therapist was always urging me to un-bottle my emotions. It might take a little time, but I think Chiara will get over the hurt.'

Vanessa put down her coffee. 'I'm sure she will. Now fill me in on everything that's been happening with Cecilia.'

So, I told her about my visit to Venice, the celebration of the Republic's victory over the Emperor, and Cecilia posing for Giorgione's *Sleeping Venus*. Then I recounted how Lodovico had been spying for the Duke of Ferrara.

'I've just remembered something,' Vanessa said. 'Luca asked me to do some research at the library for him, to find out about Ferrara's stance regarding Emperor Maximilian. I was going to tell him, but Chiara falling off her horse and breaking her leg put it out of my mind. Just a minute, I'll get my notes.'

Vanessa went to the desk in the corner of the room. She

rummaged in a drawer then padded back across the carpet. 'On 10th December 1508,' she read, 'Representatives of the Papacy, France, the Holy Roman Empire and Ferdinand I of Spain concluded the League of Cambrai against the Republic. The Marquis of Mantova and the Duke of Ferrara also joined in, thereby isolating Venice.'

My pulse jumped, and a feeling of dread overtook me.

The final rehearsal for the re-enactment over, I strolled with Luca down Via Canova toward the palazzo where he had his flat. It was a warm night, the ever-present scent of honeysuckle from the town gardens perfuming the air. We climbed the wide marble staircase, and he let us into his flat.

In the kitchen, he poured us both a glass of Prosecco. 'Cheers! How are you feeling?'

'A bit nervous, given what your mother told me about the alliance against Venice. What if Lodovico has declared his true colours and has taken Cecilia with him to Ferrara?'

He took a sip of the wine. 'Are you sure you want to go through with this?'

'Definitely,' I said, trying to sound positive.

'It's a little like conducting a séance.' He gave me a wry smile. 'Only we don't need a medium.'

'Indeed,' I said, my stomach fluttering and my bravado of earlier in danger of toppling. 'If I can, I'll tell you everything as I experience it. Then you can try and pull me out if it all starts going pear-shaped.'

'What if nothing happens? What if you don't connect?'

I smirked. 'True, we could sit here all night just staring into space.'

'Is there something you can do to... oh, you know what I mean...'

'Maybe if I think about her, maybe that'll help.'

'What about if you relaxed a little, sat back, closed your eyes?... Fern?... Fern?'

. . .

The Queen's brother is visiting again and there's the usual banquet in his honour. At least, on this occasion, he's here with only a small entourage. Lodovico and I have been placed at the top table. *Such an honour!* I watch my husband circling around Giorgio Cornaro like a moth around a flame. Lodovico refills the Queen's brother's goblet from the flagon on the table. Why did he not wait for a servant to do it? What a toad he is, and to what avail?

Spring has arrived in this year of our Lord 1509, and peach blossom fills the vases lining the side of the banqueting hall. My true love is also here, the first time I've seen him since our tryst at the hunt. Zorzo strums his lute and sings:

> *'I find no peace, but for war am not inclined;*
> *I fear, yet hope; I burn, yet am turned to ice;*
> *I soar in the heavens, but lie upon the ground;*
> *I hold nothing, though I embrace the whole world.*
> *Love has me in a prison which he neither opens nor shuts fast;*
> *he neither claims me for his own nor loosens my halter;*
> *he neither slays nor unshackles me;*
> *he would not have me live yet leaves me with my torment.*
> *Eyeless I gaze, and without a tongue I cry out;*
> *I long to perish, yet plead for succour;*
> *I hate myself, but love another.*
> *I feed on grief, yet weeping, laugh;*
> *death and life alike repel me;*
> *and to this state I am come, my lady, because of you.'*

The words are from one of Petrarch's sonnets, I know, for I have read it. Zorzo catches my eye. My heartbeat quickens as I remember that day last autumn when I let slip that he'd fathered my child.

He'd smothered me with kisses and begged to see Lorenza before Lodovico's return from Ferrara. So, I took him to the house in Asolo, and he swung her above his head just like the time when he sketched her for *The Tempest*. Then I showed him her paintings, where the mix of colours spoke of a maturity and skill beyond her years. 'She takes after you in beauty and talent,' he said, and I'd swelled with pride.

After dinner the court dances the *saltarello*. Bouncing on our toes, we appear merry. Such a farce. Pope Julius has issued an interdict against Venice and has excommunicated every citizen of the Republic for the non-restitution of the Papal States. *Excommunicated!* We are no longer to receive any of the sacraments, and, when we die, we won't go to Heaven. *Maria Santissima!* This is serious and here we are, dancing as if we didn't have a care in the world.

There's a sudden commotion at the far end of the hall. *Gesù bambino!* The Queen's brother has collapsed. A sick feeling washes through me and I shoot a glance at my husband. He's smiling. *Smiling!* Quickly, Lodovico wipes the smile from his face and goes to Giorgio Cornaro's side, helping to lift him from the floor to a chair.

The musicians have stopped playing and there's a stunned hush. 'Call my physician,' the Queen commands. People start scurrying to and fro' and the courtiers break into small groups to gossip.

I take advantage of the commotion and hurry to our quarters. My husband's travelling chest is by the window, unlocked. I rifle through it, not knowing for what I am looking. If he has poisoned Giorgio Cornaro, Lodovico wouldn't be so careless as to leave the poison lying around. Yet, I'm certain that's what he's done, for why else would the Queen's brother collapse so soon after Lodovico poured his wine?

I let out a sardonic laugh, thinking of when I slipped valerian into Lodovico's drink in Venice. The two of us are as bad as each other, although I didn't go so far as to try and poison him. I'm angry with myself, for I was supposed to keep watch over my husband and have failed in my pledge to the Queen. I need to find evidence, but where?

Lodovico's cape is hanging from a hook on the back of the door. I go to it and slip my hands into the pockets. At first, I feel nothing. Then my fingers encounter a small package. I pull it out and open it. Seeds. I take a couple from the package, which I then return to Lodovico's garment before I dart back to the hall.

Giorgio Cornaro's eyes flutter open and I cross myself. *Praise God! He's still alive.* The physician is ordering an emetic to be prepared. Clearly, he suspects poison. What should I do? Should I point my finger, or should I keep quiet? No. The future of the Republic is at stake; I need to flush out the traitor in our midst.

'I beg a word, Domina,' I say to the Queen.

'Yes, my dear. What is it?'

I show her the seeds I found in Lodovico's pocket and start to describe what I'd witnessed at the banquet. From the corner of my eye, I spot my husband watching me. One minute he's there, the next he has disappeared.

'Guards!' the Queen calls out. 'Arrest that man!'

In the meantime, the physician tastes one of the seeds. 'Apple,' he says. 'The fruit itself is perfectly harmless. However, apple seeds are poisonous and contain cyanide. If you swallow one or two seeds at a time it is unlikely you will feel anything at all. But crushed into a powdered form, they're lethal.'

I put my hand to my mouth. This is terrible. *Terrible!* Such shame my husband has brought upon us. 'Domina, I beg your forgiveness.'

'Not your fault, my dear. The fault is mine for allowing that vermin anywhere near us. When you voiced your suspicions six months ago, I thought we were too strong for him. I'm sorry, Cecilia, but I've always considered your husband such a *little* man. More like an annoying flea than anything else. How wrong I was…'

I can't help smiling at her description of Lodovico and cover my mouth with my hand.

The Queen's guards burst into the hall.

I stare at them.

Where's my husband?

'Gone, Domina. The stable-boys report that his horse is missing,' the most senior guard says.

The sound of retching comes from Domina's brother. He's vomiting. *Praise the Holy Mother of God!* The Republic needs him to live, for we are surrounded by enemies and Giorgio Cornaro is the only man with the experience to lead our army against them.

Zorzo has materialised at my elbow, his eyes wide with concern. 'How are you, *dolcezza?*'

I take in a deep breath and straighten my back. 'Ashamed of my husband and fearful of the future.'

The Queen must have overheard us, for she says, 'Fear not, Cecilia. You are under my protection.'

I drop into a deep curtsey, relief washing through me. To live in her shadow will be an honour; I shall serve her for the rest of her days. 'Thank you, Domina.' I put to the back of my mind my worries about her health.

The future will look after the future.

The Queen's brother staggers to his feet and is taken to his quarters. Domina orders the court to retire. I go to my room, and soon Zorzo comes to me.

Our lovemaking is unhurried this night. He kisses my hairline, the lobes of my ears, and my chin; his lips are soft and warm. His fingers probe my sex and then his lips are where his fingers were. It occurs to me that I should give him the same pleasure. *How?* He lets out a soft groan and runs his hands though my hair as I swirl my tongue over the tip of his manhood; it tastes of salt and of Zorzo. Then I swallow him further into the hot wetness of my mouth.

He moans and flips me over. And now we are loving each other together, and he's thrusting into me, my legs wrapped around his body, and it is so, so good to reach our joy at the same time. Zorzo kisses me deeply. 'I love you, *dolcezza.*'

My heart fair beats out of my chest with happiness, but I'm also afraid my husband will spoil everything.

'I wonder if I'll ever see Lodovico again?' I ask.

Zorzo kisses my brow. 'I expect he'll not show his face around here anymore.'

'Then you and I can love each other when we want.' A smile splits my face. 'And you can teach our daughter to paint. Make her your apprentice, when she's old enough.'

Zorzo laughs. 'And what if we have a son? Will you want that for him too?'

'If he shows talent. Why not?'

'Do you love me, *dolcezza*?'

'With all my heart, *amore mio*.'

He enfolds me in his arms, and I snuggle against him. Finally, we shall have the time for love to take a firm root in both our souls. My body relaxes and, another smile touching my lips, I drift off to sleep.

'Fern! Fern! Wake up!' Luca was shaking me gently. 'We should return to the villa.'

'With all my heart, *amore mio*.'

'Fern!'

'What?'

'The villa, we need to go.'

'What time is it?' I asked, dazed.

'Past eleven.'

'Isn't it a bit late?' I shook my head. 'We could spend the night here at your flat.'

'For you to continue your communion with Cecilia?'

'You heard me tell you everything that was happening?'

'Yes, Fern. Let's go back to the villa and recharge our batteries. Tomorrow is another day, as they say.'

'You sound worried.'

'Hmm.' He frowned. 'How did you think I would feel when you told me about making love with the painter? And the treachery of Cecilia's husband doesn't bode well.'

'It wasn't me with Zorzo, Luca. Please don't be jealous. I need to see this through.' I forced a smile. 'If I leave Italy without finding out what happened to Lorenza, Cecilia will be waiting for me when I get back from London.'

He kissed me on the forehead. 'You plan on returning?'

'I love it here, despite everything that's happened.'

'Oh? And what about loving the people?'

'Them too,' I nodded. 'Especially a certain person.'

He wrapped his arms around me and pulled me close. 'And who might that be?'

I lifted my chin and his mouth came down on mine, kissing me so thoroughly my knees began to give way. He ran warm kisses across my cheek and down my neck. 'You, of course, Luca. I love you,' I said.

And I did. I knew that now. A warm feeling spread through me. Harry would want me to be happy. It wasn't my fault that he'd died. A tragic accident that took the life of so many. I owed it to him to live mine to the full.

'Lorenza!'

My heart stuttered. 'Did you hear that?'

'Yes, *amore mio,*' Luca said.

'Cecilia wants us to see this through.'

And I would.

I'd find out what had happened to Lorenza.

Both Cecilia and I need to know the truth.

CHAPTER 24

*C*hiara was out of bed and sitting on the patio, plugged into her Walkman while Vanessa and I sorted through boxes of correspondence that the Contessa had found stored in the villa's basement. 'These date from the time when the family had its palaces on the Grand Canal,' she said. 'I never knew they were here until the other day.'

I picked up a dusty old folder. 'Do you think we'll find anything useful for your genealogical research?'

'Hopefully. Oh, and, by the way, when I was sitting with Chiara last night, I read an old book in Italian that was stored with the letters.' Her eyes glowed. 'I found out a lot more about what happened in 1509. And I've translated some of it for you.'

Without waiting for my response, she reached into her handbag and pulled out a notebook. 'This is what I've managed to translate so far.' She cleared her throat. 'Shortly after issuing his excommunication interdict against Venice,' she read, 'the Pope sent his troops to invade Romagna and seized Ravenna. They had the assistance of Alfonso d'Este, Duke of Ferrara, who proceeded to seize Rovigo, which belonged to the Republic, for himself.'

'Lodovico would have been caught up in that battle,' I exclaimed. 'He was a cavalryman.'

'Indeed.' Vanessa turned over a page and carried on reading,

'In April, Louis, the French King, left Milan at the head of his army and moved rapidly into Venetian territory. To oppose him, Venice raised what they called "the greatest and best-paid army ever seen on Italian soil", under the command of two cousins... Bartolomeo d'Alviano and Nicolo di Pitigliano.'

'That's interesting. So, Giorgio Cornaro was no longer in charge of the troops...' I put down the file I'd been holding. 'I wonder if he survived the poisoning attempt?'

'I think he did. I seem to remember he didn't die until some-time in the 1520s.' Vanessa looked down at her notes. 'Alviano and Pitigliano disagreed on how best to stop the French advance. When Louis crossed the Adda River near Brescia in early May, Alviano advanced to meet him. But Pitigliano, believing it best to avoid a pitched battle, moved away to the south.'

'With half the army?' I exclaimed, shocked.

'Yes,' Vanessa read on, 'on the fourteenth of May, Alviano confronted the French at the Battle of Agnadello. Outnumbered, he sent requests for reinforcements to his cousin, who replied with orders to break off the battle.'

I didn't like where this was going. 'What happened next?'

'Pitigliano continued heading south,' Vanessa read. 'Alviano, disregarding the new orders, carried on with the engagement and his army was eventually surrounded and destroyed.'

'How terrible!' my voice wavered.

Vanessa nodded and stared at her pad. 'Pitigliano managed to avoid encountering Louis. His troops, mercenaries, hearing of Alviano's defeat, had deserted in large numbers by the next morning, forcing him to retreat to Treviso with the remnants of the Venetian army.'

'Was there any mention of the Emperor's attack on Asolo?' I ran a shaky hand through my hair.

'This is as far as I've got, Fern. I'll translate the rest this evening, then fill you in when you get back here after the re-enactment.'

'That will be perfect, thanks, Vanessa.'

I went back to sorting through the papers. I thought about Luca and how safe he made me feel, and a finger of unease stroked my insides. Cecilia's story was coming to an end, of that I was certain. Although I had no concrete proof, I knew in my soul she was about to die. I needed to be careful I was always protected by Luca when I slipped back in time. His warning to me about not being able to return to the twentieth century if I was with Cecilia when she died had scared me.

I gave my body a shake and went back to the task at hand. The letters in the folder I held were written in ancient Italian, and there wasn't a hope in hell I'd understand them. At least I could catalogue them chronologically, which is what I did until I needed to get ready for the re-enactment of Queen Caterina's court in Asolo this evening.

Watching the parade of people strutting through the town was a little like watching the movie of a favourite novel. Not as good as the original. The woman playing the role of Caterina Cornaro was tall and dark, whereas the Queen had been short and blonde.

The costumes were only an approximation of the clothing I'd seen through Cecilia's eyes. The men wore longer doublets than those I'd known as my nemesis, not showing their codpieces, which made me doubt they wore any. The women's hair, my own included, held back in garlands, didn't display the intricate plaits woven with jewels and hair-nets with which I was more familiar. The stink of unwashed bodies that had pervaded in the past, not to mention the lack of sanitation (outside toilets were the norm), made the early sixteenth Century a much smellier period of history, however, than 1989. Only the music and dancing were authentic.

Tonight, the weather was hot and humid. Sweat trickled down my spine and legs as I moved through the steps of the dance. Masses of people had turned up to watch the performances, which was good for Asolo's cafés and restaurants... and made people aware of the history of the town. I could sense the pride of the locals in the uniqueness of their heritage.

After we'd finished our dance, Luca took me for a drink in the Caffè Centrale. We managed to find a table on the terrace, despite the crowds. Auntie, who'd said she wouldn't have missed seeing the re-enactment for the world, had sat herself down next to us. 'I'm dying of thirst,' she said. 'I'd love a fresh orange juice.'

'It seems we'll have to wait to be served.' Luca glanced around. 'Or maybe we've got lucky…' The barman, in a white jacket and black bowtie, was approaching their table.

'*Una telefonata urgente!*' he announced.

Luca leapt up. 'An urgent phone-call for me.'

Unease spiked my chest as I watched him run to the bar and pick up the receiver. He returned within a couple of minutes. 'That was the police.' His voice rasped. 'I'm needed at the villa. There's been an intruder.'

'Would you like me to come with you?' I reached for my handbag.

Luca pressed his lips together in a slight grimace. 'Better not. I want to find out what's going on and make sure Mother and Chiara are all right.'

'It would save you having to come back for me,' I insisted.

'The police officer on the phone was relaying a message from the *Commissario*. He couldn't say if they'd caught the prowler or not. I'm worried sick, and don't want to put you in any danger, Fern.'

I got to my feet and gave him a hug. 'For once, I won't call you a caveman.'

He kissed my cheek. 'I'll pick you up from Susan's as soon as I can. You'll be safe enough as long as you're not on your own.'

'Fern can stay the night at my house,' Auntie interjected. 'There's no need for you to put yourself out, Luca.'

'No, I think it's for the best if Fern comes back to the villa.' A frown creased his brow. 'Just not straight away.'

'Vanessa still needs my help with Chiara,' I said by way of explanation as Luca ran in the direction of the parking lot.

'Hmm,' Auntie tilted her head toward me. 'Is there something you're not telling me about your relationship with that young man?'

I felt the blush in my cheeks and was relieved Auntie's attention had been distracted by the arrival of our drinks. *Luca must have placed an order at the bar before he left.* I lifted my glass and drank deeply. 'He's been so kind to me,' I said to my aunt. 'We've grown close.'

'Just close?' she smiled knowingly.

I reached across the table and took her hand. 'It's early days.'

I glanced up at the gathering clouds, which were reminiscent of the sky in Giorgione's *Tempest*. 'Let's finish our juices and go home. Looks like a storm is on the way...'

An hour later, I'd changed out of my re-enactment dress into a pair of jeans and a t-shirt, and was sitting in Auntie's kitchen, a plate of biscotti in front of me and a glass of sweet wine in my hand.

'What did Luca mean when he said, *you'll be safe enough as long as you're not on your own?*' she asked, dunking her biscuit into her drink.

'Luca believes I've been regressing to the past,' I said without preamble. 'And he's worried about my safety.'

'Stuff and nonsense!' Auntie's tone was dismissive. 'I would have thought better of Luca. He seems such a sensible person...'

'God, it's hot tonight,' I said, making a snap decision to change the subject.

I'll never convince her I'm reliving Cecilia's life and there's no point even trying.

The atmosphere had turned oppressive, and I wiped the sweat from my brow.

'I think that storm is about to hit,' Auntie said. 'Do me a favour, please, love. Run upstairs and close all the window shutters. I'm suddenly feeling extremely tired.'

I did as she asked, and, when I returned to the kitchen, she'd moved to the sofa in the sitting area, Gucci Cat on her lap, and her deep, rumbling snores bore witness to the fact that she'd fallen asleep.

An ear-splitting crack of thunder split the air.

With an uneasy feeling of foreboding, I retook my seat at the table.

Luca said I shouldn't be alone. Maybe I should wake Auntie up?

But it was already too late.

That buzzing sensation was back in my head, and the world around me spun on its axis.

I hear the thunder and, through the open window catch sight of a fork of lightning. Lorenza rushes into my arms. My daughter is afraid of storms, and no matter how many kisses and cuddles I give her, she shakes like a leaf. 'It's only giants playing skittles in the sky,' I say, holding her close.

Lorenza gives me a pleading look. 'Tell the naughty giants to stop.'

I kiss her soft, warm cheek and squeeze her tight. We're at the Barco, but the court is not with us. Given the option to go with the Queen to Venice last month or remain in Asolo, I made the decision to stay here. I could not have taken my daughter with me, because of Domina's strict rule about "no children at the Venice court," and no one could have foretold the way events have unfolded.

After Lodovico's attempt to poison him, Giorgio Cornaro retired to Brescia with kidney problems. However, we all believed the magnificent army raised by the Serenissima would quell the French without difficulty. It's been the greatest shock to everyone that the Republic has lost such an important battle.

And now the Emperor has raised his flag over Asolo castle. I'm so worried about what will happen next. Maximilian and his soldiers came down the Sugana Valley, leaving a sea of devastation. How has it come to this? The Doge of Venice hasn't raised a hand to help the defence of Asolo. Our hope rests with the troops in Treviso. Zorzo has gone to fetch them and has sent word they'll be here momentarily.

These past months with my true love have been so happy. He has been with me almost all the time, teaching me about art, loving me and our daughter. The women he frequented in the past, the courtesans of Venice he also painted, are no longer in his life. Of that I am sure.

My ears prickle.

Horses are neighing in the yard below.

I hear the stamp of hooves, the jingle of harnesses and the shouts of men.

Could Zorzo be back with our soldiers already?

I go to the window, Lorenza tugging at my skirts.

Holy Mother of God! The troops aren't ours; they're Austrian. I can tell from their standards and the guttural sound of their language.

Fear grips me.

I pick my daughter up and make for the door. If I can get to Pegaso before the soldiers find us, there'll be a chance for us to escape.

A shadow crosses the floor and I step back.

A man bars our exit.

I peer at him.

Maria Santissima! Lodovico stands before me, smiling his thin-lipped smile. 'Greetings, wife! I have come to take you to safety.'

I back away. 'With you? A traitor? Never!'

'I can't leave you and Lorenza here.' He grabs my shoulders and gives me a shake. 'The Emperor's troops are half-starved, half-crazed, and set on pillage. They'll make mincemeat out of you. My job was to show them the Barco's location. I had no idea you were still here. Thank God your maid told me.'

Lorenza has burst into tears, and I put her down. She cries even more loudly when her supposed father pulls me against him. 'You are my wife. Do as I say!'

'I will not.' I lift my hands and push at his chest. The *little* man, as the Queen called him, takes hold of my wrists. Even if he is short and thin, he's stronger than I am.

'I want to you leave me…'

Zorzo is due to arrive with the troops from Treviso, I tell myself. He won't know where to find me if I go with Lodovico.

'Is that what you wish? That I should go?' He smiles again. 'With pleasure. You've been less use to me as a wife than a jouster's dummy. But my daughter comes with me.'

Before I know what's happening, he snatches Lorenza up and scurries out of the room, slamming the door. I hear the key turn in the lock. There's another crash of thunder and dark clouds obscure the sun.

My vision is blackening, and I struggle to regain my equilibrium.

'Lorenza,' I scream.

I blinked in the darkness. I had to find Lodovico and get to Lorenza. Where had the door disappeared to? I peered through the gloom but couldn't see it. I let out a gasp and doubled over with sudden shock. I was at Auntie's house, not the Barco. *And the damn lights have gone.* I could hear the storm raging outside, the thunder, the wind, the clatter of hailstones.

Where the hell is the flashlight? I felt my way to the kitchen cupboards and rummaged around. *A candle. Good.* My fingers encountered a box of matches and I struck a light.

'What's happening, love?' Auntie called out in the darkness; her voice was groggy.

'Nothing to worry about,' I said. *There's everything to worry about for Cecilia.* 'The storm has come, and the lights have gone.'

'As ever. Well, we're perfectly safe. Luca sent someone to install that conductor this afternoon.'

'Oh, he didn't tell me.'

'I expect he had other things on his mind. Talking of which, when's he coming to fetch you? It's just that I'd like to go to bed…'

'You go up, Auntie. I'll be all right.' *I hope.* 'Where's your flashlight?'

'The battery ran out and I forgot to get a new one. There's another candle in the drawer. I'll take that.'

I helped Auntie to the stairs, then sat down on the sofa.

Cecilia was clamouring in my head, and there was nothing I could do to stop her.

The television set disappeared before my eyes and my fists were suddenly pounding.

I'm hammering on the door, screaming, *Lorenza!*

But no one opens.

I go to the window and stare through the pane.

Lodovico is on his horse, my struggling daughter on the saddle in front of him. He catches my gaze and waves. Then he gallops away, leaving the soldiers rampaging in his wake.

If I jumped out of the window, I would land in the middle of the troops, and they would rape me, no question.

Madre di Dio! They might break down the door to this room; I must hide.

Trembling, I search the room for somewhere.

I look from left to right. There's a large wooden chest in the corner, half-filled with blankets. I run to it. Then I squeeze into the space beneath the layers and let the lid slam shut.

I put my hands to my ears and try to shut out the mayhem below, but the shouts of the soldiers and the screams of the kitchen maids still echo inside my head. What are those men doing to them? And what they will do if they find me?

I touch my gold necklace, cool against my skin. Hope flickers within me. The soldiers might not know I am here; they might not even come upstairs. I take a deep breath and let it out. *Keep calm!* Yet my heart beats with such force and I shake with such violence I'm sure they will discover me at any moment.

Oh, *Gesù bambino!* What's this acrid smell? This sudden warmth? This roaring sound? I move the blankets to one side and peer through a crack in the wood.

Maria Santissima!

Red tongues of fire are licking their way across the floor...

. . .

I sniffed the air. Something was burning; I was sure of it.

My entire body trembled. I remembered the smoke pouring through tunnels, the panic and the choking and the searing in my lungs.

Acrid fumes stung my eyes. A roaring sound filled my ears. I shook myself, willing my mind to be cleared of what had happened in the past. There was nothing I could do about it. The fire was at the Barco, not here.

Then why couldn't I breathe? And why were my eyes stinging? *Oh my God!* Flames were leaping across the curtains. The window must have blown open, toppling the candle onto its side and setting the fabric alight. I leapt up from the sofa.

I had to wake Auntie and get the both of us out of here…

I make the sign of the cross as a fiery wall of death dances toward me, blocking any chance of escape. Where can I go? My stricken body quakes; there's no way out.

I let out a sob and clutch at my belly. *Lorenza!* She must be terrified. Lodovico doesn't love her. He took her out of spite. What if I die here? What will become of her? *Lorenza!*

Tendrils of smoke seep through the wooden slats of the chest and curl their way down my throat, making me cough. Tears furrow my cheeks. Dear Lord, how could you let this happen to me?

Fire is about to take me from this world, from everyone I love…

My mind was whirling. *Focus, girl!* I ran up the spiral staircase. The corridor had filled with smoke; I could scarcely see. I raced to the bathroom and grabbed two hand-towels, wet them in the basin, and hurried to Auntie's room.

Through the gloom, I could make out her shape in the bed. I shook her and shouted, 'Wake up! The house is on fire. We've got to get out. Quick!'

Auntie gave me a confused look, then swung her legs from

the bed. I handed her the wet towel and said, 'Hold this over your mouth and nose. It'll allow you to breathe.' I held out my hand and Auntie slipped hers into it.

We felt our way down the stairs. The wooden kitchen cabinets were in flames now, but the way was clear to the front door and we staggered through it, Gucci Cat at our heels.

On the front step, Auntie suddenly turned around. 'My manuscript. I have to go back for it.'

'Don't worry. I'll get it.' The fire hadn't travelled that far. I could race upstairs and back in no time.

I left her standing on the garden path. 'Run next door and call the firefighters,' I yelled as I ran indoors, the lower part of my face covered in the wet towel.

Trying not to breathe in smoke, I took the steps two at a time. I remembered Auntie's manuscript was on the desk in her study, just at the top of the stairs. I pushed open the door and, peering through the smoke-filled room, spotted her old typewriter and a box of papers. I grabbed the box and hurried back outside, where I handed the manuscript to Auntie.

'I want to save my paintings,' I told her.

They're my creation, like children to me. I can't let them burn to ashes.

'Help is on the way,' Auntie said, grabbing hold of me. 'You should wait.'

I shook myself free. 'There isn't time…'

Panic-stricken, I headed back into the house. *Have to save my work.*

My makeshift studio was in the corner of the kitchen where the flames hadn't yet taken hold.

I grabbed my watercolours and a couple of canvases, then hurried toward the front door.

The wet towel was no longer wet, so I dropped it.

My mouth and nose filled with smoke.

My lungs screamed in searing agony as I took in a ragged breath.

I was back at King's Cross, staggering through the smoke-filled tunnel.

Only, this time, there wasn't a train I could get on.

This time, the fire had spread and was licking its way along the ceiling timbers. A huge bang echoed, and the joist above my head came down.

This time I really was going to die…

A crash resounds. *Maria Santissima!* The shouts outside fade. The blaze spits and crackles, and the searing heat forces my back against the wood. There's nothing I can do.

Zorzo, where are you?

You're too late.

Too late to save me.

Too late to save anyone.

I shall never see you or Lorenza again.

Never feel your warm lips on mine.

Never hold our child in my arms.

Never have the future I'd dreamed of with the two of you. Who will look after her? *Lorenza!*

Smoke fills my nostrils and I breathe it in, willing the fumes to take me before the flames do.

Heavenly Father, let this be quick!

The heat is a shock, burning my nose, my throat and my lungs. I gasp and inhale scorching air, choking and retching.

My breath is sucked from me. The bitter stench of my singed eyebrows, hair and skin fills my nostrils. The gold at my neck is too hot to bear, and a deafening sound echoes in my ears.

'*Lorenza*,' I whisper through cracked lips.

How did I manage to speak when I can't even breathe?

I sense the strange woman and know why she is here. The woman is a spirit, but a good one. She will search for Lorenza and find her… of that I am sure.

The pain is now consuming me, and I cry out in agony.

I writhe and then my head is filled with a buzzing, and then a shimmering and then…

~

Luca

I arrived at the villa, lightning zigzagging across the sky. A police car was parked out front, and I pulled up next to it. I yanked the door of my Alfa open. Through the sheeting rain, I raced up the front steps and into the sitting room, all the while the voice in my head repeating, *Too late, too late, too late.*

Chiara was perched on the grand piano stool, her leg stretched out in front of her. There was an angry-looking bruise on her left cheek. A balding police inspector with a pencil-thin moustache sat on one side, Mother on the other, and my brother Antonio stood next to them.

'What happened?' I asked.

Through stuttering breaths, Chiara told me.

'I went to check on my horse. Then I heard a rustling of the straw in the empty stall next to his.' She shook her head. 'Federico was there, demanding to know why I hadn't returned his phone-call. So, I told him to fuck off.

'He said the girl was just a fling and that he really wanted to be with me. I laughed in his face. That's when he grabbed me and knocked me to the ground. He started swearing at me and calling me a spoilt bitch. Then he punched the side of my face. At that moment I realised how much I hated him. He tried to pull off my shorts. I think he wanted to rape me. I managed to bite his hand. He was rolling around in agony, making such a fuss, what a *mammone*. I grabbed my crutches and got the hell out of there, slamming the door to the stable shut and locking him in.'

'That was so brave of you, Chiara,' I said, rushing up to her and giving her a hug. 'Thank God you're all right.'

'Yes, thank God,' Mother repeated.

Antonio huffed. 'Commissario, I hope you will arrest that *stronzo* shithead for assault.'

'*Sì, signore.*'

Another fork of lightning ripped the sky open.

I spun around, the voice in my head almost deafening, *Too late, too late, too late.*

'Oh my God, Fern!'

The hounds of hell at my heels, it seemed, I ran to my car, jumped in and raced toward Altivole.

I could see black smoke rising from the end of the road leading out of Susan's village. *Cazzo!!* I put my foot down on the accelerator. I was back in that recurring nightmare, the dream that had stalked my sleep ever since I'd met Fern. *Too late! Too late! Too late!* This was what it had all been about. My heart thudded.

I pulled up behind a fire engine, its lights strobing through the mist that had come down in the wake of the storm.

An ambulance was parked in front of it.

Firefighters were standing, hoses in their hands, spraying the blackened house.

Fuck! Fuck! Fuck!

I jumped out of my car and rushed forward.

A police officer barred my way.

'*Troppo pericoloso.*'

Too dangerous, of course, but where the hell were Fern and her aunt?

The officer pointed at the ambulance.

My heart fucking sank.

CHAPTER 25

I opened my eyes.

Sunlight slanted through a gap in the curtains.

I lifted my hands.

They were swathed in bandages.

I swivelled my gaze to the left.

Luca.

Sitting on a chair next to my bed.

Lines of worry on his face.

'Wh… wh… what happened?' I groaned.

'You're in Castelfranco Hospital, sweetheart. Your aunt's house caught fire. Thank God you're all right.' He got up from the chair and perched himself on my bed. 'The paramedics had to resuscitate you and give you oxygen.' He bent and kissed my mouth. 'They're keeping you under observation to make sure there are no aftereffects from smoke inhalation. The second degree burns to your hands should heal completely in a couple of weeks.'

'Is Auntie all right?' I asked, coughing. My lungs felt as if they'd been branded with a hot iron.

'She's fine. Checked into the Hotel Duse in Asolo with her cat. Oh, and she's got your paintings with her.' He lowered himself and kissed my mouth. 'Rest now Fern. Don't try to talk…'

I nodded and the action made me dizzy. I was tired, so very tired. Sleep overtook me quickly, I must have been on medication, and when I woke I felt much better, especially because Luca was still here with me.

'Hi,' I smiled. 'Thanks for staying.'

'I wish I hadn't let you go back to Susan's.'

'I'm glad you did,' I breathed, and there was no longer any pain. 'Auntie would have died if there'd been a fire and I hadn't been there.'

His expression darkened. 'I don't understand why you went back into that inferno,' he said sternly. 'I thought you were afraid...'

'I am, but I couldn't bear it if my paintings had been destroyed.' I paused and collected my thoughts. 'I know what happened to Lorenza.'

'She died in the fire?' His eyes met mine.

'No. Lodovico took her.'

My face crumpled and I started to cry. It was all so sad. Slowly, between sobs, I told him what had happened to Cecilia.

'I thought I was too late to save *you*,' Luca said. 'But it wasn't me, it was Zorzo who was too late to save Cecilia.' He pulled a Kleenex from the box on my bedside table and dabbed at my eyes. 'I must have been dreaming I was him. The remorse he felt for not getting to the Barco in time must have come down to me through the centuries.'

'We can't change the past, can we?' I took a deep breath, filling my lungs. 'The course of our lives can change on the tiniest decision. Cecilia resisted Lodovico. If she'd left with him, she would have saved herself. Zorzo went to fetch the army from Treviso. If he'd stayed with Cecilia, things would probably have turned out differently.'

'And if you hadn't gone into the house to rescue your paintings, you probably wouldn't be in hospital tonight. I nearly lost you, Fern.' His words came out strangled. 'History could have repeated itself in the same way that Zorzo lost Cecilia.'

'I don't suppose we'll ever find out what happened to Lorenza.' My heart felt like it was breaking. 'Poor little girl, being brought up by an uncaring father. He only took her out of spite.'

'At least she didn't have to suffer the malice of the soldiers.' Luca stroked a tear from my cheek. 'Cecilia probably wouldn't have been able to save herself and her child. So, in a way he rescued her.'

'Such a tragedy.' My breath caught on another sob. 'Shame the Queen couldn't have bent her rules and allowed Cecilia to take Lorenza to Venice.'

'I doubt it even entered her head there was any danger. The Republic thought itself infallible, and it became so again,' Luca said calmly. 'I've been reading the book Mother found. Apparently, Pope Julius soon realised that the eventual destruction of Venice would be too dangerous.'

'Oh?'

'He needed Venetian support to face up to the Kingdom of France and the Ottoman Empire.'

'The Pope's alliance with Louis ended?'

'Yep. And Pope Julius also fell out with Lodovico's duke.'

'Don't tell me he excommunicated him...'

I nodded. 'Didn't stop the Duke of Ferrara from fighting back, though. Then Maximilian switched sides and allied himself with the Pope. He wouldn't give up the territory he'd taken from Venice, though. Soon after, the Republic jumped horses and joined up with the French to combat Julius and Maximilian. Venice and France ended up dividing the whole of Northern Italy between them.'

'And the Republic endured.'

'You could say that. But the events of 1509 marked the end of Venetian expansion.'

I lay back on the pillows and closed my eyes. Sadness overwhelmed me, as if I was in mourning. Cecilia's death had affected me deeply, I realised; it would take time for me to adjust.

'How long are they keeping me in hospital?' I asked.

'Until tomorrow, all being well. A precaution. They advise against returning to London for at least a fortnight.'

'Right. More sick leave.' I exhaled slowly. 'The bank will really be fed up with me.'

'Concentrate on getting better, my love,' Luca said in a firm tone. 'Your room at the villa is waiting for you. Mother and Chiara sent their love and will come to visit this evening.'

I gave him a shaky smile. 'You didn't tell me about the intruder…'

'It was Federico. He tried to force himself on Chiara, but she managed to get away from him, thank God.' Luca went on to recount the events of last night.

'Federico behaved just like Lodovico,' I gasped, shocked. 'I didn't mention to you how much he reminded me of Cecilia's husband in case you thought it too far-fetched. But everything that has happened, has been an echo of what happened in the past, and has changed our lives forever.'

'We can't change the past,' Luca said, stroking my arm. 'But the past can change us…'

I caught my lip with my teeth. 'Oh my God! I've just thought of something. Lodovico locked Cecilia in her room, but Chiara did the opposite and locked Federico in the stable.' I burst into tears again. 'I'm sorry. Not normally such a cry baby.'

'Post-traumatic stress, my darling,' Luca said, pulling another Kleenex from the box. He wiped the snot from my nose then held me close again before kissing me tenderly on the lips.

With a sudden whoosh, the door swung open and Auntie came in, a bouquet of pink roses in one hand, and a box of *Baci* chocolates in the other.

'Sorry I set fire to your house, Auntie,' I whispered as she kissed my cheek.

'You did nothing of the sort. It was a freak accident. And it's you I have to thank for saving my life, and Gucci's. Not to mention my manuscript.'

Auntie pulled up a chair, opened the box of chocolates, and offered them. Luca took one, but I declined. He handed me the small piece of paper that had been wrapped around his chocolate.

I read to myself, *in dreams, as in love, all is possible.*

A week later, I was in the living room at the villa, waiting for Chiara to appear. I stared at my hands. They were still a vibrant shade of pink, but they were healing, and my lungs were back to normal. My greatest worry had been that I wouldn't be able to draw and paint as a result of the accident.

I blew out a long, slow breath. I was dreading going back to London. Dreading my imminent separation from Luca. I'd used up all my vacation entitlement, but we'd agreed he would visit me regularly by adding a day's leave to one weekend a month. It would have to do.

For now.

I looked up as Chiara hobbled into the room. She'd been helping me sort through the old boxes in the cellar, bringing me rolled-up maps and documents to scrutinise before cataloguing them. 'Look,' she said, holding a small oval painting in her hand. 'I think it's of one of our ancestors.'

I slipped on the cotton gloves I wore to protect my hands and reached for the cloth I'd been using to wipe the dust from parchments. I screwed up my eyes and examined the signature in the bottom right-hand corner of the picture, partly hidden by the dirt of centuries. I wiped gently, and revealed the letter L. Then an O, followed by an R. *Lorenza. Oh my God! Could it be?* My heart pounding, I carefully uncovered the rest of the signature. *Lorenza Gaspare.*

Gaspare had been Lodovico's surname. How had the girl managed to become an artist? And who was the Goredan ancestor in the portrait? 'This is fascinating,' I said to Chiara. 'Is your mother around? We must show it to her.'

Chiara was already heading out the door. 'I'll go and get her,' she said.

I held the portrait up to the light, marvelling at the fine brushwork. Within minutes Chiara had returned with Vanessa. 'Look at this,' I said, my face wreathed in smiles.

Vanessa let out a gasp. 'Incredible! Who'd have thought? I've no idea who the man in the portrait is. Where did you find it, Chiara?'

'At the bottom of the last chest. It was under another stack of those boring letters. I'll go and get them.'

A warm feeling spread through me as I watched mother and daughter search through the correspondence. They'd grown much closer. Chiara, no longer under Federico's influence, had even agreed to go back to the university. As for her ex-boyfriend, he was in jail awaiting trial. I hoped he'd be sent down for a long time.

'These letters don't tell us much,' Vanessa said eventually. 'They're mostly about buying and selling spices. Like many Venetians, our family was in the spice trade in the fifteenth and sixteenth centuries.'

Disappointment rolled though me, but I told myself not to be silly. Just because a painting signed by Lorenza had miraculously appeared, didn't mean the mystery of her life would be solved all at once. I would have to content myself with holding the miniature in my hand; I would use my imagination to fill in the gaps. Lodovico had gone some way toward redeeming himself by allowing Lorenza to pursue her artistic talents. I'd been haunted by the fear he had repressed the girl like he'd tried to repress her mother.

Lorenza probably twisted him around her little finger; she was that sort of child.

When Luca returned from the office, I showed him the portrait. 'This could be the connection between me and Giorgione,' he marvelled. 'Another reason why I dreamed about him.'

'A portrait of your ancestor. Painted by Giorgione's daughter. How amazing is that?!'

'Beyond amazing,' he said, holding me close and kissing me.

I wished I could tell Cecilia about Lorenza. But my nemesis no longer came to me in dreams and visions. She'd helped me reach out to Luca, and now we'd become a couple, she was leaving me in peace. I'd have to find somewhere associated with her, I supposed, but I couldn't face that yet.

After dinner, Luca put his arm around me and led me onto

the terrace. We sat sipping Prosecco in the warmth of the summer night. Fireflies flitted across the garden, their lights like tiny lanterns, and the air was redolent with the scent of honeysuckle.

My eyes met Luca's and I knew, I suddenly knew, what I'd say next. 'When I get back to London, I'll hand in my notice at the bank and put the flat on the market.'

He leapt from his chair and swept me up in his arms.

Then he kissed me.

A long, lingering kiss. 'I love you, Fern.'

'And I love you, Luca. With all my heart, *amore mio*.'

EPILOGUE

One Year Later

I'm in Luca's and my new home, and I can hear his Alfa coming up the driveway. We've been married for six months now, the happiest six months of my life. I love him so much. I know it's a cliché to say this, but he's taken all my broken pieces and has glued them back together again.

I also love my life in Italy. Love the beauty of the landscape and architecture, not to mention the kindness of the Italians. Thankfully, my return to London was only brief. Within a month, I was back in this country, helping Luca plan the restoration of the farmhouse where we now live. We moved in a fortnight ago and have named it, *Casa Cecilia*.

Chiara gave us her blessing, even though she went through the trauma of Federico's betrayal here. He was sentenced to three years for attempted rape, and I doubt we'll see his face again. This house is a happy place, filled with good memories of childhood picnics that far outweigh the misery she suffered for a few days. She's back at the university and has changed her course to political science. She'll fight for Veneto independence one day, she says. As an elected politician.

Luca calls out, 'I'm home,' and comes through the door, into the warmth of the kitchen, where I'm stirring a pot of soup, our six-month old black Labrador puppy Zorzo at my feet.

'You'll never believe what Mother has discovered,' he says, kissing me on the lips. 'You know that portrait painted by Lorenza of my ancestor? Well, apparently, she married him.'

My jaw drops. 'What! Married him? How do you know?'

'Mother's genealogical research. I had lunch with her at the villa and she told me she'd finally filled in the sixteenth century branch of the family from which we're descended. There's a record of the marriage in the library of San Marco in Venice.'

'Wow,' I gasp.

He bends and tickles our puppy under the chin, then straightens himself and says, 'Remember that Mother was going to go there before Chiara took that fall off the horse? Well, she's been so busy, she only got 'round to it the day before yesterday. She didn't want to tell me anything over the phone, insisting I had lunch with her, and she showed me the notes she took. Our ancestor was a nephew of the Doge. We always thought we were descended from Doge Goredan, but Mother discovered his son died in the same plague that put an end to Giorgione's life, so the line passed through the nephew instead.'

'How amazing! To think our baby will be descended from the great artist himself.' I place my hand on the swell in my belly; there's a bubble of movement under my fingers. 'Feel this.' I move Luca's hand to the small bump. 'Our daughter is pleased.'

The next morning, I take the pup for a walk down to the old chapel. June this year has been wet and chilly, and last night there was a thunderstorm, the sky like the one in *The Tempest*. Our house has a lightning conductor, smoke alarms and flash-lights in every room, just in case, but my fear of fire still makes my heart quake, albeit much less than before. At least that piece of burnt wood hasn't made a reappearance in my life, not that I've been anywhere near places associated with Cecilia recently.

At the same time as supervising the restoration of the farmhouse, Luca has overseen the rebuilding of Auntie's place, a bungalow this time. 'I won't be able to manage the stairs for much longer,' she said. 'And neither will Gucci. He's getting on in years like me.' Thankfully, Auntie was fully insured and is delighted to be moving into her new home the day after tomorrow. Also delighted at the prospect of becoming a great aunt in four months' time. My only regret is my parents live so far away, but flights between the UK and Italy are becoming cheaper; they've already visited twice since I left London. They came for the wedding, of course, which took place in Asolo with the reception at the Cipriani, and the second time only last week, to see the house.

My feet crunch on the stony path. The churchyard is up ahead, and I let the pup off his leash. There's a smell of damp vegetation as I reach for my pad. I haven't been down here since we moved into *Casa Cecilia*; I sit on the low wall in front of the church and make a start on my sketch. At Easter, I had an exhibition of my paintings in Castelfranco. They sold well; now I'm hard at work preparing for the next one.

'*Lorenza!*''

Even though I've been almost expecting the ghostly whisper, my heart jumps.

'Cecilia, thank you for helping me reach out to Luca,' I whisper in the Venetian dialect Luca has taught me to speak. 'I want you to know that your daughter became everything you wanted her to be. I'm certain, for I've seen her work. And I'm carrying her descendent. I had a premonition the baby is a girl. We've decided to call her Lorenza.'

A sigh ripples in the cypress trees behind the church. I lift a hand to my eyes.

Two figures, their arms linked, stand in the portal.

A man, dressed in a short doublet, his dark brown hair reaching to his shoulders, and a woman.

Cecilia.

The man, Giorgione, bows and the woman curtseys.

I blink, and when I look again, the figures are gone.

A crow caws in the chestnut tree on the hill behind. I put my sketchpad away, hitch my rucksack over my shoulder, whistle for the pup, and walk back up the road.

AUTHOR'S NOTE

Giorgione, Zorzo or Zorzone, was one of the most enigmatic painters in the history of Italian art. Little is known of his life, which has been romanticised by writers over the centuries.

One of the legends about Giorgione is that his true love was a young woman known as Cecilia. There is some doubt about who she was and if she actually existed. For me, she did exist and was a lady-in-waiting at the Court of Queen Caterina Cornaro. However that is only my interpretation of the myth.

The Tempest has been called the first landscape in the history of Western painting. I love this work and have enjoyed weaving its creation into my romance. *Lady of Venice* is a work of fiction, however, and just my view of how things could have been.

The creation of Giorgione's *Sleeping Venus* has also been romanticised in my novel. Although it's not obvious from an inspection of both this and *The Tempest* that they depict the same woman, I have used artistic license and imagined that they did so, and that the woman is Zorzo's true love, Cecilia.

There was a Venetian noble woman, Caterina Cornaro, who was married to the King of Cyprus and became the Sovereign of Asolo. She died in Venice on 10 July 1510, a year after the Barco, her villa of delights, was damaged by a fire set by the League of Cambrai troops. It was there that she had established a court of literary and artistic distinction and where Pietro Bembo set his platonic dialogues on love, *Gli Asolani.*

I have read the following books for inspiration and information:

Baldassare Castiglione, *The Book of the Courtier*
Herbert Cook, *Giorgione*
Peter W. Edbury, Joachim G. Joachi,. Terence Mullaly, *Caterina Cornaro Queen of Cyprus*
Antonella Gotti, *Caterina Cornaro, Regina di Cipro e Signora di Asolo*
Thomas Kabdebo, *Tracking Giorgione*
Alberto Ongarato, *Giorgione da Castelfranco, L'uomo, l'artista, il mito*

I hope you have enjoyed reading *Lady of Venice* as much as I loved writing it. Your feedback is important to me and I would love to know what you thought of Fern, Luca, Cecilia and Zorzo. I'll keep an eye out for reviews on Amazon and Goodreads, or you can drop me a line by email.

ABOUT THE AUTHOR

A lover of all things Italian, Siobhan Daiko lives in the Veneto region of northern Italy with her husband and two cats. After a life of romance and adventure in Hong Kong, Australia and the UK, Siobhan now spends her time, when she isn't writing, enjoying the sweet life near Venice. She writes steamy contemporary romance under the name SC Daiko. You can find her at www.siobhandaiko.org.

ACKNOWLEDGMENTS

I would like to thank the following people:
John Hudspith for his editing of the earlier version of this book,
Lady of Asolo.
Trenda Lundin, my current editor, for her encouragement and
advice regarding the rewriting of *Lady of Venice*.
Xavier and Rafa of Cover Kitchen for their beautiful design.
My lovely PA Helena Gant, for looking after me so brilliantly.
Ann Bennett, my writing buddy and friend, for her comments on
the first draft.
My beta readers, Fiona, Helena, Joy, Michelle, Nanette and Nico,
for sharing *Lady of Venice's* journey with me and for their
invaluable critique.
Victor, my husband, for his love and support. Our son, Paul, and
his wife, Lili, for their help with technology.
Last, but not least, I thank you, dear reader, for reading this
book.

OTHER BOOKS BY SIOBHAN DAIKO

The Orchid Tree

Veronica COURTESAN